Neville Stocks is a South African living in Cape Town. After studying to be a teacher, he taught mainly English for five years, before entering business and qualifying as a Chartered Secretary. He has over forty years' experience in financial markets. In 2005 he published his first novel. A keen traveler, he has twice visited St Helena Island, doing extensive research for *The Deciding Votes* on his second visit in 2007.

THE DECIDING VOTES

Neville Stocks

THE DECIDING VOTES

AUSTIN MACAULEY
PUBLISHERS LTD.

A CIP catalogue record for this title is available from the British Library.

ISBN 978 184963 386 4

www.austinmacauley.com

First Published (2013)
Austin Macauley Publishers Ltd.
25 Canada Square
Canary Wharf
London
E14 5LB

Printed and bound in Great Britain

Author's Note

I would like to acknowledge, and convey my grateful thanks, to all those who have given me their support, help, technical advice, time, and the sharing of their knowledge and opinions, during the creation and publication of this book. I would particularly like to mention my family, Judith, Anne, Michael and Jane; Peter and Margaret Reece; and Tania Wimberley, for discussions on mergers and acquisitions.

The internet-based story "Robin and Morgan Le Fey" by Hester NicEilidh (http://fanfic.michael-praed.org/robin_index.html) gave me the link between Morgan Le Fey and Robin Hood which I refer to in my novel.

I thank the officers and crew of *RMS St Helena*, especially Dr Ron Martin, who was the Surgeon, or ship's doctor, on my first voyage to and from St Helena.

On St Helena Island itself, the people were unfailingly friendly and helpful. I must give special mention and very grateful thanks to Mrs S Ivy Ellick, Basil George, Hensel Peters, Colin Corker, Jane John and George Benjamin. I thank those at the General Hospital, Prince Andrew School and the Consulate Hotel who answered my questions, even by telephone from Cape Town. The St Helena Tourist Office, and its many guides and publications, are mines of information, as is the Museum of St Helena, and the St Helena Herald and The St Helena Independent newspapers. I have tried to give as accurate a representation of this interesting and beautiful Island as it is possible for an "outsider" to achieve. If I have made any errors, then please forgive me.

Finally, I thank all the good people at Austin Macauley Publishers for adopting *The Deciding Votes* and bringing it to life into the hands of its readers.

1

On a Sunday afternoon in 1937, Joseph Morgen sat on the summit of Morgen Koppie and looked out across the beautiful landscape of the north-eastern Orange Free State. It was a lovely view, and he never tired of it. The grass was golden in the afternoon sunlight, and all around him were strewn the numerous sculptured hills which gave the area its special character. Each of these koppies had its own individual shape and size, crowned by an endless variety of peaks fashioned from golden krantzes and grassy tops. To the north-east lay the commanding ridge that included the Platberg, or Harrismith Mountain, and in the haze in the far distance he could see the high mountains of the Drakensberg.

On the skirts of the koppie, and extending all around it, lay Morgen Farm, to which he had proudly given his family name, as indeed he had to the koppie which formed its high point. Joseph looked down upon it with pride. He saw the avenue of young poplar trees extending from the dusty road, the neat stone and white buildings, the two small dams, and cattle dotting the lower slopes and valleys. He was very satisfied with all they had achieved, but it had been very hard work.

After struggling to make enough to live on in that Great Depression of the early nineteen-thirties, he had sought to build a new life in more secluded parts. He had left his beloved, green-eyed, full-bosomed Jessica with her parents in Johannesburg, and set out on a motorcycle over the rough and dusty roads towards the coast, seeking opportunities. He had rather liked the small dorp of Platberg, then scarcely more than a village, lying in a pleasant hollow below the high Platberg, the dominating mountain so called because of its flat top. Over a drink in the bar of the modest Grand Hotel, he had heard of a tract of farmland that was for sale. He had liked it, and so had Jessica when she had seen it. Somehow they had managed to scrounge the funds they needed to buy the farm and get it established. It had been a struggle, but little by little they had succeeded and the farm was now profitable. Jessica had also given him two fine sons during that time.

Joe had been selling milk in the surrounding towns and villages, but he was ambitious and wanted to develop his business and structure it properly. As part of that he would form a company, but he now needed a brand name so his business and its produce could become known and established in the minds of customers and the public. He mused about this as he sat on the hilltop enjoying the beauty and assessing his and Jessica's achievements thus far. "Morgen" was of course an obvious choice. "Morgen's Milk" had a good ring to it, with suggestions of morning, and morning freshness, but was it right? He stood up, took a last look around and made his way down towards the farmhouse.

By the time he had looked in to see that the milking was being done properly, and he had finished his evening rounds, the children were bathed and fed and Jessica was reading to them, as she did each evening before they went to bed. Joe poured himself a drink and rested his heavy frame in a deep, comfortable chair. He sipped his drink, relaxed and half listening as he let his mind wander over the events of the day.

Jessica was reading a version of the story of Robin Hood. Robin had been seriously injured by a soldier on horseback and his companions had been forced to leave him alone in the forest, thinking him to be dead. He was spirited away to the faerie realm and restored to health by the magical and beautiful Morgan le Fey. She fed him with milk from her own breasts. They were beautiful and her milk was magical, full of flavour…nourishing….

Joe was suddenly alert and attending to the words of the story.

"Read that again. About the milk. Please."

"'Morgan's milk was magical, full of flavour, smooth and rich and sweet, nourishing and healing.'"

"That's it! That's it! Morgen's Milk it will be – our Company and our milk!"

So it was that Morgen's Milk was born.

2

One Sunday afternoon, about seventy years later, Lucy Morgen stood on the summit of Diana's Peak on St Helena Island. That day the prevailing south-east wind was relatively light so it was not cold, but pleasantly cool, as the cloud played around the mountain-top, enveloping her, then opening up to show her glimpses of the wonderful views all around. The carved wooden board marking the summit told her she was 823 metres above sea level, the highest point on the Island. As she walked along the ridge, she loved the feeling of isolation and solitude when the mist closed in and restricted her vision to the grassy path and surrounding vegetation – ferns of all kinds, arum lilies, some flax, and especially the shapely black cabbage trees and sculptured candelabra of the tree ferns against the cloud and fading into the mist. When the views opened she could see the mountains and ridges with permanently stooping trees bent by the trade winds; the rich greens of the high land and deep valleys; villages and houses on the gentler slopes, plateaus and kindly valleys; patches of stony, sandy desert towards the coast; and the greys and browns of the rocky cliffs, beyond which was the vast Atlantic Ocean.

For this is one of the remotest places on earth, and Lucy had chosen to come here for that reason. At approximately sixteen degrees south and five degrees forty-five minutes west, St Helena is a tiny dot on the map in the Atlantic, in the tropics south of the equator. The nearest land is little Ascension Island to the north-west, 1125 kilometres away. The African coast is 1920 kilometres to the east, and South America 3260 kilometres due west. Lucy had sailed for five nights, out of sight of land, on the RMS *St Helena* to cover the 3100 kilometres from Cape Town, far away to the south-east.

Lucy found a place to sit, and looked down to Sandy Bay on the southern coast. She never tired of the beauty of this lovely island, whose unimaginable variety made it seem so much bigger than it really was. She felt at peace here. She had come to escape her previous life, and had looked to go so far away that she could not again be disturbed. She had known a little about St Helena. It was remote enough to be an effective prison for Napoleon, and to keep Boer prisoners in the Anglo-Boer war. Curiously too, the Morgen family business had at one time had some vague interest in the Island. If one wanted to escape to a new world, one need surely go no further. After her divorce, and then when Neil had also failed her, she had wanted to go as far away as possible. So she had come here just over three years ago. It was peaceful, safe and beautiful, the people were delightful and friendly, and she was very happy.

Lucy let her eyes wander down the long valley to Sandy Bay and out into the ocean. South Africa was far across the water to the south-east. Thoughts of "home" idly crossed her mind. Seeing the date earlier at home, she had remembered that it was Geoff Loman's birthday. No doubt there would be a party, and some of her family would be there. She was glad she was not one of them.

3

As Geoffrey Loman planned to have a sixtieth birthday party to outdo even that for his fiftieth birthday, he decided to celebrate his fifty-seventh modestly, with only a hundred or so guests at his home. To be fair, the occasion was also a celebration of the latest acquisition made by his Predvest company, so the guest list included, not only family and friends, but colleagues, business associates, directors of the acquired company, some captains of commerce and industry and influential political figures. Outside the property, between the high walls on both sides of the elite Sandton street, expensive cars lined the way for some distance. Smiling, uniformed guards greeted the guests and directed them to the entrance. They kept watch outside while the guests passed through the enormous metal gates and crossed the paved way to the open double doors, which gave access to an enormous entrance hall. It was all marble and mirrors, with doorways leading off it, a wide marble staircase to the right, and glass doors to the left opening onto the pool area and gardens.

As he entered the room with his wife Cathy, William (or Will as he preferred) Morgen thought once more that the public areas of the Loman property seemed more suited to a large luxury hotel than to a home. The couple had been prevailed upon to come by their daughter, Mary, who was married to Geoff Loman's son, Adrian. Tall, urbane and dignified, with mild grey-blue eyes and once brown hair mostly turned to grey, Will was Chairman of Morgen Holdings, the family business. Cathy was small, slim and vivacious, with deep brown, kindly, usually smiling eyes. At the open doors to the pool deck they were welcomed by Geoff and his wife Rachael. Geoff was tall and broad with a shock of wavy grey hair, a square, lined and ruddy face, bloodshot brown eyes and untidy grey eyebrows. Rachael was small and slim, with dark hair and eyes, dark suntanned skin and a still good, carefully maintained figure. She was a good hostess, a pleasant person, contented in her role of supporting Geoff as and whenever he demanded.

The pool was half Olympic size, with a broad, open paved area and a wide covered colonnade on both of the sides bordered by the house. Here a bar had been set up, long tables carried a sumptuous and beautifully presented buffet dinner, and guests could sit in shade or sun. Colourful umbrellas, tables and chairs were scattered around the pool deck and the immaculate lawns. The winter tracery of branches of large oaks and plane trees was softened by the formation of early spring buds on this sun-soothed, highveld day. The curves and colours of the gardens took the eye on a pleasing journey out beyond the pool, to the border of the property, and ultimately to the Magaliesberg Mountains, low and hazy in the distance. On one side of the pool a bandstand had been erected and from there a jazz band and the Soweto String Quartet alternated to provide jazz and classical music. With glasses in hand, men and women sat or stood in colourful groups.

Will surveyed the scene, summing up those already there: some political figures out for free drinks and dinner, Predvest executives summoned to pay homage to their lord and master, merchant bankers (why *do* they call themselves investment bankers?) and commercial lawyers celebrating the closing of a major deal and looking for future business. It could be a long afternoon. Cathy's survey soon located Mary sitting at a table with her cousin, Patsy, so they went over and sat down with them.

Drinks flowed and food was consumed in great quantities, while the musicians competed with the rising volume of human voices. Before the taking of desserts, Adrian – tall, with wavy, dark hair and the brown eyes of his parents – stood up on the platform in front of the band, spoke kind words about his father, and proposed a toast to him on the occasion of his birthday. As the guests sat down again, Geoff took the microphone. He thanked his son and guests, acknowledged the representatives of the newly acquired company, and promised increased earnings for Predvest and its shareholders as a result of the acquisition.

"The market has spoken again. It likes the deal. It likes what we're doing, and you've all seen the share price rising. We're not finished yet. I can promise you that the next deal will not be long in coming. Yes, Predvest will grow its present businesses, but we also need more good acquisitions to hasten our growth. We'll find them, and we will continue to reward our shareholders."

Later, as the shadows lengthened and the sharp coolness of a highveld spring evening began to steal across the garden, some of the guests began to show signs of leaving. James Bold and Stanley Vane were standing under one of the fine old oak trees, chatting as they vaguely watched the scene. James had married Patsy Morgen, Mary's cousin. He was tall and strongly built, with light brown hair, grey eyes, a round face and smooth fair skin. He was well spoken, with a confident air, often giving an impression of urbane softness, of being well fed and slightly smug. Stanley, by contrast, was short, dark and wiry, with curly, black hair, dark eyebrows and dark eyes set deeply in a face made somewhat devilish by a pointed chin. He was ambitious and ruthless, but could be very charming if he wished. Indeed, he had been married to Patsy's sister, Lucy, for a time. Both men were merger and acquisition specialists at Enduring Bank. They had worked a lot together, and were key players in the most recent Predvest acquisition. They had done much work for Geoff Loman and had benefited from his predatory approach to building his business. There were some small deals in the pipeline at Enduring, but they were now looking out for the next really big transaction – bringing, of course, enormous fees and commissions, and millions for them in bonuses.

Adrian came over to join them. He raised his glass in greeting.

"Are you planning Predvest's next takeover?" he asked.

"I hope so," said James. "After all we can't leave your predator company without prey for too long."

"Hopefully we'll be able to bring you another deal soon," said Stanley.

"A good company, that is undervalued."

"With lots of fat to be stripped out."

They looked idly about them as they sipped their drinks. A little way from them Will and Cathy stood up, preparing to leave the party. Mary and Patsy were standing saying good-bye to them. All Morgens, they made a pretty family group. Stanley watched casually; then with intense concentration.

"A company like Morgen," he said.

4

Elegant yet functional, Morgen House was set on a rise on the outskirts of the Sandton business district, north of Johannesburg. Years ago, large parts of the city's central business district had fallen into decay, and many businesses had relocated to the north, effectively building a new main business district in the formerly suburban Sandton area. Will Morgen had become Chief Executive Officer (CEO) of Morgen Holdings after the tragic death of his elder brother and previous CEO, Malcolm, in a road accident. Soon after, he had moved Morgen's head office northwards into the new building developed by their Property Division. It had been a good move, and, for the executives at least, one closer to their homes, situated mainly in the wealthy northern suburbs.

Will had recently relinquished the position of CEO, to become Executive Chairman, in order to create the space and opportunity for the two Morgen sons, Malcolm's son Mark, and his own son Robert (or Rob), to become joint Managing Directors, each in charge of a number of the Group's many businesses. For Morgen had grown over the years and now comprised far more than the Milk Division, though that was still cherished for its role in the origin of the Group.

Will had reserved for himself a large corner office on the top, ninth floor of Morgen House. It was comfortably, though not too luxuriously furnished, it had fine views to the north and west. He was there on the Wednesday after Geoff Loman's party. It proved to be a very busy day, so Will was slightly irritated to be interrupted by a phone call from Geoff.

"Hi, Will. Sorry to trouble you. I need to talk to you. Can you make lunch tomorrow?"

"I'm afraid not, Geoff. It's a busy week. There's a lot going on."

"I need to talk to you."

"About what? I saw you on Sunday. Nice party, by the way. Thanks."

"I want to buy Morgen."

"*You* want to buy *Morgen*?"

"Predvest wants to make an offer for Morgen Holdings."

"Morgen's not for sale."

"Let's talk."

"There's nothing to talk about. Morgen's not for sale."

"If we do make an offer, you'll have to put it to your shareholders. *They* might want to sell, so I think we should talk."

"OK, if you insist, but we're not for sale. Come here at six this evening."

Geoff Loman was an aggressive and impatient driver. The roads of Sandton were, as usual, still very busy at six o'clock in the evening. Geoff was driving in the fast lane, but frustrated by the slowness of the traffic. The entrance to Morgen House was upon him earlier than expected, so he swung the steering wheel to cross to the inside lane, cutting off another vehicle which came to a sudden halt, narrowly missing being run into from behind as well. Jennifer Rogan uttered an expletive as she slammed her foot on the brakes, seeing a white 7-series BMW with four men in it cross her path. A moment later it turned into the entrance to Morgen House, and she saw the registration plate: GEOFF 1. Her journalistic instincts were immediately aroused. She knew the car and the driver, and, despite the dusk, thought she glimpsed James Bold as one of the passengers. Her anger died as she moved her car forward again, still watchful of the traffic but thinking of the possible implications: Morgen House, Geoff Loman and an M and A specialist from Enduring Bank. She knew well not to read too much into a small occurrence, but decided to watch carefully for any developments.

Geoff had brought with him his son Adrian, who was Financial Director of Predvest, as well as James Bold and

Stanley Vane from Enduring Bank. These three had brought the idea of buying Morgen to him on Monday morning. Despite some family connections, it seemed to make perfect business sense. He wondered why he had not thought of it himself. The four men were checked through security at the ground floor reception desk and taken up to the ninth floor by Will Morgen's ever-pleasant secretary, Judy Lane. They were a few minutes late, so Will and three other Morgen executives were already there, waiting for them: Joint Managing Directors Mark and Rob Morgen, and Neil Harrier, who was responsible for a number of functions and bore the title of Operations Director. Mark and Rob were both tall, like their fathers, but Mark was broader-shouldered with brown hair and green eyes, while Rob was blue-eyed with dark hair. Neil was also tall, but lean and athletic-looking, with dark wavy hair and striking dark bushy eyebrows above deep blue eyes.

Greetings and introductions were informal and brief as each knew the others at least a little. There was some small talk while Judy – tall, fair, grey-eyed, efficient, and graceful and charming as ever – poured drinks for them, and then left the office. The men seated themselves at the round conference table at one end of the spacious room. Will opened the meeting by repeating that Morgen was not for sale, but asked Geoff to state his business.

"Will, I've brought James and Stanley along with us as they've already done quite a lot of work on this, and we would like to move rather quickly with it. Of course we'd prefer to do a friendly merger if possible. We'll pay a good price, so it'll be in everyone's interest."

"Geoff, Morgen is a family business – "

"But quoted on the Stock Exchange."

" – run by the family."

"Who only own a minority of the shares. There're a great many people out there who'd be more than happy to sell to Predvest – to exchange their Morgen shares for shares in Predvest."

"Geoff, this is not friendly at all. It's like attacking your own family. Look around this table. Adrian is married to Mary, and James to Patsy. Stanley and Lucy are no longer married, but Stanley was also part of the family."

"Well, we can bring the family businesses together. We should've done it long ago. Perhaps it was too close to see, but it's been under our eyes all the time. It's a perfect fit – you must see that. Morgen's share price has been in the doldrums, as the business has been producing no better than ordinary results. It seems to us that Morgen is carrying a lot of fat that can be shed. We'll see to that."

"Mark and Rob are already working on a cost-saving plan."

"We'll ensure that a great amount of potential value will be realised – it's our speciality. Return on capital, earnings, shareholder value, you name it, can be improved very quickly."

"How?"

"We should easily be able to take out a few hundred million a year of costs. Look at this head office – most of that can go. Of course we'd guarantee places in the new organization for the four of you here, as well as a few other key people. Then your milk business is not performing. That would be scaled down or sold."

"You can't expect the cows to produce very much milk in a drought. When Morgen's Milk does well, it does quite well enough. Besides which, it's the heart of the Morgen Group. The Group was born out of the milk business."

"Sentimental rubbish! Like Morgen Farm. That must cost a packet to keep going."

"It's great for our image, and our marketing."

"Can you show me a return on that investment?"

"Goodwill, image – the benefits spread to the whole group."

"And the cash return?"

"Some intangibles can't be expressed in purely monetary terms."

"Then we would sell or close it, and reinvest where we'll make a good profit."

"Geoff, your ways are not our ways. We can improve Morgen's profitability ourselves, in our own way, and preserve the character and culture of the Group. We value our heritage" – gesturing towards the portrait of Joe Morgen on the wall – "and value our people."

"More than profits?" asked Adrian.

"Sometimes more than profits, as long as we also produce respectable earnings."

Neil had been listening quietly to the exchange, but now asked: "If you do decide to go ahead with an offer, what will you propose?"

"An exchange of shares," replied Geoff. "Predvest is currently trading around 1000 cents, with Morgen around 750. If we offer one Predvest share for each Morgen share, that will give you a premium of around thirty-three per cent above Morgen's market price. That's very generous."

"No it is not," said Will emphatically. "That will greatly undervalue Morgen. Morgen is intrinsically worth far more."

"That's not what the market is saying. It will need a lot of work to realise the latent value in Morgen. We think most Morgen shareholders will jump at the offer. They'll get an immediate thirty-three per cent above a languishing share price. They'll also participate in the future growth of Predvest, which has a spectacular track record. If you think Morgen has upside potential, then help us to achieve it. You'll benefit immediately through the price we're prepared to pay, and subsequently through holding Predvest shares."

"How do you propose to go about making such an offer?" asked Neil.

"Obviously there are a number of ways to do it, but we want one hundred per cent of Morgen. We don't want any minorities to hinder our operations, and that includes the family. So we'll propose a scheme of arrangement in terms of section 311 of the Companies Act. In that way, if we get seventy-five per cent of the votes at the shareholders' meeting, the deal will be binding on all shareholders."

"You can't possibly get seventy-five per cent," said Will. "The family has twenty-five per cent already. They'll all vote against the deal."

"Are you quite sure?" asked Geoff.

"Mary is now a Loman as well as a Morgen," said Adrian. "She'll vote as I tell her. She'll follow the money, and she sees the Predvest share price rising all the time, while the Morgen price does nothing."

"Morgen has given her a good living," Will reminded him.

"And Predvest a better one; and if we realise the value we think we can in Morgen, the earnings and share price of Predvest will increase further."

James entered the conversation: "Patsy will never stand in my way. She knows what's good for her, and will vote for the deal if I tell her to. In any case, she has no great love for Morgen. 'The business, the business, the business' was all she grew up with. She hardly saw her father, he was so busy running the business – and then it took his life."

"That's hardly fair," said Will.

"So that only leaves you, at best, with nineteen per cent of the votes," said Geoff. "As we understand it, Mary and Patsy each hold three per cent of Morgen. Lucy has another three per cent. Mark, and you, Rob, each own four per cent, while you, Will, have about eight per cent."

"That's more or less correct."

"I will vote against such a deal," said Mark.

"And I will too," said Rob.

Neil turned to Will and asked: "Do you have in place a shareholders' agreement covering the family shares?"

"No," replied Will, "we've never needed one – until now it seems."

5

Will immediately called a family meeting – or rather, a meeting of the family shareholders in Morgen Holdings. This was a relatively rare occurrence, but Mark, Rob, Patsy and Mary all came to Will and Cathy's home in the pleasant and expensive suburb of Hyde Park the next evening. Lucy, of course, was far away on St Helena Island and could not be there.

As the chill of a clear spring evening did not permit sitting out, they settled themselves comfortably in the main lounge. It was a large but welcoming and harmonious room, with cream walls, curtains and carpets in shades of blue, comfortable blue-grey leather couches and armchairs, a warm stone fireplace and coffee tables of cherry wood and glass. Beautiful South African landscapes on the walls – by Dmitry Nikashin, Peter Bonney, Hannes du Plessis, John Meyer and others – provided an irresistible feast for the wandering eyes.

After drinks had been served, Will described the meeting of the previous day and outlined the merger proposal that could be expected from Predvest Limited.

"If the offer does in fact go ahead," said Will in conclusion, "there'll have to be a meeting of shareholders of Morgen Holdings. Predvest will need seventy-five per cent of the votes at the meeting in order to succeed. As a family, we control twenty-five per cent of the votes, so if we all vote against the deal it cannot go ahead. Indeed, we can stop this thing right now by all of us, including Lucy who I'm trying to contact, committing ourselves immediately to vote against any such resolution. If I can convey that to Geoff Loman he'll hardly incur the costs of going ahead when he knows he cannot win. I trust I can rely on all of you in this matter."

"I'll definitely oppose any offer from Predvest," said Rob.

"And I will too," agreed Mark.

Will turned enquiringly to his daughter Mary, who looked uncomfortable. Both she and Patsy had been sternly briefed by their respective husbands.

"I've discussed things with Adrian," said Mary after a pause. "It seems to be a very good offer. My shares will be worth a third more if I convert them into Predvest ones – and Predvest's been doing really well. Adrian should know better than anyone. His whole life is bound up with Predvest. Dad, I know this will disappoint you, but Adrian will not be at all happy if I vote against him. Things could become very, very difficult at home."

"I can't vote against a deal that'll bring more than a million in bonuses to James," said Patsy. "If it were a bad deal it would be difficult enough, but he's explained to me that it's a very good one for everyone. He's already insanely jealous that I'm so much richer than he is. He's very ambitious, as you know. I hate to think what would happen if I went against him. He scares me sometimes."

"We surely don't all have to vote the same way, do we?" asked Mary.

"But, darling, the family always has," intervened Cathy. "It's an unwritten law."

"James says there's no reason I can't vote as I please," said Patsy. "He says there's no written agreement to force me to vote in a certain way."

"We've never needed an agreement," said Will. "The family has never had a problem voting together for what is in the interests of Morgen. This is now clearly the case. If Geoffrey Loman takes control, Morgen will effectively cease to exist. Parts may survive, but parts will be sold or closed down, and very many jobs will be lost. The caring culture established by Big Joe Morgen will be totally destroyed. So will everything the family has worked so hard to build up over so many years."

"Morgen, Morgen, Morgen. That's all I've heard about my life through," said Patsy. "Morgen was all my father ever thought about – and then he was killed coming back from a

Morgen function. I have no reason to love Morgen more than Predvest."

"Adrian says Morgen is not doing well and Predvest will get it right," said Mary.

"Perhaps we should have been more alert and started remedial action sooner," admitted Will. "Maybe we've been too complacent, and been satisfied with a rate of growth that was too low for these times. But Morgen is still profitable, and Mark and Rob now have matters in hand. We are well able to make any changes needed in our own way – and with a much kinder face."

"Adrian promises they'll do things in as gentle a way as possible."

"But that is not the Loman way, Mary," said Rob. "With all due respect to your father-in-law, Geoff has a terrible record. The last business he built up also flourished, but then collapsed. People lost hundreds of millions. He's doing the same thing all over again: buying undervalued, profitable businesses like Morgen with expensive paper – that is by paying with overpriced shares. He has to depend on that to increase profits. Predvest's shares are grossly overvalued. It's an illusion that in the long run you'll do better with them than with Morgen's. When the party's over and Predvest can't find any more such deals to do, the share price will collapse, as the market sees that their growth can't continue."

"Also no one really knows the true value of Predvest," added Mark. "Talk to some of the analysts. They'll tell you that Predvest's accounting methods change every year. Comparisons with previous year's earnings are nearly always impossible. Some believe their results are being manipulated to keep the market happy and the share price high."

The discussion continued, and became more and more heated, but Will could not persuade the two younger ladies to commit their votes against their respective husbands' interests.

6

Lucy had been fortunate to find a comfortable home to move into not long after her arrival on St Helena Island. It had only needed minor alterations, some renovating and the tidying up of the garden, and she had settled very happily there. It was situated at the head of a leafy valley high up in St Paul's. Facing northwards, it was sheltered from the prevailing south-east trades, and Lucy loved to sit on the covered front veranda, never tiring of the beautiful view. She could look down towards Jamestown and Rupert's Bay, though the latter was discretely hidden and Jamestown Valley took a turn to the left out of sight near Briars. Below her, Prince Andrew School, where she taught English, lay on Francis Plain. To the left she could just see High Knoll Fort seated on top of its brown hill; the green wooded slopes to her right were Alarm Forest; and in the distance she looked across Deadwood Plain to Flagstaff Hill. Lucy loved to watch the ever-changing shades of light and colour, varied infinitely by season, time of day and night, sun and moon, cloud and mist. On this balmy evening she had taken her school work onto the veranda, sitting at a table there so she could feel the peace of the Island and look up every now and again to appreciate the subtleties of the softly deepening dusk. Lights were beginning to twinkle in the distance when her telephone rang.

It was her Uncle William. Mary feared bad news, as he had not phoned her in St Helena before, though Aunt Cathy had phoned at Christmas and on her birthday.

Will sounded tired. They exchanged pleasantries, and then he explained the reason for his call and outlined the details of the proposed Predvest offer for Morgen. "Lucy, we need your votes to stave off this attack. I hope I can count on your support."

"Uncle William, I'm sorry about these developments, and I can see that they're awkward for you. I'm sure you'll get enough votes to stop this without me. I've no interest in the matter, and don't want to become involved. I won't be voting at all."

"Lucy, Morgen has provided you – still provides you – with a very good living."

"I'm grateful for that. My holding in Morgen provides me with all I need here, and more."

"Predvest shares, if the offer succeeds, will give you a lesser income."

"But the capital will be more. In any event, my needs are relatively simple here. I like it like that."

"Lucy, you must understand that Morgen as we know it is at risk – the family business. Think of your grandfather and your father, and all they put into it."

"My father gave his life to Morgen, and Morgen took his life."

"That's not fair."

"I sometimes feel I hardly knew him he was so involved with the Company. After my mother died he threw everything, even more than before, into the business. I know it was to help him get over the grief of her loss. But later he was too busy even to come to my twenty-first birthday party: he was called away on business at the last moment. Then he died in a car crash, but he was returning from a Company conference."

"Lucy, I'm sure he would want you to vote to keep Morgen as he knew it and intended it to be. Predvest will pull it to pieces – jobs will be lost, parts sold off or closed: its very soul will be torn out and destroyed."

"I hear you, Uncle William. But you must understand that I came here to escape from all of that – from a world where such things can happen, where money is all, and it means nothing to destroy lives to make a few more millions. I've left all that behind me. I don't want it to follow me here, so please don't expect me to get involved – or to vote – in this matter."

The following afternoon, soon after Lucy had arrived home from school, her telephone rang again. The voice was deceptively smooth and urbane.

"Hello, Lucy. It's James here – James Bold."

"Hello, James."

"Just thought I would phone and see how you are getting along. Are you enjoying it there?"

"James, you did not phone for that reason. You have not been interested in me at all."

"Well, you did promise to make love to me once."

"That was only to keep you at bay – and before you married my sister."

"I sometimes dream of taking you up on that promise."

"Liar! Let me guess. You're involved in the Morgen-Predvest matter."

"Well, it did occur to me to mention the subject. I see you've been told about it."

"My Uncle William phoned last night. I told him I don't want to be involved."

"Lucy, you own three per cent of Morgen. That's a big chunk of the votes. If you won't vote against the deal, I want to persuade you to vote for it."

"I'm not interested."

"Lucy, it may be that they are the deciding votes. They could be very important."

"I've left all that behind me, James. Please leave me alone."

7

Predvest's initial approach to Morgen had stirred up a hive of furious but secret activity. The chief executives of both groups spoke to their directors, trusted close colleagues and advisors. Plans for attack and defence were discussed and formulated. Advisors scrambled to obtain the most up to date details from the share registers of both companies. Key shareholders would be consulted and approvals obtained. Written undertakings to vote for or against the proposed deal would need to be sought in due course.

On the Friday morning Morgen Holdings held a board meeting. As Will Morgen had not been able to garner enough family votes to stop the proposal at once, it was expected that Morgen would have to prepare to fight off what all the directors agreed was a very unwelcome and hostile attack. As good practice required, a subcommittee of non-executive directors was set up to evaluate any formal offer that would be received and to advise Morgan's "minority" shareholders. Professional advisors were also appointed to help evaluate an offer, to provide relevant advice to the Board, to help stave off the offer, and to see to legal matters.

By Friday afternoon Geoff Loman had spoken to all of Predvest's directors and obtained their approval to proceed with the pursuit of Morgen. The matter could be dealt with formally at the next Board meeting. At the most recent annual general meeting of the company, the shareholders had placed the un-issued shares of the company under the control of the directors. There were more than sufficient to issue to pay for Morgen, so a shareholders' meeting could probably be avoided.

All of this activity was conducted with the utmost secrecy, as it was not permissible for market-sensitive information to leak out and cause changes to the share prices of the two companies, with those in the know profiting at the expense of those who had not been informed of what was happening. However, a paragraph in Jennifer Rogan's column in that Saturday's *Business Weekend* set some speculative tongues wagging. She mentioned that she had nearly been run down by a car bearing the registration "GEOFF 1" as it turned into the entrance to Morgen House. "If that Geoff was one Geoffrey Loman, could it be that he is also trying to run down an undervalued and relatively neglected Morgen Holdings?"

On Monday morning the Morgen share price began to rise. The Stock Exchange asked some polite but pointed questions, and Predvest and Morgen immediately issued separate cautionary announcements via SENS, the Stock Exchange News Service, and in the press on Tuesday morning. Both said they were in discussions which could affect the prices of the company shares, and shareholders were therefore advised to exercise caution in dealing with their shares.

8

Suddenly, it seemed to Lucy as though everyone in South Africa wanted to speak to her. After the telephone calls from her Uncle William and from James Bold, she soon had calls from her sister and brother, Patsy and Mark, from her cousins, Rob and Mary, and from others. Everyone wanted to talk about Morgen and the expected Predvest offer, and to persuade her to vote for or against the deal, depending upon that person's view. Fortunately she had no Internet connection or e-mail address, but even the humble telephone reminded her how the world was shrinking, and seemed to bring her previous existence alarmingly close to her remote retreat. She could not refuse to answer the phone, for the school or colleagues or Island friends might need or want to talk to her, but she began to make it clear that she would not speak to anyone about the Morgen-Predvest deal. She simply put the phone down if the matter was raised. The calls became fewer, and then she was left alone, but the unwelcome intrusions into her remote and peaceful new world unsettled her deeply. She could not keep out thoughts of her previous life, no matter how hard she tried.

Lucy was born and spent the early part of her life in and around Platberg. She loved the pretty little country town, set in its bowl below the beautiful mountain, ever changing in the varying light and cloud conditions. She loved the open streets wide enough to turn a wagon drawn by a full team of oxen, the self-important old red-brick public buildings, the spired churches, and the shopping streets with interesting old buildings whose fretwork decorated canopies extended over the sidewalks to provide shade and shelter for pedestrians. It was a good place to grow up, with clear country air, safe places to play, good schools, and the mountain, company farm and beautiful countryside to explore.

Platberg was very dependent on Morgen for its prosperity. Morgen's Milk had a big factory there and was by far the largest employer in the area. Lucy's father, Malcolm, ran the company's milk business when Lucy was young and, as the factory manager (and company director), was one of the most important people in the town. Lucy grew up in an environment where her family had a certain status.

In 1938 "Big Joe" Morgen had started a small milk factory in Platberg, taking in and processing milk both from his own farm, and from the local farmers who until then had not had a ready outlet for their produce. He encouraged them to increase their milk production, helping them with technical advice, and gradually extended the range from which he could receive milk into the factory, which itself was gradually extended. Eventually Joe had opened vast areas to milk production, with some of his milk trucks travelling hundreds of kilometres daily to collect milk from farmers who were now assured of a market for what to them was a cash product as they were paid monthly. In more recent times Morgen's Milk had assisted its farmer-suppliers to install cooling tanks on their farms, which not only helped to preserve the condition of the milk, but enabled the trucks collecting milk churns to be replaced by huge articulated tankers.

Joe had first sent fresh milk to the big city dairies, but had soon established his own dairies and milk distribution infrastructure. Later he began to produce yoghurts. South Africa was a land of variable climate, so milk was a difficult industry of scarcity or plenty. When milk was in oversupply, and he could not afford to turn it away from farmers who would be hurt by that and would then not be there to supply him in times of drought and low production, he turned it into cheese; then, after expanding the factory, also into powdered milk and skim-milk powder. After that Morgen began to make baby foods, based on milk.

Joe was proud of the growth of the company, but also of the good it had done for that part of the country. The development of milk farming provided a valuable food resource, but also led to the creation of farm and factory jobs and the uplifting of people of all races. He employed qualified agricultural experts to advise his farmers, so improving their productivity and profitability and the quality of their produce. Joe established a medical clinic next to the factory, open to all employees and the townsfolk. Later, under Lucy's father, two mobile clinics travelled into more remote parts, providing free medical help and teaching basic healthcare to the simple country people who needed it. Joe always believed that a successful business should be trusted to provide good quality products at fair prices, but also that it should have a kindly face and be of genuine service to its customers and the community. He never underestimated the value of the goodwill so achieved, and Morgen's Milk was held in high esteem. Though profitability in the milk industry could be variable, as the industry went through its cycles, the company had generally done well. In recent years it had moved into other businesses, partly to protect itself from that volatility, but, as the Milk Division of the enlarged Morgen Group, Morgen's Milk was still regarded, not only sentimentally, as an important component of the group.

Lucy could not remember a time in her youth when her life was not in some way connected to the company. Her parents lived in a comfortable home close to the site of the factory, where her father had his office, so he could be quickly available if needed at any time. She remembered her father saying that he could always hear, often subconsciously, the sounds of the factory both from home and in his office. On two or three occasions she remembered that he had awoken at night for no apparent reason, pulled on some clothes and made off to the factory. Even in his sleep he had become aware of some subtle change in the low background sounds, and knew that something was wrong that needed his attention.

Lucy remembered her grandfather and grandmother with affection. She had been a little in awe of her grandfather who was a big man in every way. Known as "Big Joe" in and around the town, he was tall and heavily built and towered over her as a little girl – a giant topped with wavy grey hair, but whose cool grey-blue eyes suddenly warmed as his face wrinkled into a smile for her. Her grandmother Jessica was smiling and kind and loving as all grandmothers should be. She had then a round, motherly figure, and, Lucy remembered, green eyes like her own.

As the company had grown, offices had been opened in Johannesburg near to the centre of commerce, so Joe and Jessica alternated between their home in Johannesburg and Morgen Farm. Lucy loved to spend time on the farm, often sleeping over there. There was so much to see and do. Morgen Koppie was initially a challenge to climb, but even now she remembered conquering it for the first time, and how she had loved to sit up there and enjoy the stillness and the views all around her.

The original farm still held an important place in the affections of the family and the company. It was still a working farm, but had been turned into a model farm, with research and teaching being undertaken under the guidance of the professors at the Agriculture Faculty of the University of KwaZulu Natal in Pietermaritzburg to the south. There were some "cottages" (actually really good family homes) where members of the family could stay if and when they wished, the first of which had been built by Joe and Jessica for their own use when they moved out of the original farmhouse.

Morgen Farm had played a significant part in the marketing of the company, and its milk products in particular. It was a living traditional image which combined with modern research to produce "real country goodness" of high quality. The farm became a stopping-off place for travellers or tourists passing on their way through the mountains between the highveld of the interior and KwaZulu Natal and the coast. They could eat at one of the two restaurants, enjoy a picnic in the shady, colourful gardens, visit the food and company museum in the restored original farmhouse, or, of course, buy the company's and other products in the farm shop.

Lucy had been sorry to leave Platberg when, at the age of eleven, her family had moved to Johannesburg. Her grandfather had gradually been handing over his responsibilities in the company to his sons, Malcolm and William, and Malcolm moved to Johannesburg to take over as CEO at what had by then become the company's head office. Lucy entered a completely different environment, living in a comfortable home in the wealthy northern suburbs, attending an excellent private school, obtaining an arts degree at the University of the Witwatersrand, training to be a teacher and then taking up a teaching post in one of the better Johannesburg high schools.

While Lucy adapted reasonably well to the change, she always remembered that her teenage years also brought great sadness. The death of her grandfather, when she was fifteen, was a big blow, and that sad time was unfortunately extended by her grandmother's death soon afterwards. About that time her mother was found to have cancer, and, despite the best treatment available, and her cheerful and positive disposition, she gradually wasted away and died tragically when Lucy was seventeen. Her father, even more than the children, was devastated with grief.

Malcolm had grown up in the family business and had devoted himself to it. He had always worked long hours and his duties often called him away from home. With the death of his beloved wife Margaret, he threw himself into a frenzy of activity, devoting himself even more intensively and over even longer hours to the company and its business, hoping in that way to occupy his mind and shield himself from his grief. He was hardly ever at home and his children saw even less of him than before. This intensive activity became a habit, and the company became an obsession and his main priority. Lucy always remembered how her father had been called away on business on the morning of her twenty-first birthday party and had not been there to share that important occasion with her. He *had* attended her university graduation ceremony, and had been proud of her, but two years later he had tragically been killed in a car crash on his way home from a company function. Lucy felt his loss as a double blow: not only had she suddenly lost her father in tragic circumstances, but she also felt a deep underlying sadness that she had had so little of him over the years. Her burgeoning resentment towards the company hardened.

9

James Bold's telephone call disturbed Lucy in other ways. They had indeed been close to one another at one time, but her memories were not entirely happy.

Lucy knew that she would not generally be classified as a beauty, but that she could be very pretty and had a good figure. With auburn hair and green eyes, an oval face, quaintly upturned nose, and full lips which curved up enchantingly when she smiled, she knew that she could be very attractive. Of course she had admirers, but some basic insecurity deep within her always made her wonder whether she was courted for herself or for her money. Her family was wealthy, which counted for much in that materialistic society, and, after her father's death, Lucy was wealthy in her own right, having inherited from him a substantial legacy, including a large number of Morgen shares. She had had many friendships with men, and had even briefly experimented sexually, but she had never allowed any of them to develop fully, so her would-be admirers had usually drifted away.

As Lucy approached her mid-twenties, she found that she was attending more and more weddings, as many of her friends, former fellow students and young colleagues were marrying. It seemed to be the thing to do, and Lucy began to feel a subtle social pressure pushing her in the direction of marriage. At about the age of twenty-six, it seemed that those around her were expecting her to marry, and she was often asked when she was going to allow someone to put a ring on her finger. It was about this time that she met James Bold. When contemplating marriage a choice is made from those available at that time – like buying a house, Lucy thought in later years – and James seemed to fit the requirement as well as anyone.

They had met at a mutual friend's wedding. He had asked her to dance, they had danced well together, had enjoyed each other's company, and had agreed to meet again. James was then a young investment banker, not at all wealthy, but well educated and, she later discovered, intensely ambitious. Lucy liked his tall, strong figure, the grey eyes that smiled at her, his confident air, smooth educated voice and urbane manner. Initially at least, Lucy did wonder if he were not a little too smooth, and about the extent to which her wealth contributed to her attractiveness in his eyes, but she liked him well enough. They saw a lot of each other, and even began to discuss the possibilities and practicalities of getting married. Here James was particularly persuasive, and even urgent, but Lucy remained cautious and was prepared to bide her time a little longer before making a final commitment, though she did feel that she was beginning to love him.

Three or four times James suggested that they should go away together, for a few days or at least a weekend, but Lucy declined as she felt that she was not yet ready for the level of intimacy that that implied. On the last such occasion, he had proposed a weekend in the country at a luxury resort in the Magaliesburg area, only a short drive to the west of Johannesburg.

"I don't think we should do that," said Lucy.

"But we're going to be married, aren't we?"

"Perhaps."

"So what difference does it make if we go away together?"

"I don't feel ready for it yet."

"Come. We'll have fun together, and it'll help you make up your mind about getting engaged and setting a wedding date."

"James, I need more time to be quite sure. Please bear with me for just a little longer."

"OK, then let's go for a day. I'll pick you up on Saturday morning."

So they set out on the pleasant drive into the country. Lucy listened to James painting a picture of their future together, where they would live ("a good address is *so* important"), and his ambition to start his own business.

"Have you the money for all that?" she inquired gently.

"No, not immediately, as you know, but you said you wanted to buy a house, and perhaps you'd also like to invest in my new business, until I'm properly established. Then I could pay you back if you wished, but you might like to stay invested in a good business."

It was a beautiful day, calm and sunny, so they sat outside on the immaculate lawn under colourful umbrellas and enjoyed a leisurely lunch. James was especially attentive, and Lucy noticed that he was solicitous about keeping her wine glass topped up. When a slight light-headedness added itself to her relaxed and mellow mood, she let her glass stand full, admiring the lit yellow and golden tones through the sparkling cut crystal.

After lunch they decided to walk a little along one of the short trails in and around the hotel grounds. They held hands, and Lucy felt a warm glow of pleasure and a gentle intimacy with James as they paused to admire the view of surrounding hills and the little town in the valley below. James led them down a steep, stony path into a narrow, shady gorge through which a little river ran. Soon they were alone, taking the path which followed the stream. It was pleasantly cool there, with a feeling of privacy created by the sheer stone walls of the gorge, the dense green canopy of the trees and the rushing, bubbly music of the stream. At places where the path widened they walked side by side, holding hands. Two or three times James put his arm around her and kissed her briefly.

At the end of the gorge it opened a little, and they stood on a platform of flattish brown rock to watch a waterfall plunge down the steep cliff into a clear pool, from which the stream was fed. They took in the beauty of the place, and it seemed natural to put their arms around each other and hold the embrace. Lucy felt James's strong body pressing against hers, noticed the grey eyes and smooth lips close to her face, then closed her eyes as they kissed.

"What a lovely moment to treasure," she thought.

Then suddenly James thrust his tongue into her mouth and began pulling at her clothing, seeking all at once, it seemed, to expose her breasts and pull down her jeans. She tried to pull away, but he held her with one strong arm while the hand of the other clutched at her breasts.

"No!"

"Come on. Make love to me. No one will see us here."

"Leave me alone. Take your hands off me. Someone might come." She managed to free herself, and stood facing him, panting hard. "You frightened me."

"Don't you want to make love to me?"

"Not like this. Not here. What about some tenderness and privacy, at the right time?"

"Well, then, come to the hotel. I have a room. We can make love on a beautiful bed in private."

"You have a room!"

"Oh, yes, I checked in last night. I thought we might need it, even though you didn't want to come for the weekend."

"You planned this. You brought me here for the sole purpose of having sex with me, of getting me into bed."

"I thought it would help you decide to marry me, to be fully committed to me once we had done that."

"You obviously don't know me, James Bold. Let's get out of here, so you can take me home. I don't suppose I'll find a taxi from here."

She made to move past him onto the path, but he stood in her way and held her so tightly that she could not move.

"You will stay here until you promise to make love to me. I love you, and I want you."

"No!"

"Promise. It can't be too difficult. You gave all the signs of loving me. Promise."

Lucy could not move. She thought of her options, clamped in his arms.

"OK, I promise."

"When?"

"James, I don't know. When the time is right. You're hurting me. Let me go, and let's go back home. Please."

He let her go and led the way along the little path.

Lucy remembered a quiet and strained walk back to the car, and a silent drive to Johannesburg. She asked him to drop her off at her gate, and did not invite him in. The next day she phoned him and ended their relationship.

Perhaps James felt one Morgen sister might suit him as well as another. Three months later he married Lucy's younger sister, Patsy.

10

On Friday, 21st September announcements appeared in the main financial newspapers, and were disseminated through news agencies and the stock exchange news service, to the effect that the directors of Morgen Holdings had received formal written notice of the firm intention of Predvest Ltd to make an offer to acquire all the shares of Morgen Holdings. In technical terms, Predvest would propose a scheme of arrangement between Morgen and its shareholders under section 311 of the Companies Act. In essence, Predvest would offer to exchange each Morgen share for one Predvest share. In terms of the applicable legislation formal offer documents would have to be mailed to Morgen shareholders within thirty days, the Morgen board of directors would have to inform shareholders of its views regarding the fairness of the offer, and give them their advice, within fourteen days of the posting of the offer documents. The High Court would be asked to convene a meeting of Morgen shareholders to consider and vote on the offer. If a majority, representing three-fourths of the votes exercisable by shareholders present and voting either in person or by proxy at the meeting, voted in favour of the scheme, it would be approved by the Court and would be binding on all members of the company. If such a majority were not achieved, the scheme would fail, and Predvest would not be allowed to make another offer for Morgen for at least a year thereafter. The offer was now a reality, and its terms were known. The timetable had been set, and the clock was ticking.

After the cautionary notices issued by both companies ten days earlier, there had been some discussion and speculation in the media and amongst investment analysts and portfolio managers. The Morgen share price had risen from 750 to 820 cents in expectation of a possible bid for all or part of the company. However, once the announcement of the terms of the offer had been made, the price jumped to 980 cents, just below the 1000 cents around which Predvest was still trading.

As if a giant boulder had been dropped into a pool, the announcement set off waves of feverish activity, speculation, greed and anxiety. Share traders closely watched the markets in both shares and looked for opportunities. Their buying had of course caused the price of the previously relatively neglected Morgen shares to rise. Would the offer succeed or fail? Would the offer "price" be raised to more than one Predvest per Morgen share? Would the price of Predvest shares rise or fall or hold steady? They sought possible answers to all these questions.

In offices around the country, and especially in the main financial centres, stockbrokers, financial analysts and investment portfolio managers were studying the available information about both companies, trying to obtain more information, assessing the fairness or otherwise of Predvest's offer, and analysing the possible effects the proposed transaction would have on each company and their respective share prices. Should they buy or sell or await developments? How should they advise their clients?

Meanwhile large and expensive teams of commercial lawyers and investment bankers were frantically working to influence them, and to prepare the voluminous documentation, required by law, about the offer and the two companies involved, so shareholders and other interested parties would be in a position, theoretically at least, to make informed decisions. The High Court was petitioned to call the necessary Morgen shareholders' meeting, so the time and place and other details could be sent to shareholders together with the formal offer documentation. The Morgen and Predvest boards each instructed theoretically independent teams of experts to evaluate the terms of the proposed transaction, and to report to them on whether or not they considered the terms to be fair to their shareholders. Teams from both Predvest and Morgen, with their respective advisors, set off on "roadshows", visiting and making presentations to major shareholders of Morgen, trying to persuade them to vote for or against the proposed deal, and trying to elicit from them written undertakings to vote a certain way.

Inevitably, the arguments remained essentially the same, but were repeated again and again, in various ways and with supporting evidence and numbers, to further the case of each side. Predvest argued that Morgen was an old family business, trundling along inefficiently, carrying costs of all kinds which should be removed. Morgen operations would be made far more profitable, and value would also be realised by the sale of some businesses and assets. Morgen shareholders had already seen a substantial increase in their share-price, and would benefit further from the continued growth of the successful Predvest group. On the other hand, Morgen argued that it was already improving the efficiency of its operations, and that it could itself continue to become more profitable without the wholesale loss of jobs, sales of assets and loss of identity which would tear out the soul of the group and effectively destroy it. Moreover, it believed that the current value and long-term potential of the Morgen Group was far greater than implied by the price offered by Predvest, which was trying to pay for Morgen by issuing expensive shares whose price could fall, as had indeed happened in Geoff Loman's previous venture, which had left him with a tarnished reputation.

The story was a big one in the financial media. There was much analysis and comment, and some human interest stories too, as events unfolded. Geoff Loman and Will Morgen were interviewed on television, radio and for the print media, as were prominent analysts and market commentators who knew the companies well.

Inevitably the waves washed over the whole Morgen organization and its contacts, causing much stress, anxiety and fear, particularly about possible losses of jobs and business opportunities, amongst its management, general staff, suppliers, customers, and the communities in which its factories and branches operated.

11

James Bold and Stanley Vane were both heavily involved in the task of procuring undertakings from Morgen shareholders to vote in favour of the Predvest scheme. Inevitably the question of the shares held by Lucy Morgen, and the votes they carried (there was one vote for each share), came up for discussion. Though she had already told James that she did not want to be involved in the matter, they agreed that Stanley, as her former husband, should at least try to persuade her to vote for them, as three per cent of the votes was a relatively large holding.

Lucy put the phone down on him as soon as she realised the purpose of his call, but had, in any event, no desire to talk to him. However Stanley was persistent, and he kept calling and making such a nuisance of himself, that at last she decided to hear him out.

"Lucy, this is a good deal. Patsy and Mary are voting for it, so why not you?"

"I told you I'm not interested."

"Well then, won't you just do it for me – for old time's sake?"

"Stanley, that would be the last reason for me to vote for the deal. Now that I've heard you, please leave me alone."

"We shouldn't need your votes if all goes well, but it was worth a try. But I don't like your attitude, Lucy, so I think you should know that I intend to see this deal through. I'll enjoy making money out of Morgen, and seeing it dismantled."

Lucy put the phone down, shaking. She made herself some coffee – the Island grew some of the best in the world – and sat on her front veranda, looking out across the Island and trying to relax. However, she could not keep the past from her thoughts.

She had met Stanley soon after breaking off her relationship with James. Though wary after that failed encounter, she had naively been attracted to the smaller and darker Stanley, mainly because he seemed so different from James. However, there had been a lull in business at that time, so Stanley, with little to do and in search of a rich wife, had devoted much time to her, and had been very attentive and charming. Then twenty-seven, she had found it easy to persuade herself that she was in love and agreed to marry him.

After an all too brief period of happiness, things began to go wrong. She found that, while Stanley could be charming when he chose to be, he was also ruthless, and increasingly malicious and spiteful. He was intensely ambitious, and he hated the fact that she was far richer than he, and that she was more protective of her wealth than he felt she should be. He was fanatical about having an heir, but she failed him by twice miscarrying. Increasingly he neglected her, often pleading pressure of work. When she discovered that he had a mistress, she decided to leave him, after only four years of marriage.

Exhausted, mentally and emotionally bruised, and disillusioned with a materialistic society that seemed to revolve around the pursuit of wealth, Lucy retreated to her roots. She returned to Platberg to seek peace, and a healing of mind, body and soul. She purchased a pleasant and comfortable house, in a peaceful, tree-lined road, with a beautiful view of the mountain. There she could rest and let the peace and beauty wash over her, refreshing her mind and seeping into the depths of her being. She climbed the mountain, and took long walks in the beautiful countryside to distract herself from the inevitable pain and feelings of failure while her divorce proceedings continued. She went to Morgen Farm, recalling her childhood as she walked there, and again climbed Morgen Koppie and admired the surrounding view. Eventually she felt the need to work, and to help others, so she began to teach English at the local high school.

She was thus happily settled when she began to see Neil.

12

Neil Harrier was four years older than Lucy. He had begun his career in the Morgen organization as a promising young graduate, had risen to be one of its most senior managers and was now an executive director. Lucy had first met him in her late teens and had liked him. She thought him good-looking, with his lean athletic face and figure, pronounced features and full sensuous lips, while the smiling deep blue eyes below his dark eyebrows also suggested kindness. He obviously liked her and they chatted in a friendly way. They met a few times at company functions and at her home, for her father often invited company managers there. Neil had been very sympathetic when Lucy's father died, and he and his young wife, Meg, had invited Lucy to their home for dinner on three or four occasions. Over the following years they had bumped into each other from time to time, even meeting for coffee occasionally. Lucy found that Neil was a sympathetic listener, and she had found comfort in talking to him as her marriage became increasingly unhappy.

For some months after Lucy's move to Platberg she heard nothing from Neil, and indeed thought little, if anything, about him. He was bound up with the past she sought to escape. Then one day he phoned her.

"Lucy, I'm coming to Platberg on business next week. It would be good to see you again. Would you like to have dinner with me?"

"Oh, I don't think that would be a good idea," was Lucy's instinctive response. She was still emotionally bruised, did not feel the need for male company after her failed marriage, and Neil was a married man, she rationalised later.

Neil did not press the matter. They talked briefly and wished each other well. He respected her feelings, and so did not contact her again, despite having to make regular business visits to Platberg. It would be pleasant to have the company of a Lucy, but instead he dined alone, and worked alone in his hotel room, on evenings when he was not involved with the factory management, whose private lives he also respected.

Perhaps eighteen months passed before Neil and Lucy saw each other again, at Morgen Farm as it happened. It was school holidays and Lucy was approaching the entrance to the Coffee Shop, the smaller and more intimate of the two restaurants there, when she saw Neil approaching from the other direction.

"Neil, what are you doing here? How lovely to see you," she said, with a delighted smile.

"I've been in Platberg on business. Just popped in here to say hello and see if all is well. Thought I'd have coffee before getting onto the road. I must be back in Jo'burg this evening. Will you join me?"

They stepped inside and instinctively found a corner table where they could be relatively private. Dark wooden walls, wooden beams across the ceiling and polished wooden tables all combined with curtains and carpets of warm reds and blues to create a feeling of cosy comfort, but with a brightness from polished brass utensils on the wall nearest the kitchen, paintings of local artists hung hopefully for sale on the other walls, and windows looking out onto the attractive sunlit gardens. The seductive smell of coffee was heavy in the air as they sat down.

They ordered coffee and eats, for the baking done on the premises was renowned. They had been greeted with big smiles, and Lucy could not help noticing how pleased the staff were to see Neil. He was obviously well-liked, and not simply a manager from head office to be polite to, or ignored.

"How long have you been here? Why didn't you tell me you would be in town?" Lucy asked as soon as they were alone.

"You told me you didn't want to see me," said Neil, answering the second question first.

"I would never have done that."

"I asked you to dinner, and I distinctly remember you saying that you did not think that was a good idea."

"Oh, I seem to remember something vaguely. I'm sorry, Neil. I must have still been disillusioned and vulnerable after my divorce – and you are, or were, a married man."

"I'm still married. I'll tell Meg I've seen you, but I won't say how wonderful you're looking. She'd be jealous."

"I'm better now. I love it here. I'm making a new life for myself. It's good to see you though – I've always thought of you as a good friend I could talk to, even though we never saw very much of each other. How long have you been here? What do you do when you're not working?"

"I'm usually here for two nights when I need to come to Platberg. Daytime is for work, mainly at the factory of course. I usually spend one evening with Andries, our local manager, and perhaps some of his senior people. The other evening I usually eat alone, and then work in my hotel room. Andries would willingly look after me, but I think he is secretly relieved that he can be off-duty with his family those nights."

There was a pause, and then Neil added: "I have sometimes thought it would be nicer to have dinner with you than on my own. I've often been aware that you were not far from me."

"Neil, please let me know before you come here again. That is if you feel you would like to see me. I'm sure that having dinner together will not hurt your marriage in any way. I wouldn't want to do that, but I would like to see you."

They chatted for a while, catching up on each other's news. Lucy told him how she had become active in some of the projects encouraged by the company and based at Morgen Farm. In her spare time she was teaching English there, as well as basic literacy, mainly to adults who had not had the privilege of a proper education. She was also helping with the organization and financing of a project through which people in the surrounding areas were encouraged and assisted to produce traditional articles and curios for sale in the Farm Shop and elsewhere.

"I came here this morning to do some work for that project," said Lucy, "otherwise we'd have missed each other. But there's also been some bad news. Joseph Dlamini, who has worked here for at least forty years, died yesterday of pneumonia."

"They told me about that. I am really sad to hear it. Joseph was always cheerful, always hard-working, and very loyal to the company," said Neil.

"I saw his niece, Patience, this morning. She is absolutely distraught, not only about Joseph's death, but also about money. Joseph's daughter and son-in-law died of AIDS some time ago, leaving two children Patience has been caring for. Joseph – do you know his wife died? – has been supporting the three of them, and now he is gone. She went off to Platberg earlier this morning to see Terry Walters, your Human Resources Manager, to tell him herself about Joseph, and to see if the company can help her, especially with the children."

"Terry and Andries will know what to do. I hope he nominated his niece, and/or the grandchildren, as his dependents to receive a death benefit from the pension fund."

"I hope so. But Neil, I'm worried that the benefit may not be enough. He'd already worked for many years before his category of employee was able to join a pension fund. Neil, please can you get the company to help?"

"I'll look into the matter when I get back to Jo'burg. The company has a policy of granting ex-gratia benefits out of its profits, in special cases, and where the benefits from the pension funds fall short of certain minimum standards. Terry and the pensions people at head office will know what to do, and what case, if any, should be made to the directors."

"Thank you, Neil. I am so worried about them."

"The company looks after its loyal servants. It does do many good things, Lucy."

A few weeks later Neil again needed to be in Platberg on business. He telephoned Lucy in advance, and this time they agreed to have dinner together. A little after seven o'clock Neil called for her at her home and drove them to Susanna's restaurant, which they both liked. It was situated in a complex on the edge of the town, beside one of the two access points onto and off the main north-south national road, and designed to service both the traveller and local residents. There was a busy and profitable filling station owned by Susanna's husband, Kobus, as well as shops to lure the tourist-traveller, fast food and take-away restaurants, a children's playground next to a large field with ostriches and farm animals, and a good motel with views of the mountain where Neil usually stayed. Susanna had started her restaurant when her children had left home. She loved cooking and catering, and contact with people, and aimed at something more special than the, admittedly good and well patronised, fast food restaurants offered. So Susanna's was patronised by guests at the motel and by locals when looking for something more special than usual.

There was mist on the mountain and a chill in the air, but the carpeted, curtained and softly lit interior of the restaurant was warm and comfortable. Susanna's welcome was cheerful, and they were smilingly shown to a quiet table beside the far wall. Two perfectly formed deep red roses in a glass vase made an accent of colour against the snow-white table cloth. A candle lamp cast a soft intimate light on the table.

"This is nice," said Lucy as they settled themselves comfortably at the table. "Thank you, Neil. It's a long time since I've had dinner alone with a man."

"Would you like some wine?" he asked presently. "Red or white?"

"I'll have red. Men usually like red don't they? I don't mind red."

"I asked you which *you* would like, not what you think 'men' might want. I want you to be happy, and have what you would like."

"Well that's a new experience," said Lucy, "and I appreciate it. Stanley always told me what I should have. He always wanted everything his way."

They settled on a good blanc de noir. They held their glasses up to the candle flame to admire the wine's glowing pink-red colour, and then raised their glasses to each other in a silent toast.

"Thank you for helping Patience and Joseph's two grandchildren," said Lucy as they ate their starters. "She's very relieved."

"Joseph nominated his two grandchildren to receive his death benefit. As the amount was relatively small, because he had only been a member of the pension fund for about half his years of service, it has been supplemented by the company. As the children are young minors, the benefit will be paid monthly to Patience for the benefit of the children until the younger reaches the age of twenty. That's how we usually deal with such cases."

"And we've persuaded Patience to join our home crafts project – so she'll be able to work from home to sell through the Farm Shop."

Their main course was served and the conversation drifted on to other topics. They found much to talk about and were enjoying each other's company. After taking her last mouthful Lucy put her knife and fork together on her plate, sat back and sighed contentedly. She watched Neil as he continued to eat. In the low light his hair and eyebrows were dark, and his eyes a deep blue when he glanced up at her.

"I enjoyed that," she said. "It's nice not to have to cook, but, much more than that, I think I'd forgotten what it's like to enjoy this sort of company: a good friend to be happy and comfortable with, and to able to talk to without complications."

After a pause Lucy asked, "Does Meg know you are with me? What does she feel about it?"

Neil sat back and looked at her. He thought again how lovely she was. Her eyes were a darker green in the subdued light, and the candle flame seemed to rekindle the reds in her auburn hair. She wore a gold chain around her neck, where her skin seemed smooth and creamy. Just a glimpse of cleavage suggested the softness and curves of a shapely bosom.

"I told her we'd be having dinner together tonight. She didn't comment. To be honest I don't think she cares one way or another. She doesn't really care very much for me any more."

Lucy was not sure what to say.

"I'm sorry, Lucy. I shouldn't have said that. It just slipped out. I'm not asking you for sympathy or anything. Perhaps I'll tell you some day. But meanwhile let's just enjoy being together, and sharing each other's company as we've been doing – without complications, as you put it."

They dropped the subject and spoke of other things. They lingered over coffee, so it was quite late when Neil drove Lucy home. He got out and opened the car door for her, then waited at her front door while she unlocked it, to be sure she could enter the house safely before he left her – a big city security habit, he told himself wryly. He did not expect to be invited in. Lucy turned, quickly thanked him and wished him goodnight. She threw her arms around him, hugged him tightly, and was gone almost before he could respond.

So it was that Lucy and Neil began to meet. It became an established pattern that they would have dinner together on one of the nights that Neil was in Platberg. When the summer came and the evenings grew longer, they would meet earlier. Sometimes they would sit and have a drink on the veranda of Lucy's home, chatting idly while watching the changing moods of the mountain. On other occasions they would go for a walk together, through the suburb, or, if there was time, along one of the roads that soon took them into the open countryside.

Following Lucy's lead at the end of their first evening out, they hugged closely but briefly when meeting and parting. One evening, after four or five meetings, Neil was watching Lucy doing something in her kitchen, prior to their going out for dinner. Prompted by the desire to hug her again, he put his arms around her, but was instantly surprised to find her fiercely fighting him off. Startled, he drew himself away, and they went out to the restaurant in a strained silence. As soon as they had sat down Neil apologised.

"Lucy, I'm sorry if I offended you. I just wanted to be close to you again. I promise I will never willingly hurt you or do anything you do not want me to do. I do value our times together, and I don't want to spoil them, or have you feeling you need to be defensive."

"Well at least that's settled," said Lucy. "I acted instinctively. I didn't mean to hurt you, Neil, but I have been hurt before, and you *are* a married man."

They were careful in public, as many of the townsfolk were company employees, but that was not difficult in a platonic relationship. They wondered whether they were not being seen too often at Susanna's, and whether they should not rather eat at Lucy's home. They decided there could be little harm in meeting in public, and that Neil's car parked at Lucy's front gate could even more easily be misconstrued by any who cared to take a mischievous interest. Eventually they decided they did not care, and sometimes ate out, while at other times Lucy reciprocated by cooking for them, which she enjoyed doing.

After dinner they would sit on the couch in Lucy's lounge, often close together, and chat, watch television, or even read to each other snippets they had saved since their previous meeting, while they sipped coffee or a liqueur. On one occasion Neil tried to put his arms around her, but Lucy continued to sit back so he could not. He stroked her gently and tried to kiss her, but she sat demurely, looking straight ahead and with her legs crossed. She took his hands and placed them on his lap.

"I can't respond," she said.

13

The shock waves set off by Predvest's announcement that it would bid for Morgen Holdings continued to find their way into every part of the Morgen organization, washing into every factory, warehouse and office, finding every representative in the field, every place where Morgen did business, every customer and supplier, and every community it served, even creating ripples for Lucy as far away as remote St Helena Island.

At the head of the Morgen organisation, Will, Mark and Rob instituted immediate damage limitation communications (beyond those to shareholders and the financial markets and media), including to staff, suppliers and customers. The offer from Predvest was only an offer, and no more than that. It was unwelcome, and would very likely be rejected by shareholders. Business would continue as usual. However, in the strange way of such things, these well-meant and necessary communications also helped to promote uncertainty, because they were necessary at all, and in some quarters raised questions and provoked fear. The television, radio and print-media news reports and analysts' discussions all added to these uncertainties and fears.

However, it was a private meeting between the Predvest side and the investment team of Gilt Assurance Investment Management (or "GAIM"), a subsidiary, and the investment management arm, of Gilt Assurance, one of the largest life and pension fund institutions in the country, that, ironically, did the most damage. As part of their roadshow to garner votes in favour of the offer, Geoff Loman had gone to the offices of GAIM, accompanied by his main Enduring Bank advisors, James Bold and Stanley Vane. For their policy-holders, Gilt owned shares in Morgen Holdings. The formal prepared presentation seemed to go off well, with Geoff doing all of the talking, as was his wont. However, certain of GAIM's analysts and portfolio managers were rather persistent in their questioning. What about the differences between the cultures of the two groups? Was the price offered not too low, given the value of Morgen's assets and its prospects? How could the merger take place without the destruction of value? What would Predvest actually do to extract value from Morgen, and what estimates of cost savings were they making?

Geoff answered in his customary smooth way, but was somewhat evasive. He could not in fact quantify the expected benefits, but pronounced them to be considerable. He referred to his track record which showed the success of previous deals. He became slightly irritated as the probing questions continued.

"I'm not sure what you can do that Morgen can't do on their own," said Joy September, GAIM's senior industrial analyst. "What *specifically* will you do if you acquire them?"

Stanley, who could be impulsive at times, had been growing more and more irritated. He burst angrily into the conversation:

"Can't you see? We'll fire the staff and keep the businesses, of course. Even some of the businesses must go. The milk division is making next to nothing. Morgan Farm is a pretty toy with no return on investment. Some of their property projects are ludicrous – imagine thinking of a hotel on St Helena Island. Does anyone even know where that is? The pension fund has an enormous surplus: we can liberate that pretty soon. Then they have a whole lot of ex-gratia pensions they pay, and they provide free health services around the country: they do these things because they want to, not because they have to. We can soon put a stop to all unnecessary expenditure."

There was a stunned silence as Stanley paused for breath.

"Hold your horses, Stanley," said Geoff, trying to smooth things over. "We'll have to evaluate everything once we get control of the company."

"But these are some of the things you may do?" asked Joy.

"I suppose so."

"What about loss of good will?"

"That's most difficult to assess, as you well know," responded Geoff smoothly. "I can't be too specific at this point in time. We will need to evaluate things and do our sums, and will then do what we must for the benefit of our shareholders."

The conversation continued, but damage had been done.

Somehow details of the meeting were leaked to Jennifer Rogan. Her report appeared on the front page of the influential *Daily Business* a day or two later:

PREDVEST TO BE RUTHLESS WITH MORGEN

Predvest is likely to take drastic steps to prune expenses and extract value from the Morgen Group should its current bid to acquire control of Morgen Holdings succeed. *Daily Business* has learnt from reliable sources that representatives of Predvest this week told a meeting of interested parties that they would, in line with their usual practice when acquiring 'underperforming' companies, take immediate action to create value for Predvest shareholders, and increase their earnings per share. Such steps are likely to include large-scale retrenchments of staff, the closing down or sale of businesses showing poor profitability, and the sale of 'underproductive' assets. This appears to place at risk the future of the milk division, which has been through a difficult period of drought and low milk intakes in the past two years, as well as the iconic Morgen Farm, which Predvest apparently views as a 'nice-to-have' which generates no real return on investment. Certain projects of Morgen's property division will be reviewed, and assets are likely to be sold. Predvest is also eyeing the surplus in the Morgen Pension Fund, which is believed to be substantial. Sources also say that all expenditure regarded as non-essential will be eliminated, and that this could include the free health services Morgen supplies in some country areas, and certain voluntary or non-contractual pension payments.

When approached for comment, Goeffrey Loman of Predvest would only say that Predvest would carefully evaluate all actions, but would act in the best interests of Predvest shareholders, who would in time also include present holders of Morgen shares once those shares were exchanged as the result of a successful takeover bid.

William Morgen, speaking as Chairman of the company which bears the family name, said that, if true, the possible future actions attributed to Predvest confirmed his personal view that a takeover of Morgen would be detrimental to all its stakeholders. He felt that Morgen shareholders should reject the offer.

In almost no time at all the report and its contents were circulated, and spread by word of mouth, throughout the Morgen organization and the world it inhabited.

14

Lucy and Neil continued to see each other every few weeks. Almost imperceptibly they grew closer and closer to one another. Each found that, when they were not occupied by their work, more and more of their thoughts were of the other. They looked forward eagerly to their next meetings as important events not to be missed. They began to speak to each other on the phone occasionally between meetings. In a subtle way, they gradually began to depend on one another.

Although they did not talk much about it, preferring to concentrate on their own friendship when together, Lucy gathered that Neil's marriage was not happy. After the birth of twin girls when they had been married for less than a year, Neil and Meg had had no more children. It had been a hard time looking after two tiny babies, but they had managed. Though Neil believed he had been a good husband and father, Meg apparently resented the long hours he had to devote to his work. Whether through fatigue or resentment or both, she began to neglect him sexually and in other ways, and bound herself more and more to her children, who became her real priorities in life. Staying mainly for the sake of the children, Neil had more and more to lower his expectations from his marriage. He said he lived a life of compromise, "which means 'lower your standards'", so far as his married life was concerned. Thus Neil and Meg appeared to outsiders to be reasonably well suited to each other, and seemed to manage well enough most of the time. However, Lucy was aware that Neil was not really happy at home. She also knew that the happiness he found with her was gradually filling the void in his life, as indeed the happiness she found in her relationship with Neil was filling the void in hers. Physically she still kept him largely at bay, for Lucy had no wish to be the cause of a break-up of his marriage, no matter that it was an unsatisfactory compromise, and that she herself had reason to be cynical about that institution. However, she did occasionally catch herself longing for him to put his arms around her.

One day at Morgen House, when Neil was working with Andries the Platberg factory manager, Andries asked him, as he was leaving the office on the completion of their business, whether Neil had heard that Lucy was planning to leave Platberg. Neil had not, and found it difficult to believe, but the thought of losing Lucy troubled him and intruded on his thoughts for the rest of the day. On his way home that evening he parked his car in a quiet place and phoned her.

"Lucy, what's this about you leaving Platberg? Andries told me there's a rumour that you're going away. Where will you go? You wouldn't come back here would you?"

"No, I wouldn't, but I don't think I'll be leaving. I've been ill and had a few very bad days at school, when my resistance was low. I didn't phone you, as I knew you were very busy and I didn't want to worry you. There was a big problem, and I did give in my notice, but it's been solved now and I've agreed to stay on."

"Thank goodness for that! I've been worried all day. I honestly don't know what I would do without you, Lucy. It's just so wonderful to know there's a loving friend out there who really cares about me."

However, the thought of losing Lucy took root in Neil's mind and persistently worried away there. It led to other thoughts, which he shared with her two or three days later when next he telephoned her.

"Lucy, the thought of losing you has led me to think a lot about us. I know I'm married and that troubles you. But in a strange way, because you're giving me some of the things I should find in my marriage, but don't, you're helping me to compensate, and making it easier for me to stay married. If I'm down, I think of you, of our times together, and how fond we are of each other. I then feel better, and able to carry on, even if things are not what they should be at home.

"But what if I lost you? I'd remember you still, but the memory wouldn't be complete. That's been all right when I know I'll be seeing you again in a few days or weeks, but not if you went where I couldn't be with you again. I told you long ago I would want to make love to you if the circumstances were right. I do dream of that, and I can play it out in my mind, but only up to a point, because I don't actually know if you really like making love, or would like it with me. We've hugged a little. I've put my arms around you a few times. I remember holding you that cold day in the mist on the mountain, but you were wrapped up – untouchable and tamper proof – in warm clothes and anorak. I know you so well, yet I don't know the *feel* of you. I want to touch you, and hold you, and know the shape of you, and what it feels like to be physically close to you. We haven't even kissed properly – by which I suppose I mean improperly!"

"I do like the physical side of love, Neil. It's just that you're married, and it hasn't seemed right, even if your marriage is not as it should be."

"Please will you think about these things, Lucy?"

The next time they met happened to be on a Sunday morning. Neil had to be in Platberg for a conference at the factory. The conference programme included all of Saturday, and Saturday night, but Neil arranged to spend the Sunday morning with Lucy, before driving home that afternoon. He called for her at her home, fairly early in the morning, and drove her to Morgen Farm, where they had a cosy, relaxed breakfast at the Coffee Shop.

They had decided to go for a walk on the farm after breakfast, and so they set off towards Morgen Koppie, carrying drinks and a picnic lunch in their light rucksacks. To extend their walk, they took a path that wound its way around the farm, before eventually joining up with one that took them up the steep slopes of the little mountain. When their path narrowed, and they could no longer walk beside each other, Neil let Lucy go ahead. As it was a warm, sunny day, Lucy was wearing a short-sleeved T-shirt and, unusually, shorts instead of her customary jeans. Neil was able to admire her shapely figure, the attractive way her hips and bottom moved as she walked, and the creamy smoothness of her bare legs and arms. As if sensing his gaze, Lucy stopped and turned to him. He saw himself reflected in the lenses of her dark glasses below a wide-brimmed sun hat.

"You go ahead," said Lucy.

"I was admiring the view. You look lovely."

Neil put his arms around her. She did not resist, but after a few seconds placed her hands on his arms and took them gently but firmly away from her.

"Not here," she murmured. "Somebody might be able to see us from down there, or someone might come along the path. They could be my pupils or your staff. You take the lead. Then I can watch you for a change."

Neil went ahead and they slowly made their way to the top of the koppie. Arriving somewhat breathless, they took off their rucksacks and dropped them on the ground. Breathing deeply, they admired again the wonderful view. They never tired of it. It was a glorious day, with only a few cotton wool clouds in the sky. The air was clear after recent rain, so it seemed they could see for ever in all directions.

Neil stood behind Lucy, folded his arms around her and pulled her close to him, holding her with a hand cupped around each breast.

"Trying to learn something of the feel of you," he said softly.

"I feel too exposed here," said Lucy. "Let's go down the other side for a bit. I know a place that looks away from the farm buildings and the road. We'll be less likely to be seen there."

With Lucy leading, they went down a little way, and found a place where two flat rocks, close together, made reasonably comfortable seats. There was also some shelter, and a little shade, as a large boulder guarded one side of an overhang of the rock caused by the faster erosion of part of the sandstone cliff.

"Here it is," said Lucy. "I've often sat here in my youth. It's partly sheltered, but still has a lovely view. I'm hungry, so let's eat."

She sat down on one of the flat rocks and started to lay out their picnic lunch. Neil looked out across the golden, rocky-crowned koppies to the high mountains of the Drakensberg far to the south. It was a beautiful place. He sat on the rock beside Lucy's. They had brought fruit juice, crusty bread rolls, and what they called good "hiking food" – dried fruit, nuts, biscuits and chocolate. They ate well, relaxing, enjoying the view and chatting, but all the while intensely aware of each other's physical presence.

Still sitting, Neil began to touch and stroke Lucy, gently and tentatively at first, then more confidently and adventurously as she made no move to stop him. He leant forward and kissed her gently on the lips. Holding the kiss, he put his hands under her T-shirt and stroked her back and midriff. Gradually he worked his hands into her bra to hold first one and then both breasts. They were wonderfully shaped, smooth and soft and heavy all at the same time. He began to stroke her thigh, a little at first, then moving higher and higher along her leg, appreciating her smooth shapeliness. She thought he would make a wonderful lover.

"I think you've just about reached your limit now," she said at last.

They stood up and held each other closely, kissing intimately and passionately for the first time. They grew still, but continued to hold each other.

"Can you hear the silence?" Lucy asked. "I always love the special stillness of the mountains, when you are far above the sounds of the streams."

"I can hear it, but also the beating of your heart."

Reluctantly they made their way down the mountainside. They spoke of each other and their wonderful closeness. Neil had begun to know the feel of the Lucy he loved. Lucy had had a moment of revelation.

"You really do love me, Neil, don't you? And I think you must be a beautiful lover. Suddenly I know I love you too. I probably have for a long time, but have not admitted it, even to myself. We've avoided the truth by using words like 'being fond of one another', and 'loving friendship', but I know now we have something much, much deeper."

Without expressing it in words, Lucy and Neil both knew that they would make love the next time they were together. It was quite late by the time Neil finished his work, so there was little chance of a walk before dinner. He returned to his hotel, showered and changed into more casual clothes, and then drove the short distance to Lucy's home. She had invited him to dinner.

Lucy had also had a busy day's work, and had in addition spent most of the late afternoon preparing dinner, but he found her relaxed, welcoming, fragrant and beautiful. She poured each of them a drink and they sat on the veranda watching the last light fading from the mountain. As darkness quietly enfolded them, a slight chill in the air sent them to the warmth and soft light inside. The dinner table was beautifully set, with two tall candles in elegant silver holders, and crystal glasses from which they sipped excellent Cape wine which glowed a deep red against the candlelight. In the soft light it seemed to Neil that Lucy's eyes caught and held a deeper green from her silky, emerald-coloured blouse, and a sparkle from her diamond and emerald ear-rings. Her eyes shone as she spoke animatedly, sometimes looking intently into the deep blue of his, trying to plumb the depth of his thoughts and feelings.

After the main course, Neil helped Lucy carry the dishes to the kitchen. They put them down, and then Lucy turned to him, put her arms around him, and said softly: "I have some dessert for you if you want it now, but it'll keep. Perhaps you would like to sit in the lounge instead, or go to the bedroom?"

"I first need to go to the bathroom for a moment."

"You use this one. I'll use the other. I'll see you in the bedroom," said Lucy.

Neill expected Lucy to be nervous and shy, so he thought he would find her in bed covered to the neck. However, when he opened the bathroom door, she was waiting for him at the end of the passage. She took his hand and led him into her bedroom, which was softly illuminated by two candles on the dressing table. They stopped in the space between the door and the bed and hugged. Lucy again surprised him:

"You take off something, then I will. We'll go turn and turn about. Take off your shoes."

"I'll be undressed before you. I'm sure I'm wearing fewer items than you," said Neil as he obeyed.

So they played an undressing game, and without any of the embarrassment Neil had feared. Those beautiful breasts he had felt on the mountain were a marvel when fully displayed, as indeed was the whole of her as she slowly revealed herself to him.

"You're well endowed," Lucy said.

"You're a miracle," said Neil. "Turn around slowly so I can appreciate all of you", which she did calmly and without embarrassment.

So they learnt about each other's bodies: feasting their long-starved eyes; being oh so close together; touching, stroking, kissing, exploring with hands and lips and tongues; stimulating, rousing to passion, calming and caressing.

"You *are* a beautiful lover, Neil. I thought you would be."

"You are a miracle," he repeated. "Not only of beauty, but the way you are comfortable with your body, and in making love."

"And now do you know the feel of me?" she asked mischievously as she snuggled even closer to him.

Lucy remembered that time as possibly the happiest of her life. She and Neil were lovers for nearly two years after that memorable evening. Neil's car was often parked outside her house, and if tongues wagged they did not care.

"Sex with you is so lovely," she told him once. "You make me feel so good. And you're caring and patient and understanding. Stanley was always peremptory and demanding. Once he'd had his way, he left me to my own devices. It was demeaning in a way, as though I was just a thing to satisfy him."

She also told him about her contact with James Bold. "He only wanted my money, and so did Stanley really. I've never known whether men have been more interested in me or my money. But I don't feel that with you, Neil. You don't want to leave your wife to marry me, and I understand that you have to worry about your children, but you do show you value and care for *me* as a person. I do love you."

They enjoyed their times together, and began to speak to each other on the phone almost every day in between. They found more and more ingenious ways to be with each other more often. Neil sometimes arranged his work so he could be away from home over weekends. Then they would drive down the Oliviershoek mountain pass into Kwa-Zulu Natal and stay at one of the beautiful hotels in or near the Drakensberg Mountains.

Lucy particularly remembered their first weekend away. They stayed at the Champagne Castle Hotel, in a valley close to the high mountains. They arrived at twilight, put their luggage in their room and sat on the terrace in front of the lounge, sipping their drinks, absorbing the peace and beauty, and watching the coming of evening. They walked across the grassy terraces in front of the hotel to a rustic wooden railing at the edge of the mown lawn. There was a meadow with grazing horses in front of them, with darkling trout dams beyond. All around them the mountains rose to great heights, holding them securely in this sheltered valley, but also inspiring awe and wonder at their great size and beauty.

The names of the mountains tripped off Neil's tongue: Champagne Castle glimpsed as a right angle on the main escarpment; the ridge formed by the burly Cathkin Peak, the twin peaks of Sterkhorn, then Turret, Amplett and so down to Hlatikulu Nek. Behind it was a further ridge, but its Dragon's Back fused to seem part of the nearer one as the whole darkened to a glorious silhouette against the last lingering light of the twilight sky.

Neil stood behind Lucy with his arms around her, not needing to pull her close as she pressed herself against him.

"I've always dreamed of being here, holding – close like this – someone who really loved me, as we watched all of this: then to celebrate both love and beauty by taking her into my warm room and making love."

"Let's go to dinner first, and then we can do that," she said.

The next day dawned sunny and clear. The mountain silhouettes of the evening before had acquired depths and colour, and in every direction the soaring mountains drew their eyes skywards. Before breakfast they strolled down to the nearest trout dam, and saw a fringe of forest and an upside-down mirror image of the highest mountains in the still water. After breakfast they put on their day packs and went on one of Neil's favourite walks. Lucy remembered a steep climb up the ridge behind the hotel, the path winding its way at times in the open and at times through damp, shady patches of indigenous forest with ferns and yellow-wood trees; a stop on top looking down on the hotel; then walking along the broad grassy ridge towards the high mountains. They stopped at a point where the path began to descend onto a broad plateau which stretched out before them for two or three kilometres to the base of Cathkin Peak, rising more than a thousand metres from the grassy plain. The high mountains of the main escarpment swept away to the left, and the mountains of the Cathkin Peak ridge and those beyond curved away to the right. They found places to sit a little away from the path, and marvelled at the splendour of it all.

"This is one of my favourite places," said Neil. "It's wonderful to share it with you."

There were some baboons barking on the ridge rising to the left; over to the right were a family of grey rhebok, alert, running short distances with rocking-horse motion, then stopping to look at them again; in the air they saw jackal buzzards and what they thought was a lone black eagle. When Lucy closed her eyes and kept very quiet she could feel the stillness of the mountains that she loved so much.

As they had time, they descended onto the plateau and walked to Blind Man's Corner where the main Contour Path ran along the foot of the high mountains. There they turned back, returning across the plateau and descending by another path past streams and waterfalls, lichen-stained sandstone cliffs, areas of protea tree savannah, the large rocky feature named the Sphinx, and natural and planted forest, to reach their hotel tired, exhilarated and very much in love.

These experiences were wonderful, and Lucy and Neil loved sharing them and spending time together. However, the deeper their love, the more they shared and the more they came to depend on each other, the more it hurt when they had to part. Lucy particularly felt the wrench of parting, and Neil began to worry that he was hurting her by keeping so close. They discussed the matter, and decided that the positives they drew from their relationship outweighed the hurt, but Lucy continued to be miserable for a few days after each parting.

"Why don't you leave her?" she asked. "Why do you stay with Meg if she doesn't love you, and basically only tolerates you?"

"I promised to stay when I married her," Neil replied. "I know I'm not being faithful to her by seeing you, but it somehow seems wrong to leave after all these years. Perhaps if we had no children it might be different, but I need to stay to give them a stable home."

One night at Lucy's home they were lying in bed lazily talking after making love, when Neil mentioned he would be going away for Christmas, still some months away.

"I have to be in London on Company business, so I'll stay on for a few days with Meg, and we'll come back early in January."

"And do you know where *I* will be and what *I'll* be doing?" said Lucy, in a strangled voice, sitting bolt upright and pulling the bed clothes with her. "I'll be here on my own, probably having Christmas dinner all alone. Oh, Neil, it's too much! I don't think I can continue to live like that. You really must decide whether you want to stay married to Meg, or whether you want to be mine."

They discussed matters at length, and eventually parted unhappily, with both of them agreeing to review their situation. They both had a few very unhappy days, and some further discussions.

"Lucy, I *am* sorry. I simply can't make myself leave home in the current circumstances. Can't we continue as we have been?"

"I'm sorry, Neil. It's simply hurting too much. I understand about your children, but you could still arrange to see them. If you truly loved me enough you would come to me and be mine. I can no longer keep hurting like this. I'm afraid that I cannot let you see me any more," she ended with a breaking voice.

Lucy could also not bear to live in a town where she knew Neil would often be. She decided in her deep depression to leave, this time to go as far away from her previous life as possible, and start all over again.

A few months later she was on St Helena Island.

15

Susie Mack recognised Geoff Loman's voice as soon as he spoke.

"Susie, why are you selling our shares?"

"Hell-oo Geoffie. Lovely to hear your voice. How are you, my dear?"

Susie was Senior Dealer at Bullion Asset Management Limited, often shortened to BAM, a subsidiary and the investment arm of Bullion Insurance Holdings, whose marketing punchline was "Whatever we touch turns to gold". The busy dealing room was situated high up in the gold and brown BIH Building in Sandton. Susie's desk was at the end of a row of dealers, all seated in front of computer screens, following every minute change in the endlessly moving financial markets, placing trades, and receiving and giving instructions and information by telephone. From her position near the large plate-glass window Susie could look out onto the cluster of modern high-rise buildings of the Sandton business district. She could see the domed top of the glass and concrete Predvest Building, from where Geoff was presumably calling her.

"I'm fine, Susie, but I want to know why you're selling our shares."

"Client orders, I'm afraid. They think Predvest's expensive and want us to take some profit."

"Can't you keep them off the market? Absorb them yourselves in other portfolios?"

"I need orders for that."

"That analyst of yours – Ted – he should talk to your clients and tell them Predvest is still good value. I can't have sellers coming onto the market and pushing down the price of Predvest with this Morgen deal on the go. The lower our share price the lower the price Morgen shareholders will see they're being offered. I need your help."

"Perhaps you should talk to David and Harry."

"I'll set up a meeting. Will you put me through to David?"

"I'm doing that. Bye, my darling" – the last in the baby voice she sometimes affected, with telling results on susceptible males.

David Goldberg was BAM's Managing Director, and Harry Naidoo its Head of Trading and Susie's direct boss. BAM managed the investments of the life insurance company and all the other entities in the Bullion group, as well as numerous portfolios for other clients. Geoff Loman was a major client, for BAM managed all the investments of the large and growing Predvest Retirement Fund, as well as several other family and business portfolios for him.

Susie had joined the staff of BAM three or four years previously, and had rapidly established herself as a competent dealer. She carefully cultivated the goodwill of her superiors, and got on reasonably well with her fellow dealers and the various portfolio managers who placed orders to buy and sell investments with the dealers in the dealing room. Susie was in charge of dealing in equities. Orders were placed on the Johannesburg stock exchange through broker-members of the exchange, and Susie had built up a network of relationships with brokers' staff.

Susie was physically very attractive, of medium height and voluptuous proportions. She had dark hair and deep brown eyes, contrasting fair skin, a round face and full lips. She had emerged from a modest background and was determined to make her way in the world. If her sexual attractiveness could help her, she was quite prepared to use it. She played up to those she felt could be of use to her.

About a year previously Susie had been the guest of Predvest at a conference-cum-entertainment weekend they had organised for some of their business contacts. She had kept as close as possible to Geoff Loman, subtly exuding sweetness and delight, and by dress, movement and manner suggesting her charms and their possible availability to him. On the second night he had come to her room, and they had made love. Though generally content with his small, slim wife Rachael, Geoff was not averse to some variety in his life. He continued to see Susie discretely from time to time, and bought her presents, sometimes suggested by Susie herself. In business he sometimes found her useful, and contacted her directly when he needed information about the stock market, or wanted certain jobs to be done. Her superiors at BAM were happy, so long as their important client was looked after and brought them business.

They had more misgivings about some of Susie's relationships with the stockbrokers they dealt with. Brokers were paid for their services, including for research provided by them, by the commissions they made for each trade they transacted. The proportion of business to be allocated to each broker was carefully allocated by BAM at the beginning of each year in accordance with the assessed value of each broker's services to the company, and business was placed with each broker largely according to that allocation during the course of the year. However, Susie often gave the impression that she had more power to allocate business to brokers than was the case in reality. That meant she was able to have many brokers dancing attendance on her, and paying her special attention in order to secure a greater share of BAM's business.

"I'm a bit concerned about Susie again," Head of Trading Harry Naidoo confided to Managing Director David Goldberg. "Mike O'Reilly invited me to lunch at LDT Broking yesterday. We had a good chat. Obviously they want more business from us if possible, but he also asked me what part Susie played in that. He was a bit embarrassed to ask, but it seems that she's given one or two of their young dealers the impression that she plays the major role. If they look after her, they'll get business – that kind of thing. We've had it before as you know. Of course I reassured him and explained how we do things, but I'm not sure what to do, if anything, about Susie."

"I'd say, leave it alone, so long as she's not a major embarrassment. Her relationships can be useful, and, on the other side, she does bring in business."

Shortly after Susie's arrival at BAM, the married David had, unwisely in retrospect, allowed himself to succumb to her charms. He had enjoyed the experience, but now had no wish to ruffle her feathers and risk exposure by confronting her, unless it became really essential to do so.

A day or two later Geoff and Adrian Loman went to meet David and Harry at the BAM offices.

"Why are you selling our shares? You should be buying them," said Geoff once the opening pleasantries were over.

"Clients' orders, I'm afraid, Geoff," responded David.

"Surely you can persuade them Predvest is good value and they should hold on to them? Otherwise, can't you put them into other portfolios instead of selling them on the market?"

"That's a sensitive issue," said Harry. "Some of our portfolio managers object to being told to take certain shares into their portfolios – after all they're responsible for the investment performance they achieve."

"I'd have thought Predvest would enhance investment performance. Listen," continued Geoff, "I can't afford to let the Predvest share price slide in the current situation. I may need help to support it. I need a strong buyer, or buyers, in the market."

"We're not allowed to manipulate share prices, Geoff," David reminded him.

"I know that. But you *can* buy our shares. Do it discretely, if you must. Buy them with your shareholders' funds if necessary, as a strategic investment. That'll strengthen our partnership. We could become your industrial arm."

"I'm not sure the group's thinking about an industrial arm," responded David mildly.

"Then think about it. Please understand that I give you a lot of business, including the Predvest Retirement Fund. Many others out there would love to have that business. And there'll be more behind it, much more. I know you've been pitching to manage the Morgen Pension Fund. If we win, you'll get it, one way or another. But I need your support."

"Leave it with me, Geoff," said David. "We'll have to see what we can do."

16

Paul Lowe had invited Susie Mack to lunch at the stockbroking firm of Rosenberg and Levine on Tuesday, 2nd October. Paul had fairly recently joined that medium-sized firm, which had done only small amounts of business with Bullion Asset Management in the past. He had had some previous dealings with Susie and BAM, and was naturally eager to use those contacts to bring in increased business to his new firm, especially as he discovered that trading volumes were down and such business was sorely needed. David Goldberg and Harry Naidoo had also been invited, but had declined the invitations, leaving Susie to go on her own.

Rosenberg and Levine had their offices high up in one of the taller Sandton buildings, a short walk from Bullion's offices. From the wood-panelled entertaining room, with a carved wooden bar counter along one wall, a round dining table and some comfortable chairs, there was a pleasant view over the Sandton business district southwards to the cluster of Johannesburg sky-scrapers in the distance. The room was made interesting by memorabilia of the past, including photographs of old Johannesburg and its earliest goldmines. There were also framed share certificates of businesses long since dead, each no doubt representing someone's long past dream of wealth.

Senior partners Hymie Rosenberg and Solly Levine joined Paul and Susie for lunch. The conversation ranged widely, included recent political and economic developments, the share markets and, inevitably, the recent decline in trading volumes experienced by some firms.

"Susie, it's ridiculous that we don't do more business with BAM," said Solly at one point. "What do you want us to do in order to increase that business?"

"I'm sure I can do something to help you," Susie responded. "Shall I stay in touch with Paul, so we can see what happens? I've a feeling something may come up soon."

Susie was sometimes a little silly, and even rather noisy, after two or three glasses of wine at a business lunch, but this was mostly ignored by her colleagues in the busy dealing room at BAM. Later that afternoon, Harry was passing Susie's desk and could not help overhearing her speaking, in her little girl voice, on the telephone: "Sweetie that was a lovely lunch. Thank you very much. What about a little drink at Charging Bulls tomorrow evening after the market closes? Good, I'll see you there." Then, in a more normal, business-like voice, "I've a small order for you...."

"No, leave it alone, as advised," thought Harry as he moved on to more pressing matters.

Charging Bulls was a pub and restaurant situated close to the JSE Securities Exchange and frequented by many traders, financial analysts and portfolio managers working in the investment world. On one wall was an enormous mural depicting a giant bull charging a fleeing bear: investors always preferred bull markets, when prices rose, to bear markets which saw them fall. Susie arrived at the door just in time to see the tall muscular figure and blond hair of Paul Lowe coming along the pavement from the opposite direction. His bright blue eyes and wide mouth smiled attractively at her in greeting from above his regulation dark business suit, neat collar and bold tie. They found a place to sit and ordered drinks, but were soon joined by others and a noisy party developed. However, Susie made sure she kept Paul's attention. She occasionally gazed flatteringly into his eyes, compelling his awareness of the deep brown depths of her own, and she frequently leaned forward to show off curves and cleavage and the promises suggested by her shapely full breasts. Later she sat with her thigh pressed against his. As people began to drift away, Susie invited Paul to her home for supper, which she said she had already prepared. He demurred, but she became insistent, so he telephoned his wife to say that he was being detained by work and would only be home much later.

Susie lived in a comfortable modern house in a walled residential complex not far away. Their two cars passed through the security at the large gates into the development, and Paul parked outside Susie's front door while she put her car into its garage for the night. She asked Paul to open a bottle of wine while she dished up the meal which had been cooking slowly all day and was delicious. Her home was comfortably and tastefully furnished. After dinner she showed him around. The main wall in the entrance hall was almost bare.

"This space is reserved for a beautiful wooden dresser. I've been looking for a long time, and now I've seen just what I want at Willoughby's. It would make a lovely special feature, for everyone to see when coming into the house. See, here it is, in this brochure. It's the one I've marked. I've checked and they do have it in stock." Then, in the little girl voice: "It would be *so* nice to have it soon."

They passed on to her bedroom. She placed her arms around him and hugged. "You're so sweet, my darling," she said, again in her little girl voice. "I just know we'll be able to work together."

Susie gazed into his eyes, again making him aware of the deep dark pools of hers. She kept her body close to his so he could feel her voluptuous curves all the way down. She could be irresistible when she chose, but Paul was in no mood to resist. They soon found themselves on her bed with no clothes on.

Susie's voice became deep and sensual: "Ooh, that's nice. You're so big and strong, my dear. Let me ride you."

17

Early one dank October evening Lucy was cosy in her Island home. It had been cloudy for most of the day, and the wind and rain had come in squalls. Lucy had been glad to reach the shelter of her home after work and some necessary shopping. The rain spattered noisily on her roof, but it was warm and dry and comfortable inside. She was just finishing her supper when the telephone rang.

"Hello, Lucy. How are you?"

"Neil. This is unexpected." His voice was as familiar as ever. However, since she had been on the Island, they had hardly spoken to one another other than when he had telephoned her briefly at Christmas and on her birthdays. Lucy continued:

"It's good to hear your voice on a cold wet evening, but I hope you're not phoning about Morgen and Predvest. I've told everyone I don't want to be involved."

"No, Lucy, this is not about that. It would be nice to have your votes, but I think the whole thing will soon blow over. I can't see Geoff getting enough votes to carry it through. No, this is more personal. I have two pieces of news I want to tell you."

"Tell me."

"The first is that I'm in the process of divorce. I have left Meg and she is suing me for divorce. I know it's three or four years too late, but I wanted you to know."

"I thought you never would leave her. I'm sorry for you, Neil. Are you all right?"

"Yes, I am. But it's been quite difficult packing up my old life to make a new start. You know better than anyone that I really tried to make my marriage last. However, a time eventually comes when one must count the cost of doing what is supposed to be one's duty. Losing you was a big part of that cost. I've done a lot of thinking. People change, and it's been sad for me to realise that the woman I was living with is now no longer the woman I married, let alone the one I thought I was marrying nineteen years ago. Meg hasn't wanted to make love to me for a long time, but she's been seeing someone else for the past few months, so that made the decision easier – and also the fact that the twins are now eighteen and have left school. I think you know they're away in Europe, taking a gap year. Oh Lucy, I wish I'd allowed you to persuade me to leave her, when I hurt you so much all that time ago, but I simply couldn't bring myself to do it then."

"I know that, Neil. Also that it hurt you as well as me. I really do wish you well, and hope you'll find happiness again soon. At least you still have your work to do, with good people around you."

"Thank you, Lucy. I'm going to be taking leave soon, to give myself a really good holiday – which brings me to my second piece of news. I'm coming to St Helena. I've booked to leave Cape Town on the fourth of November, and should reach the Island on Sunday the eleventh. I hope you'll let me see you."

"Oh dear! Is this wise? It's a small island, so I don't know how I could avoid seeing you. In some ways it would be nice to meet again, but I came here to get over you, and to recover from the pain. I'm settled now, and feeling good again with a new life in a new environment. I don't want to open old wounds, and I certainly can't see myself ever leaving St Helena. Your life and work are far away in South Africa. Our trying to get together again will simply not work."

"I understand, Lucy, and I promise I'll respect that. However, I would love to see you again, just as a friend, if you'll let me. The holiday will do me good – two quiet weeks at sea and a week on the Island. Perhaps you could show me places you like. We could go for a walk and you could have dinner with me. Please think about it. I won't be a nuisance, and I don't expect anything permanent, though I hope we can still be friends."

18

After hearing Neil speaking of packing up his old life to make a new start, Lucy's thoughts were inevitably drawn back to Platberg. She had wonderful memories of her times with Neil and would always treasure them. For a brief moment the news of his being free from his marriage had made her heart jump, and had sparked the idea of returning to him, but immediately she knew, as she had told him, that that was now something she could not seriously consider. Her memories of Neil related to a wonderful period of her life, which, she believed, could not have continued without ever-deepening hurt to herself, and so was over. She kept those memories to be cherished, but would not now allow them to trigger painful regrets, or to form a platform on which to build fruitless hopes. She had packed up that life, moved on, and was now happily settled on the Island. She had twice run away – to Platberg, and then to St Helena. The second time she had fled to one of the remotest of places, and she did not want to risk a necessity to move on again. Running away sounded negative and cowardly, but was it wrong or silly to move away from pain or sadness? Also, it had taken courage to accept the need for change and to translate that into, what became for her, positive action.

In truth Lucy's memories of her transition from Platberg to the Island were mixed, sometimes clear and sometimes vague. It had begun with deep hurt and great unhappiness. She had not tried to contact Neil once she had made up her mind to end their relationship. However, he had tried several times to persuade her to change her mind. She would have done so if he had been prepared to leave Meg, but he had not then been able to bring himself to do that, so sadly Lucy had continued with her preparations to move on.

Perhaps there had been some talk in the little town when Neil's car was no longer parked outside her house at night, and when they were no longer seen together at Susanna's restaurant, where Neil now dined alone. Lucy put her house up for sale, resigned her teaching post, and prepared to give up her adult education class and her part in the home crafts project based at Morgen's Farm. She was moved by the regrets at her leaving expressed by her school colleagues, many of her pupils and her adult students. Some of the home crafts participants were also very upset about her imminent departure, none more so than Patience Dlamini:

"Oh what will we do without you, Mrs Lucy? Who will we be able to talk to, and who will look after us?" she cried, tears in her eyes.

"You'll do very well, Patience," Lucy replied. "I'll miss you. I'll miss you all, but I know Morgen will look after you and help keep the project going."

As it happened, Lucy did not spend Christmas on her own. After finishing what she needed to do in Platberg, she drove to Johannesburg, stayed with her brother Mark and his wife Melody for a few days, enjoying Christmas with them and making farewell visits to her sister, cousins and friends. She also took care to brief, and leave her affairs in South Africa in the hands of, Abe Levy, the avuncular attorney who, like his father before him, had represented the Company and many members of the Morgen family for years.

After Christmas Lucy flew to Cape Town, stayed there for a day or two, and then boarded the RMS *St Helena*, bound for St Helena Island. They departed in the late afternoon of a beautiful summer day. The sky was cloudless and the sea calm as Lucy stood on deck and watched, with a mixture of regret and hope, the splendid view of Table Mountain and its range gradually diminishing as the ship churned her way past Robben Island, low and undistinguished but redolent with history, and made for the open sea.

The voyage was a direct one to the Island, so they were out of sight of land for four days and five nights. The weather was wonderful, with blue skies and calm seas every day, and to

Lucy that seemed a good omen. So too was the south-east trade wind which blew in friendly fashion from behind to help speed them in the direction they wished to go. At first Lucy kept mainly to herself, reading, letting her thoughts wander, or simply resting in her comfortable cabin, in the day-time calm of the main lounge, or in a quiet, sheltered corner on one of the decks. She also spent long periods watching the ship pushing her foaming way through the deep blue sea during day-time, and the dark or moon-touched waves at night. The ship moved with a relentless purpose, which promoted positive feelings. The long journey out of sight of land was both a symbolic and a physical manifestation of change occurring. Soon Lucy found that she preferred to watch the bows cutting their way forward, rather than the churning wake they were leaving behind.

Gradually Lucy came to know many of her fellow passengers, and, in so doing, almost unconsciously began to pick up the threads of her new life. Many passengers were Saint Helenians, or "Saints" as they often called themselves, returning to the Island after the Christmas holidays, or going to visit family and friends there. They tended to gather in the informal Sun Lounge, just forward of the open Sun Deck at the stern of the ship, and were very friendly. Lucy began to talk with them and get to know them. She had of course tried to learn as much as possible about the Island before deciding to go there, but they could give her first-hand knowledge of what would be her new home. They were interested in the fact that she had been contracted to teach English to senior classes at the Prince Andrew School.

The other passengers seemed to be a mixture of British, South African and a few French and other nationals seeking to enjoy an unusual holiday adventure, with the sea voyage on a relatively small ship in the tradition of the old Union Castle Royal Mail service; with a beautiful island and unique species of bird, plant and other life; and with a redolence of five centuries of human history, including the exile and death of Napoleon Bonaparte, which made it a place of special interest, and even of pilgrimage, to the French.

In the elegant dining room Lucy was placed at the ship's doctor's table, and became very glad of that. He was a lean and fit elderly Scot with greying hair and erect carriage. He was semi-retired from private medical practice, and each year contracted to be medical officer for a few voyages because of his great love of the sea. Lucy thought him the perfect gentleman, friendly, civilised, erudite, well-spoken, and with an always interesting range of conversation. Perhaps he sensed her initial mood of strain and unease, for he gently drew her into conversation and into some of the activities aboard ship, so helping her to emerge from within herself. He was also very fond of, and knowledgeable about, the Island, and so through him she gained further insights into her future home.

One of Lucy's companions at the doctor's table was a cheerful, round-faced, young Englishman with fair skin, curly blond hair and blue eyes. His name was Colin Brown, and he was returning to the Island after a short holiday in and around Cape Town. Lucy was delighted when she discovered that he had been teaching English at Prince Andrew School for the past year or more, so they would be professional colleagues. It would be good to know someone at the School before she arrived there. She would feel less strange. He was able to tell her about the School and, of course, the Island. Gradually they chatted, spent some time together, and became friends.

Their third night at sea was New Year's Eve. Lucy felt that the symbolism of casting off the old and bringing in the new was of special relevance to her, particularly as it marked approximately the halfway point on their long voyage. The evening was marked by a special festive dinner, followed by a dance in the main lounge. Lucy had not particularly noticed that there was a Christmas tree tied to the railing on the Sun Deck, and that the public rooms and spaces on the ship were decorated for Christmas and the festive season. They would be so, as tradition demanded, until 6th January, twelfth night. At dinner she found herself liking the decorations and festive atmosphere in the dining room. The doctor and Colin persuaded her to go to the dance, and, a little to her surprise, she enjoyed herself. As midnight neared she looked around the room for the doctor, but could not see him.

Lucy knew that the ending of a watch aboard ship was signalled by the ringing of "eight bells", but she now discovered that "sixteen bells" were struck at the midnight which brought in a new year. A ship's bell had been placed in the lounge. The doctor, barely recognizable in the stooping figure of an old man, all shrouded in white and carrying a scythe, appeared and rang the bell eight times to signal the end of the watch and the old year. Then a beautiful young lady member of the ship's crew, with a sash on which was sewn the number of the coming year, stepped forward and rang the bell a further eight times to signal the beginning of the New Year. *Auld Lang Syne* was sung, and people wished one another future happiness. When the dance music restarted, Colin took Lucy in his arms and they danced together for a long while. He hugged her when the music paused and Lucy said she needed to rest. Later, they stood quietly together on deck, watching the movement of the ship through the water, and looking at the moon and stars above them.

"I've had a lovely evening, Colin," said Lucy softly. "Thank you for that. I feel hopeful now about my future. But please be careful. I've been badly hurt and am going into exile in a sense to escape from that. I don't want to hurt you."

19

"This place is like a madhouse," said Andries, shortly after Neil entered his office at the Morgen Milk factory in Platberg. It was the first week in October, and just after the publication of Jennifer Rogan's "Predvest to be ruthless with Morgen" article in *Daily Business*.

"I can well believe it, Andries," said Neil. He had travelled from Johannesburg late the day before, and had breakfasted at Susanna's. "Even Susanna was onto me this morning about the bid. She's worried about her business if the factory closes down. Platberg could become a ghost town. Her husband's service station will still have passing motorists coming off the national road, but the business we give him to service our vehicles would suffer. Even the waiters and waitresses wanted to know whether they need to worry about their jobs."

"What did you tell them?"

"That I think it'll soon blow over, and they shouldn't worry. Honestly, Andries, I can't see Predvest finding enough votes to win this thing. But what else can we say? We have to say it's 'business as usual'."

"Well, you'll have to sound convincing. I've set up a whole series of meetings for you, along the lines we discussed: factory management first, then the other staff in groups so we don't have to shut down the factory. I thought we could have a quick lunch at Morgen Farm. Then this afternoon we meet the Mayor, and later the local Chamber of Business. It looks like a heavy day."

So it turned out to be.

The Mayor, local business people, and the townsfolk in general, were all concerned about serious damage to the local economy if the factory closed down, or even if there were wholesale retrenchments. Jennifer Rogan's article, in particular, had caused initial concerns to become great anxiety, and Neil was surprised how widely and how fast it had been spread, and its contents further disseminated by word of mouth. At the Morgen factory, management, staff and trade union representatives all asked serious questions about the security of their jobs. They also feared a possible raid on the surplus in the pension fund, a consequent reduction in future benefits, and the risk that Company-paid pensions could be stopped. Terry Walters and Israel Mkhize, the two human resources managers, both spoke of numerous queries they had received about these matters. Israel told of an elderly pensioner who, the previous day, had walked fifteen kilometres into town to ask why his pension was being stopped. They had also had to reassure the staff, and some other users, about the company-sponsored health services.

Willie van Jaarsveld, the Morgen agricultural extension officer, had had several panic telephone calls from farmer-suppliers, who feared for their milk businesses. He was arranging extensive visits to farms to reassure their owners by explaining the current situation.

At Morgen Farm Neil met the staff to answer their questions and try to calm their fears about the rumoured closure of the farm and its operations. As he and Andries made their way to lunch at the Coffee Shop, they were approached by a tearful Patience Dlamini:

"Oh, Mister Harrier, is it true they will take away the money for Joseph's children? I don't know how I will manage to keep them at school and look after them properly if they do."

To all, Neil could only give assurance that the bid was being fought, and in the meantime everything would continue as usual. Pensions would not be reduced and jobs were secure. Morgen's cost-cutting programme would continue, as it was necessary, but jobs would only be lost by natural attrition if at all possible. He could not answer for a new owner of the Company, but he was sure Morgen would prevail.

20

Geoff Loman called a meeting on Monday, 8th October, to review progress with regard to Predvest's bid for Morgen. James Bold and Stanley Vane from Enduring Bank met Geoff, Adrian and other key executives and members of the bid team in Geoff's office early that afternoon. The spacious corner office was situated on the top floor of Predvest Building. Two walls were really windows with magnificent views to the north and west. One wall was dominated by a large and splendid Hannes du Plessis painting of a leopard reclining along the branch of a tree. To one side of the door was a bronze sculpture by Camilla le May of a cheetah, a beautiful animal, seemingly in motion with only two feet on the ground. There were several folders and papers on the wide polished wooden desk at one end of the room, which also had a round conference table and a corner with four or five comfortable chairs and a coffee table.

The Predvest "roadshow" had by now visited most of the major Morgen shareholders, as well as investment managers and investment advisors, giving presentations and trying to secure written undertakings to vote in favour of the Predvest bid at the shareholders' meeting, whose date had still to be set. Meanwhile, others had been working the telephones, endeavouring to contact the numerous smaller shareholders, trying to secure their votes as well. Geoff was presented with a tally of the contacts made and the success or otherwise in securing undertakings to vote in favour of the bid.

Stanley concluded, "It's an uphill battle, as you've seen for yourself, Geoff. We've only got signed undertakings for about nineteen per cent of the votes, which is disappointing. Obviously, we'll get more after the official bid documents have been sent to shareholders, but we think we're not likely to end up with enough votes on the present terms."

James said, "We may need to increase the bid price. I think many are holding out just in case that happens, but a good number of fairly substantial shareholders really believe Morgen is worth more than we're offering, and won't agree to the present terms. We know our offer price is a bit cheeky, so we can afford to raise it and still do well with Morgen. Also, there've been some sellers of Predvest on the market, and the share price has quite often fallen below a thousand cents. That's a psychologically significant figure, but also does mean a lower implied price to Morgan shareholders."

These matters were discussed in detail and at some length.

"What should we increase our bid to, if we decide to do that?" asked Geoff, after listening to the discussions.

With one Predvest share offered for one Morgen, Predvest were offering the equivalent of 1000 cents, so long as Predvest traded at that price. Giving 1.1 Predvest per Morgen share implied a price of 1100 cents, but that was not deemed to be sufficient, especially if the Predvest share price weakened. Eventually, the consensus was that a ratio of 1.2 (an implied price of 1200 cents) would be sufficient to entice Morgen shareholders to support the bid, and that a deal at that price would still be good for Predvest. However, it was important for the Predvest share price to remain stable, preferably at or above 1000 cents.

Geoff concluded the meeting by saying, "Okay, I agree we need to go up to a ratio of 1.2 Predvest per Morgen. I'll take the proposal to the Board."

Susie Mack was awake early as usual on the morning of Wednesday, 10th October. Passing from the bedroom to the kitchen to make herself some coffee, she could not help stopping to admire the new cherry-wood dresser in the entrance hall. It was indeed a beautiful piece of furniture, a feature in itself, but enhanced by a bowl of pink roses on the table top, and the interesting ornaments, porcelain figures and china plates shown off on the display shelves. The dresser had been delivered on Saturday morning, and she had immediately telephoned Paul to thank him.

"It was such a lovely surprise, my darling, and it looks really beautiful in its place. You must come and see it soon."

Susie's telephone rang just after six o'clock as she was starting her breakfast of muesli and coffee. She was surprised to hear the voice of Geoff Loman.

"Good morning, Susie. I'm sorry to ring you so early, but I need your help, and at your home I know we can talk privately and this call won't be recorded."

"I'm just having breakfast. What can I do for you?"

"With this Morgen deal on, I must have the Predvest share price at or above 1000 cents – at least at critical times. I want you to manage the process. I know I can trust you to do it, and to be discrete."

"Geoff, I'd need ammunition – orders."

"You'll have all of that. I spoke to David Goldberg last night, and BAM has agreed, off the record of course, to help us. He'll give you details of the moneys available to you. Most will come from Bullion group shareholders and other funds to be invested. If the price falls below a thousand during the day, or at odd times, don't worry, but try to close the day at that level if you can, especially at critical times. We'll let you know when those are. The first is tomorrow. There'll be an announcement after the market closes: I can't say more. I want Predvest to close no lower the a thousand cents tomorrow and on Friday."

"I think that can be done, Geoff. The usual trading volumes in Predvest are not so great as to make it impossible. Can I choose my broker? I think I know who'll do it for us."

"Do whatever you want. I don't want to know anything about it. This conversation has never taken place. If BAM wants to buy Predvest shares, that's fine and good. It's a good investment."

"I understand."

"Thank you, Susie. And I won't forget you."

"I know you won't, my dear."

Later in the morning, and after a private discussion with David Goldberg and Harry Naidoo, Susie asked Paul Lowe to meet her for a quick cup of coffee.

"I've got some interesting business for you, Paul," she began as soon as they had placed their orders with the waitress. "I'll let you have orders through the usual channels, but there are aspects which I can't talk about on phone calls that will be overheard or recorded."

"I don't like the sound of that," said Paul.

"Paul, I said I would find you business, so here it is. There's no risk involved. You know all about Predvest's bid for Morgen? Good. In brief, Geoff Loman wants the Predvest price not to fall below 1000 cents at critical times. I'll give you the orders, and your job will be to see that it does not. The price must close at 1000 cents this afternoon and again tomorrow."

"Susie, we're not allowed to manipulate share prices."

"All that is happening is that BAM is making investments. There should be no investigations if we do it right."

"We want BAM's business, but I'm not sure about this."

In her little girl voice, Susie said, "You did like our time together, my darling? Don't I make you feel good? It's our little secret, and we both want it to stay just between us, don't we?"

Paul remained silent.

"I'll let you have the first orders when I get back to my desk," said Susie.

Paul nodded.

"Thank you my darling. I just knew you would help."

After the stock exchange closed on Thursday, Predvest announced that it was increasing its bid price for each Morgen share to 1.2 Predvest shares. That evening Predvest had closed trading at exactly 1000 cents, implying a bid price of 1200 cents. On Friday it again finished the day at the same price, despite some weakness during morning trading. In the markets and in the press the increased price was favourably received.

There was a general feeling that the bid was now likely to succeed. Jennifer Rogan's *Business Weekend* column quoted several analysts who believed that the price was now much fairer and that Morgen shareholders would most likely accept the revised offer.

On Wednesday, 17th October, there was a brief hearing in the High Court, which resulted in the Court issuing an order to convene a meeting of Morgen shareholders for 10:00 a.m. on Friday, 16th November, to consider the Predvest offer. Two days later, the formal offer documents were mailed to Morgen shareholders.

21

Early on the fifth morning of Lucy's voyage to St Helena Island she dressed quickly and went out on deck. Looking into the distance over the bows she could see a low land mass just above the horizon – her first view of her new home. She felt the excitement of a landfall, but was apprehensive at the same time. She could not distinguish any features at that distance, but the Island looked small and insignificant in the vast spaces of an ocean blue-grey under an early morning cloud covering. The clouds extended to the Island and beyond, but were just high enough to leave it untouched.

Lucy went into the Sun Lounge and had a hurried breakfast from the casual buffet provided there for those who did not want to have a full breakfast in the dining room. In her cabin she quickly packed a few remaining items in readiness to disembark, and then went up onto the highest deck near the bridge to watch the Island gradually growing larger as they approached it. They were coming from the south, and the Captain followed a course which took them quite close to the Island's southern shore, before turning east, and following the coast as it turned northwards and then westwards as they sailed to their anchorage on the more sheltered northern coast. The passengers were delighted to be given this tour of so much of the Island's coastline. Lucy had heard of St Helena described as an emerald set in bronze, but there was little of green to be seen on this morning. Here was a spectacular but hostile and forbidding coastline of high rocky cliffs and peaks, mostly in darker and lighter shades of grey, with touches of brown – a fortress against the rolling Atlantic swells which broke in white where its stone cliffs rose from the sea.

RMS *St Helena* slowed as she neared her anchorage. The Island had no harbour, so they had to anchor off Jamestown, its main town. As they approached it, Lucy saw first one and then a second narrow valley opening up to her view. Someone identified these for her as the valleys behind Rupert Bay and James Bay. Jamestown lay in the latter, and Lucy began to see buildings, houses and some patches of green. With increasing excitement she tried to identify features of the small town nestling between the steep slopes of its valley. There was a wharf with buildings on it to one side of the waterfront, with a roadway extending from them along the entire seafront. Many cars were parked there, and numbers of people already stood along the railings beside the water to watch the arrival of the ship, to greet loved ones or to meet visitors. The ship dropped anchor behind a sprinkling of small craft in the bay, and sent the sound of its horn booming up the valley to announce its arrival to the Island.

While waiting for her turn to disembark, Lucy stayed on deck to watch as various official vessels approached the ship, came alongside, and went off again about their business. She watched the "air-taxi" – actually a cage in which the elderly or infirm, unable to manage the usual way of disembarking, could be taken safely ashore – being lifted by one of the ship's derricks and placed onto a small barge, to be ferried to the landing wharf. For Lucy, disembarkation became a confused collage of having her name called, being encased in a red life jacket, being surrounded by a sea of red as she waited for her turn to leave the ship, then going precariously down a gangway and into a crowded red-filled passenger launch, to be sped away from her home of the past few days, helped up the steps onto the wharf, relieved of her life jacket and shepherded onto a bus which took her and fellow passengers a short way to where they were speedily helped through the necessary customs and other formalities. She had booked a place for herself at the Consulate Hotel for a few days, while she sorted out her affairs on the Island. She was met by a friendly hotel representative and taken by minibus along the waterfront, under an arched gateway, and up the main street to the hotel. There she went through the registration formalities and was taken to her room, to await the arrival of her luggage.

For a moment Lucy felt a little bewildered and stranded, as if thrown up from the sea onto a strange new shore. She sat on the bed and looked around her room. It was modestly furnished but spacious, comfortable and clean. Its only window looked out over a jumble of roofs, but let the light in so the room was bright and cheerful. It was on an upper floor, and later Lucy would count forty-three steps from the road to her room. She had a quiet cup of tea, and then set out to explore.

Lucy went down the narrow carpeted stairs, poked her head into a comfortable lounge, and continued down to ground level. Her brief look around the hotel told her that it was much larger than it seemed from its relatively narrow frontage onto the main road. It extended quite a long way back, with a large courtyard and a number of public rooms and gardens. Lucy stepped down from the front veranda onto the road. The hotel was a mid-eighteenth century building, with a modest light-coloured facade and attractive wrought iron railings along its ground and first floor verandas and on either side of the two short sets of steps from the lower veranda to the roadside. A large picture of a red-robed Father Christmas was hung on the front of the hotel, and coloured lights for the festive season were still suspended above the wide main road down to the waterfront. Lucy began to walk down the road, whose elderly Georgian and Victorian buildings still gave it what she felt was an old world feeling, despite the motor cars parked down its centre.

Suddenly Lucy felt elated, with an exciting sense of history. Here she was walking in the footsteps of so many famous people. Here Napoleon Bonaparte had walked when exiled to the Island; so too, ten years before him, had the Duke of Wellington, while still Sir Arthur Wellesley; here walked Captain Bligh of the *Bounty*, Captain James Cook, Halley the astronomer, Charles Darwin, and no doubt many others. Not long before, in 2002, St Helena had celebrated its five hundredth anniversary, and Lucy found herself remembering aspects of the Island's history as she strolled down the main street, which opened to form the broad square named the Grand Parade. St James Church was notable on her left, and behind it a steep stairway, called Jacob's Ladder, climbed all the way out of the valley up to the fort on top of Ladder Hill. To her right was the Castle, which was effectively the seat of Government, and the attractive Castle Gardens. Straight ahead the road went by way of the Archway through the remains of old fortifications to the waterfront.

The Island was uninhabited when it was discovered by the Portuguese navigator, Joao da Nova Castella, on 21st May, 1502. He named the Island "Saint Helena" as that day was the feast day of Saint Helena, the mother of Emperor Constantine. The site of the present Jamestown was a natural landing place, being sheltered from the southeast trade winds, and having a fertile wooded valley with a stream running down it. It was used as a refreshment station by the Portuguese on their voyages to and from the Far East. The Island was "discovered" by the English (Thomas Cavendish) and the Dutch (Jan Hughen van Linschoten) in 1588 and 1589 respectively, but was eventually taken possession of and settled by the English East India Company in 1659. Except for a brief period of Dutch occupation, in 1672-3, the Island remained under the English East India Company until 1834, when the administration was transferred to the British Government, and St Helena became a Crown Colony. For centuries the Island's main importance was derived from its position on the shipping route from Europe, around the Cape of Good Hope to the East. This importance diminished considerably after the opening of the Suez Canal in 1869. The resulting economic decline was counteracted in various ways, including the establishment in 1907 of an industry based on the growing and processing of New Zealand flax, which was relatively successful until about 1966, when the British Post Office (one of the main customers) decided to use artificial instead of natural fibres for the tying up of bundles of letters. For some periods the Island economy was boosted by the presence of prisoners, with their retinues and guards, kept there because of its extreme isolation: Napoleon Bonaparte from 1815 until his death in 1821; the Zulu chief, Dinizulu, for seven years from 1890; and, between 1900 and 1903, General Cronje and up to six thousand Boer prisoners-of-war, taken in the Anglo-Boer War in South Africa around the turn of the century.

Lucy turned into the pretty Castle Gardens. The clouds had broken up and the sun was shining. It was pleasantly warm. She enjoyed meandering between the colourful flower-beds and under the tall old trees. On the far side was a small building, and Lucy read on it a plaque which recorded that one Joshua Slocum had given a lecture there, more than a century earlier.

"He was an interesting character, and was the first person to sail single-handed around the world – in a little boat named the *Spray*," said a voice beside her.

It was the ship's doctor, and Lucy greeted him with delight. "I'm glad to see you with some time off," she said.

"I always enjoy wandering around the Island, but I must soon make my way up to the Hospital, to pay a courtesy visit. We always help each other when we can."

When the doctor strode off up the main road, Lucy wandered in the other direction, through the Archway to the waterfront. She leant against the white-painted railing and watched the waves rushing into a white fringe against the dark rocks and concrete steps below her, then retreating with a roar of water and underlying clatter of rolling stones. There were numerous small craft in the bay, with the dark, white and yellow of RMS *St Helena* at anchor further out and dominating the scene. Lucy strolled, first one way and then the other, along the waterfront, eagerly noting details of her new environment. The road was backed by a wall of the old fortifications, with the remains of a moat between wall and road. A white cenotaph stood as a memorial to Saints who had lost their lives in wars. Further on was a restaurant with umbrellas and outdoor tables and chairs from where one could enjoy the sea view. Then there were rocks and rock-pools under a towering dark cliff. After standing there for a while watching the waves crashing onto the rocks and spilling into pools, Lucy turned and walked the other way. At one point she stopped to admire a gloriously flowering bougainvillea forming a pinkish mauve canopy over a bench set back from, but facing, the sea.

"That is the Honeymoon Chair. Are you planning to use it?" asked a cheerful voice behind her.

"I think I'm past that," she said as she turned to Colin, who looked relaxed, casually dressed, and with blond hair blowing in the breeze.

"You never know." His blue eyes held hers for a moment before he continued. "I thought I'd find you somewhere around here. You weren't at the hotel so I came on to look for you. I've been home and unpacked already. Come and have a cup of coffee."

He led her back through the Arch and to their right onto a green lawn, on which were wooden table-and-bench units, and which had shade provided by some tall trees. At one end, a small building housed a kitchen. It had serving windows, with a "Coffee Shop" sign over one. They ordered coffee and something sweet to eat and found an empty table. It really was a pleasant spot to relax in fine weather. Lucy sat with her back to the towering brown and grey cliff, which marked one side of the valley, and enjoyed the open views around her. To her left she could see across the moat to the bay, with RMS *St Helena* in the distance. Their coffee was brought to them, and it was delicious.

"It's grown on the Island, and really is some of the best in the world," Colin told her proudly. "Some of it's exported to exclusive buyers, like Harrod's in London, I believe, but unfortunately only small quantities are available."

Colin asked Lucy what her immediate plans were. There were still a few days before the school term would begin, so Lucy wanted to make the most of them. She needed to see the "estate agent" she had spoken to from South Africa, as she had to find a new home for herself. She also wanted to buy a car. She wanted to visit Prince Andrew School as soon as possible, to introduce herself, and to become familiar with her new working environment. Then there was work to do in preparing lessons for the new term. However, she was also determined to be a tourist for a few days, to see as much of the Island as possible. She had already booked herself to go on some tours which would be available for visitors in the coming week, before RMS *St Helena* returned from Ascension Island to take them back to Cape Town.

"I'll help you all I can, if you'll let me," Colin offered. "I could take you to the School and show you around. I'm sure the Head and office staff, at least, will be there. I'd love to show you the Island too, perhaps also some things you may not see on your tours. Would you like to go for a drive now? We could take a picnic lunch and I'll give you a quick orientation tour."

"Thank you, Colin. That would be lovely. It's good to have a friend to help me find my feet here."

22

"Why are you selling our shares?"

Geoff Loman was speaking to some of the most senior investment people at Gilt Assurance Investment Management. It was late afternoon on Monday, 22nd October. That morning Geoff had requested an urgent meeting with them, following a conversation with Susie Mack the day before.

On Sunday morning Susie had answered Geoff's summons to meet him for coffee at his home. They had sat in the shade beside the large swimming pool, the morning peace pleasantly broken by the sound of water playing and gently falling from a fountain into the pool. They looked lazily out into the garden, where the great oaks and planes were still in early spring leaf. Susie thought Geoff's eyes looked tired, and his wavy hair more wild than usual, but there was no doubt about his continuing business drive. He wanted to know from Susie the state of the stock markets, and more especially the markets in Predvest and Morgan shares, and how the management of the Predvest share price was proceeding.

"It's going well, by and large," said Susie, "but we're having to absorb quite a large number of Predvest shares to hold the price up. We're pretty sure that GAIM is the main seller."

"The changes to our share register, which I watch as you may know, confirm that," said Geoff.

"And I'm a little worried that they may be detecting a pattern in the Predvest trade. The greater volumes come into the market near the end of the day, when we're offering to buy at or near one thousand."

"Okay, Susie. Hold off for a few days. The next critical period will be before 2nd November, which is the last day to trade for shareholders to be entitled to vote at the meeting on the sixteenth. So we need to be sure the Predvest price holds up again from, say Wednesday, 31st October, until the meeting. It may also be a good idea to use more than one broker, if that's possible, to make any pattern less obvious."

"I've been thinking about that too. I have some ideas."

"Good. Meanwhile, I think I'll have a chat with GAIM."

On Monday morning Geoff had telephoned Imtiaz Patel, the Managing Director of GAIM, and they had agreed to meet in GAIM's boardroom that afternoon. Geoff had taken Adrian with him, while GAIM's Head of Research, Thabo Ndlovu, and their senior industrial analyst, Joy September, were also present. They were part of a good team that worked well together. Both Imtiaz and Thabo were small, dark and brown-eyed. Incongruously, Joy was tall, slim and elegant, with dark hair, amber eyes and olive complexion. The room was dominated by a long wooden boardroom table, but was comfortable and pleasantly decorated, with two large Peter Bonney landscapes of the Little Karoo occupying two of the walls. Morgen was a major client of GAIM, which managed the investments of the Morgen Pension Fund. Their persistent questioning at Predvest's "roadshow" meeting with them had led to Stanley's outburst and Jennifer Rogan's damaging article.

"Why are you selling our shares?" asked Geoff. "You should be buying; Predvest is good value."

There was a brief silence; then Imtiaz answered. "Predvest has done quite well for us, Geoff, but not everyone would agree that it's good value at current prices. Some of our clients want us to take some profits, while some of our portfolio managers are also reducing the holdings of Predvest in their portfolios."

"Rubbish, you should be buying, not selling."

"Our research suggests that Predvest is quite expensive," said Thabo.

"I always give you analysts all the information you could possibly need about our group. It should be obvious Predvest is good value."

"We're grateful for that," said Joy, "but I still think your shares now are rather expensive, relative to other possible investments."

"Selling now is not good for us, with the Morgen deal depending on the level of our share price."

Imtiaz said mildly, "It's not for us to determine market prices. We must deal as we see fit for our clients."

"I know that. But you could get closer to us. Buy more of our shares. Exchange your Morgen holdings for Predvest. We could even become your industrial arm."

"I'm not sure we would do that," said Imtiaz.

"We could bring you a lot of business. You manage the Morgen Pension Fund. Many other investment houses would like that business. If we win control of Morgen we could make sure you keep it. You *are* going to vote for the deal?"

"We should have the offer documents in a day or two," responded Imtiaz. "Joy will study them and we'll decide after that."

"You have a large holding in Morgen. I would like your votes. What do you need from me to persuade you to vote for us?"

"I think we have everything," said Thabo.

"Joy?"

"I think we have all we need, Geoff. We'll look carefully at the offer documents, but it's only fair to say that at present we feel Morgen is potentially worth more on its own than if sold to Predvest, even at the new offer price."

23

Lucy was a little surprised at how quickly and how well she settled into her new life on St Helena Island. She expected far more difficulty, more regrets about the past she had left behind, and especially about her loss of Neil. Later she believed that she adapted so well because she had travelled so far during her transition, partly through what seemed a long void of ocean and sky, and because her new environment was so very different from anywhere she had lived before. She simply had to adapt, and there was little if anything on the Island to remind her of her past life. Moreover, exploring and discovering were exciting, and almost everyone she met seemed to make it easier for her to feel welcome, to settle down and feel at home. She had found a friend in Colin, and her other colleagues at Prince Andrew School made her very welcome, but it also seemed that all the Saints she met were friendly and happy to see her. Even strangers she passed in the street greeted her, and she found herself continuously responding in kind to smiles and waves from passing motorists.

Lucy was fortunate to find a home for herself very easily. She fell in love with only the second house she was shown. It was high up at the head of a valley in St Paul's. She was entranced by the view, as far as the eye could see to the north, and almost a hundred and eighty degrees from High Knoll Fort on her left to Alarm Forest on her right. From her veranda she could also look down onto Prince Andrew School on Francis Plain. Re-painting and some minor renovations did not take long, she located enough furniture with which to manage until some treasured or necessary items would be shipped to her from South Africa, and not very long after the school term began she moved in.

Lucy had purchased a small second-hand car, which was all she needed on the narrow, twisting roads, where the usual speed limit was thirty miles per hour. She loved to drive around the Island, often going nowhere in particular, but exploring as the fancy took her, and frequently stopping to walk in interesting places. She loved the short scenic drive to school, and truly enjoyed this transition between home and work. She would take the winding, green-wooded road down from St Paul's, and, after crossing a pretty stream, turn left into Francis Plain Road and drive down Harper's Valley. Here the way followed a stream, which ran into a dam in an agricultural area below her on her left, until she turned right into the entrance to the School.

Prince Andrew School was a community high school, and the only school on the Island offering secondary education, which it did to children from about twelve to eighteen years of age. The education system was based broadly on the English system. Children entered the high school after attending local "first schools" (for the first four years) and then "middle schools", and school attendance was compulsory until the age of fifteen. From sixteen to eighteen years, education had a strongly vocational emphasis, but with an academic stream also provided. The school had something over three hundred pupils, a number to which, Lucy discovered, it had fallen with the erosion of the Island's population from around five thousand to about four thousand people.

Lucy was happy at the School from the moment she first entered the grounds. The grey-roofed, white buildings were set in pleasant gardens; and her first impression, when entering the foyer of the main building, was of bright white walls and gleaming polished blue floors. The facilities were excellent, with a good working library and well equipped special rooms for computer learning, domestic science, woodwork, metalwork and more. There were spacious playing fields and, with no large buildings close by, the School seemed to be set in a pleasant rural environment. There were extensive open views in an arc beyond the sports grounds. Flagstaff Hill rose to a point on the horizon towards the right end of the arc, while to the left the fortress-topped, grey and speckled-green bulk of High Knoll Hill rose from the adjacent valley and brooded over them. So, even at work, Lucy was continuously reminded of the beauty and history of the Island.

Lucy's initial exploration of St Helena had been somewhat frantic. She had been eager to discover as much as possible as soon as possible. Colin had shown her a lot to begin with, but she had also made herself a tourist for a few days. With other visitors who had shared her voyage to the Island, she walked through the historic old part of Jamestown with Basil George, she toured in Colin Corker's ancient open charabanc, she followed the story of Napoleon from his residences in Briars and Longwood to his valley grave, and she spent a day with George Benjamin to learn about the flora of the Island. Later, she began to explore and enjoy things in a more detailed and unhurried manner. It was like a new love affair, she thought later on. First came the excited, frantic desire to discover and experience as much as possible in no time at all; then a calmer, deeper, more detailed exploration of every physical aspect and shade of personality.

Some of her exploration was done alone, but often she was accompanied by Colin. They enjoyed working together as colleagues, and indeed between them they taught most of the English in the School, but their friendship also continued to grow outside of their work. Lucy was grateful for his help in settling down, but she also enjoyed his company, his conversation and his cheery, boyish manner. He was a few years younger than she, and Lucy began to feel an almost maternal affection for him. She soon had no doubt that he was very fond of her. They went for walks together, ate out or at one or other of their homes, and often sat up late into the night discussing all manner of topics. He held her hand occasionally in private, when the path they walked was wide enough to go side-by-side, or across the dinner table, but for some months made no other attempt to be closer to her. Perhaps he was giving her time to recover from Neil, she wondered, content to leave things as they were.

One day they drove out to the George Benjamin Arboretum and parked the car nearby. They spent some time there, strolling amongst the trees. Then they walked along the road to High Peak, and made the short, steep climb to the summit. There they seemed to be alone together near the top of the world. Clouds played around them, so they were alternately in mist, or able to see, in one direction or another, down the long green ridges and valleys to the desert-like coastal ring and the open sea. It seemed a privilege to be there together, and they were each intensely aware of the other's physical presence. At one moment, when the mist parted like stage curtains, they caught their breaths and exclaimed at the revelation of a stunning view, all the way down to the sea. Colin was standing just behind Lucy, and he put his arms around her midriff and pulled her close to him. Her immediate thought was of Neill on the top of Morgen Koppie; then that that time was past, and these were other arms and this was a very different view. She kept still while they continued under the spell of the beauty before them. Emboldened, he moved his hands higher to cup her breasts, or rather the swell of them under her layers of warm clothing, and somehow the intimacy seemed right and comforting. As the mist closed in again, he turned her to face him and kissed her on the mouth.

"I want you," he said.

"Colin, I'm very fond of you, and I love your company, but I don't want to hurt you. I don't think it'll work. In a year and a bit you'll be gone, and I won't follow you. It's madness to get too close to one another."

"I know you've warned me to be careful, Lucy, and I understand we only have limited time here together. But I'd like us to make the best use of that time. Surely we could be close, keeping in mind that I'll be leaving next year, and maybe with some rules so we don't hurt each other – for I don't want you to be hurt again either."

Lucy shivered. "Let's talk about it later. The mist's thickening and it's getting colder. It's time to go back."

They held hands as they walked along the road to the car, now below the level of the mist. Lucy did not speak as she felt she needed to think. It was clear, though, that some important dynamic in their relationship had changed.

Colin went to Lucy's home for dinner that evening, as they had previously arranged. They talked of school and other neutral subjects, but both knew that their conversation on High Peak lingered, incomplete, in the background. After dinner they went to the lounge to drink their coffee. Lucy sat down first, on her long, comfortable couch, partly to see what he would do. Colin seated himself very close to her, so their thighs and shoulders touched. After a while he put his cup down, placed his hand on her thigh, and broke the silence.

"I love you, Lucy, and I want you so very much."

Lucy remained silent, but made no effort to move away. He leant across and kissed her, his eyes bright and appealing.

The maternal part of her thought he was like a little boy pleading for a sweet; but to another part of her he was an attractive young man, who was a close friend and for whom she had developed a genuine fondness. "It would be so easy to make him happy," she thought, "and perhaps it would be good for me to have someone to be close to after all this time."

"Remember you have been warned," she said gently but firmly. "And we will need to make some rules, not least because we work together."

"I understand. I promise I won't be a nuisance, and I won't hurt you either."

Lucy stood up and took him by the hand. "Come."

She led him to her bedroom, where she began to switch off lights. "Shall I leave this little one on?" she asked.

"Please. I want to see you."

They kissed and hugged, and Lucy felt him trembling. She began to loosen the buttons of his shirt, whereupon he knelt down to take off his shoes, beginning to undress himself. Lucy slipped off her clothes and lay on the bed, watching and waiting. He looked at her in eager admiration, then climbed onto the bed and knelt over her. He touched and stroked her, quivering with excitement. She sensed an uncertainty about him, so she came to his aid and helped him.

"Oh, you're so beautiful, and I love you so very much," he said soon after, still breathing heavily.

"You're crushing the breath out of me, Colin. Come and lie next to me so we can cuddle up together." After a few minutes of lying quietly close to each other, she asked gently: "Have you ever done this before?"

"No."

"Why didn't you tell me?"

"I thought you might say no. Two or three times before, when I've been close friends with good, but experienced, women, they've suddenly decided they didn't want to corrupt me, when they realised I was innocent and inexperienced. I've longed to make love, physically, in the fullest way, but I never wanted it to be a commercial transaction. When I discovered you, and began to love you, I so wanted the first time to be with you. I tried to keep my longing from showing, as I knew you'd been hurt and needed time to recover, but I couldn't help myself on the mountain this afternoon. My feelings were so full, they simply overflowed."

"Have you anyone waiting for you at home in England? What will you tell her?"

"I've one or two good friends, but no commitments. I don't think they'll wait for me. Perhaps I'll become a better lover now." He paused. "I haven't told you, but I was engaged to be married, before I came out here. She was beautiful, and I loved her dearly, but she cancelled the engagement just after I'd ordered the ring. Teachers don't usually have money, and she found a better prospect."

"So you also came here to escape!" Lucy exclaimed. "I'm sad for you, Colin. I'd never have known it – you always seem so sunny and cheerful."

"That's how I try to be, and I have now basically recovered. This is a wonderful place for that – and you have also helped me, far more than you can ever know."

They lay close together for a while longer, in sympathetic silence. Then Lucy pulled away slightly and said. "Let's make love some more. We've hardly begun. You've helped me to explore the Island. Now, if you want, you can explore me, and

I'll show you lots of lovely things you can do with me. Then, perhaps, the lady you'll find for yourself after you get home to England will become very happy indeed."

Later, he joked: "At least when I teach literature now, and there are love scenes, and poets all lyrical about spring and their lady loves, I'll have a better appreciation of what they're going on about."

Lucy thought to herself: "It really is good to have someone to be close to sometimes."

24

It became clear to Will Morgen that, once Predvest had increased the price it was willing to offer Morgen shareholders for their shares, the tide had turned against Morgen in its fight to remain independent. Will, Mark and Rob, together with their senior executives, Investor Relations Department, and numerous advisors, worked tirelessly to put Morgen's case, both directly with their shareholders and indirectly by contacting opinion-makers such as financial analysts and media journalists. They were met with courtesy by most of Morgen's larger shareholders, but hardly any would commit themselves to vote against the offer. While one or two seemed genuinely undecided, it became clear that Predvest was obtaining more and more undertakings to vote for the deal.

With the offer documents being published and mailed on 19th October, the Morgen directors were obliged by law to inform their shareholders, within two weeks of that date, whether they considered the offer to be fair or not. They had no doubt about their determination to repel the Predvest raiders, as they saw them, and had been preparing and conducting their defence. However, they had also been following the established proper procedures. They had formed a subcommittee of their theoretically independent non-executive directors, charged with the duty to examine the offer and form an opinion as to its fairness or otherwise. To assist and advise them, the Morgen board had appointed two firms of investment banking advisers – one of the major international names and a smaller local company – to evaluate the offer and express their opinions as to whether or not it was fair to Morgen shareholders. A cynic would say that the results of these evaluations were as expected. While Predvest's advisers had expressed the view that the proposed transaction was fair to both Predvest and Morgen shareholders, both of Morgen's advisers were of the opinion that the offer price was too low and not at all in the best interests of the holders of Morgen shares. With that opinion the subcommittee of non-executive directors agreed, and advised the full Morgen board accordingly. Morgen's formal rejection of the Predvest offer, and their board's advice to their shareholders to vote against the deal, were published after the market closed on Friday, 26th October, in time to catch the weekend press.

Meanwhile Will and Morgen and their advisers were trying to pursue all other possible means of defence. Was it possible, for example to find a friendly "white knight", that is a party who would make a better offer for Morgen shares or, in some other way, protect Morgen from Predvest? The smaller of Morgen's main advisers, Ingwe Investment Bank, worked especially hard to find such a party.

Ingwe had been formed a few years before by two friends, John Tshabalala and Nancy Kawa, who greatly respected each other's work and who felt the need for a black-led institution of the kind in a changing society which was encouraging black economic empowerment. They were both still in their late thirties, but were well experienced and highly respected in the business world. They complemented each other well: John was tall, broadly-built, overtly dynamic, direct and out-going; Nancy was smaller, calm, serene, always seemingly unruffled, and seductively persuasive. They both genuinely believed that the Predvest deal was a bad one, that Morgan had great potential, and that it should survive to achieve it, while retaining the essential goodness of the organization and the way in which it operated. They helped to facilitate a meeting, on Wednesday, 24th October, between top executives of Morgen, Gilt Assurance and GAIM. The purpose was to explore ways in which the insurance group and its investment management company could help save Morgen, and the GAIM boardroom was nearly full for the meeting. Morgen was an important client, but, following their meeting with Geoff Loman and a final study of the offer documents, Joy September and GAIM's research team had also decided independently to recommend that GAIM should vote to reject the Predvest offer.

It soon became clear that it was not practical for the Gilt group, or any party for that matter, to be a white knight for Morgen.

"It would be silly to try to outbid Predvest now, with a higher offer," said Joy. "If the current offer is defeated, it's almost certain the price of Morgen will fall. It's being held up artificially now by the Predvest price, which we also think is far too expensive."

Thabo added, "We believe, but can't prove, that Geoff Loman has somehow found a way of supporting the Predvest price. Rosenberg and Levine are doing a lot of buying, we think for Bullion. Geoff's important to them, so he may be behind it. But, of course they may simply be doing normal buying for their client portfolios. They'll certainly argue that."

"What we *will* do," said Imtiaz, "is give you an undertaking to vote against the deal. We've only just under one per cent of Morgen, but that should help."

"It certainly will," said Will.

Imtiaz continued, "The offer needs to be defeated, so you need to find at least twenty-five per cent of the votes. Then Predvest won't be allowed, by law, to make another offer for Morgan for a year. The Morgan share price will fall closer to previous levels. Then we, and no doubt others, would be willing buyers of Morgan, provided you continue your rationalization programmes within the businesses. That will be the time to put together a friendly deal, which could leave control of Morgen in family and other friendly hands. We agree with Ingwe that that'll also be the ideal time to introduce a black partner into the business. We would participate in a deal like that, like the one Ingwe has described."

"I think we all agree that that is the way to go," said Will, "and I thank you all for your support. Now we need to find enough votes to stop Predvest."

That night part of the Morgen Milk factory in Platberg burnt down. A worker was apprehended by factory security as he tried to cut his way through the boundary fence in the confusion caused by the blaze. He had been drinking heavily in a local shebeen. There had been heated discussions about the possible takeover of Morgen, the fear of resulting job losses and even a closure of the factory. The worker had recently been given a formal warning for being drunk at work, and grew more and more agitated.

"I'll be first to be thrown out," he said repeatedly. "But I'll get even. Soon we'll all be out of work. If I'm going down I'll take everyone and the company with me."

He managed to be admitted to the factory premises while the night shift was in progress, and started the fire in a storeroom which contained inflammable materials. The town and factory fire and emergency systems worked well, so no-one was injured, but a fair amount of damage was done before the fire was put out. Neil Harrier was in Platberg that night and was called to the scene by Andries, the factory manager. They were able to ascertain that the damage was mainly to storage and warehouse facilities. It would be inconvenient, and expensive to repair, but production would not be badly affected.

"This man's been in trouble before," Andries told Neil, "so there may be mixed motives. Of course we'll have to investigate the matter properly, but it does show that there's a lot of bad feeling around. We need to get this Predvest thing behind us as soon as possible."

"I agree, Andries, but I can never understand how people think it will help to destroy things, especially things that offer them services or jobs."

In the morning Neil telephoned Will, as early as he felt he could, to inform him of developments.

"Everything's under control now, Will, and we'll keep you properly informed of course. This is a symptom, though perhaps extreme, of a lot of unhappiness here while the fear of losing jobs continues. Do you think I should cancel my trip to St Helena and stay around until the Predvest matter is settled?"

There was only a brief pause.

"I think you should go, Neil. I'm sure we'll manage without you, and you do deserve a holiday. But the most important thing now is to get the votes we need to stop Predvest and save this company and all it stands for. I don't think we can do that without Lucy's votes. She holds three per cent, as you know. She won't talk to me or anybody about it. Perhaps she'll listen to you if you're there, face to face. So go, Neil, and see if you can persuade her to vote for us."

25

Lucy later realised that her initial efforts to explore St Helena Island, once she had landed there, were directed mainly towards its physical features – places, sights, geography. Of course she was interested in the people she met and began to work with, but as time went by she came to know more of the Island people, more about them, and more about the prevailing economic and social circumstances.

The St Helenians, or "Saints", were a distillation of many races from a number of countries and cultures, including Malay, Chinese, African, British and Boer. Lucy found the people almost unfailingly friendly, and she never tired of hearing their lilting English accent. British influence was very strong, for the Island had been a British possession, one way or another, since 1659. The Islanders were very proud of their British citizenship, which was granted by Royal Charter in 1673, taken away from them in 1981 when Hong Kong was returned to China, but thankfully and rightfully restored again in 2002 when St Helena celebrated its five hundredth anniversary.

St Helena was a British Dependent Territory and had for many years depended on the British government for subsidies, both for the administration of the territory and for their tenuous RMS *St Helena* sea link with the rest of the world. Historically the Island had been used as a staging post on the long Atlantic sea routes, so it had seldom or never been financially and economically independent. Many efforts had been made to help the Island towards economic self-sufficiency, the twentieth century flax industry being perhaps the most obvious. However, that had collapsed after 1966, leaving a legacy of ruined mills, and thousands of remaining flax plants, which gave the Island vegetation a distinctive characteristic, but which became almost impossible to eradicate on some very steep mountain slopes. More recently, the Island gained external revenues from tourism, philatelic services (for St Helena postage stamps were sought after by collectors), and the export of coffee and tuna. However, these activities were all relatively small, with various constraints. Of course there was economic activity, and work for people, in other areas such as agriculture (including maize, potatoes, vegetables and many varieties of tropical and sub-tropical fruit), fishing other than tuna, hotels, shops, restaurants, communications, transport, education, medical and government services and more. However, about sixty per cent of the work force was employed by the government, wages were low, and many Saints were forced to seek employment abroad. Lucy discovered that contract employees, such as herself, who were recruited from overseas to fill important gaps in areas such as education and health services, were paid more than locals (because they had to be attracted to the Island) and that that caused understandable unhappiness.

"Have you noticed how many of the pupils at the School have relations working abroad?" Lucy asked Colin one day. "About a quarter of those in my classes have a father, an elder brother or sister, an uncle and aunt, or whoever, away from the Island."

"Yes, that's true. Many are on Ascension Island and the Falklands, but also in South Africa and the UK. There simply aren't enough opportunities here. It's mostly the young who move away, so the remaining population consists mainly of the very young and the old. One of the most important sources of income for the Island is the remittances those migrant workers send home here."

"It must put a big strain on family life."

"Yes, and the more so because it's so difficult for relatives working abroad to come home to visit their families. It can take up to three weeks, and a lot of expense, to travel from Cape Town and back, in order to spend only a week at home here. That's one reason there's so much debate about the need for an airport on the Island."

"Oh, I shudder to think of it," said Lucy. "It would open up the Island to the outside world and surely spoil its unique culture. I love its remoteness and special character."

"It would make it easier for family members here and abroad to visit each other," said Colin. "Also, better access to the Island would help the tourist industry to grow, and that would create more jobs, so more young people might be able to remain here to work. An air service would also be invaluable in cases of serious illness, where a patient needs to be sent to Cape Town for emergency treatment we can't provide here."

"I suppose so. Perhaps I'm selfish, but I know of many Saints who share my view. I hope it doesn't come. I wouldn't like this beautiful place to change."

"Maybe we need the right kind of change, Lucy. Not too dramatic, perhaps, but moving in the right direction, without losing the good there is to love and admire here." He paused. "You know, I've noticed subtle, almost silly changes, but they're important in a way. When I first came here I wondered how we could ever have a successful tourist industry, because of the attitude of some of the people. There was a restaurant in the main street of Jamestown which closed down at lunchtime, so the staff could have their lunch between one and two, just when their customers would want them to be open! I also got a terrible lambasting at Ann's Place once because I'd forgotten to book for dinner before six o'clock – but there were only a few people in the restaurant that night. Now you see these places as friendly, efficient and caring to serve their customers. Also, there was nothing in the shops for tourists to buy – to tempt them to spend money, for a souvenir or whatever. Now there's much more on offer."

Lucy listened to the debates about the possibility and desirability of building an airport on the Island, but did not pay too much attention. It seemed to be some years away, and deep down, although she understood the intellectual arguments in favour of it, she secretly hoped it would not happen. There also seemed to be various proposed projects, directly or indirectly connected with the airport, to build a big hotel, or hotels, on the Island. However, she *did* pay attention when she heard the name of Morgen in relation to one such proposal. That was the only time that she herself initiated any contact with Neil.

"Neil, I hear Morgen is involved in a property venture here on St Helena Island. I dimly recall hearing something a long time ago, but had forgotten it. Neil you can't let them build an airport and luxury hotel on this Island. It's sacrilege! It will desecrate the place."

She had much more to say, along the same lines, and Neil listened until she had finished.

"Lucy, I don't know much of what they're planning in our Property Division. Eugene Roux is very imaginative in some of his projects. I know he's been to St Helena a few times, and he loves the Island, so he may be planning something. But I can't see any private organization carrying the cost of an airport in so remote a place and making a profit out of it. Perhaps a hotel, if enough people could get to the Island? I don't know. I'll talk to Eugene if you like, and I'll let you know if anything is about to happen soon."

So matters seemed to rest for a long time.

Meanwhile Lucy continued to work, to explore, to make friends on the Island, and to love. She was very happy, and Colin contributed in great measure to that. It was wonderful to have someone to be close to at times. She could honestly say that she came to love him, so it was a wrench when his contract came to an end and she had to say good-bye. She made a special dinner for him at her home on their last night together. It was a calm and balmy evening and they ate on the veranda, with lights of the Island twinkling below them and a clear starry sky above.

"You don't want to change your mind about not following me to England?" Colin asked hopefully.

"No, my dear Colin. Much as I love you, and much as I'll always treasure the times we've had together, I'm happy here. I don't want to move. Remember the rules? Also, we know I'm older than you, and I'll not want to have children now, as you will. It's hard for me too, but it won't make sense for me to follow you."

"I know, Lucy, but I thought I'd try anyway."

"Perhaps you could visit me sometimes?"

"Not easy, with no airport. But we'll see. I can't make promises I may not be able to keep."

They made love beautifully and slept in each other's arms that night. Then, the next day, Lucy stood on the waterfront, with a heart full of happiness for their shared past and sadness at his departure, as she watched RMS *St Helena* take Colin away on the first stage of his long journey to pick up again the threads of his life in England.

It was the beginning of October, more than a year later, when Lucy heard from Neil that he was in the process of divorce, and that he would be arriving on St Helena for a short stay in the following month. Lucy had misgivings about seeing Neil, but, on Wednesday, 24th October, something happened to make her contact him, and even believe that there could be some purpose to his time on the Island.

That evening Lucy attended a presentation and discussion at the School about proposals for the airport and other developments on the Island. It seemed that the airport was now likely to be built by the government. "Neil was right," she thought. "The cost is much too much for a commercial venture." However, there was a presentation by the representative of a consortium which planned to build a large luxury hotel on the Island, as well as an adjacent eighteen-hole golf course. It was an imaginative scheme, and opinions about it were divided, but Lucy was horrified. "This will begin to change the whole culture and character of the Island for the worse," she thought. When she heard that the Morgen Property Division had an important share of the consortium, she determined to phone Neil.

She only managed to make contact with him on the Friday evening, two days later. He seemed tired, but she launched into her speech nonetheless:

"Neil, Morgen is a big part of a consortium planning to build a large hotel and golf course on St Helena. It's awful. You must stop them. It'll be like bringing the Durban beachfront to this place, where it doesn't belong. It'll be a disaster. I'll show you when you come here. You must stop them."

Neil listened to her for some time, and again promised to speak to Eugene Roux to discover what was happening.

"But, Lucy, I don't think Morgen will be actively pursuing such a project at the moment. Everything is directed to fighting off this Predvest takeover bid. Things are getting nasty. On Wednesday night someone burnt down part of our Platberg factory."

26

Susie Mack was on the prowl again. This time her target was Nick Hunter of Benchmark Stockbrokers, who was sitting next to her, and paying her particular attention, in the firm's private suite at the famous Wanderers cricket ground in the northern suburbs of Johannesburg.

Benchmark was a medium-sized broking firm whose main partners were the founders, Ben Marais and Mark Baynes. These two, together with one of their dealers, Nick Hunter, had called on David Goldberg and Harry Naidoo at Bullion Asset Management a few days before. Of course, the purpose of the meeting was to try to persuade BAM to give them a greater portion of BAM's business, of which they currently received only very small and infrequent orders. David and Harry explained how BAM allocated its business on the basis of the services given to them by their brokers, and a discussion ensued. David was diplomatic as usual.

"Keep in touch with us and we'll see what we can do," he said.

Susie was called into the meeting, and it was agreed that she and Nick, who already knew each other fairly well, should remain in contact.

After their visitors had gone, Susie said quietly, "Geoff wants another broker on his project. I think I could use Nick – unless you object."

David and Harry looked uncomfortably at one another for a moment.

"Okay, Susie," said David, "but for heaven's sake be careful."

Nick had then begun to telephone Susie each day, with market news and to keep in touch – as indeed did many others with whom BAM did business. Then Nick had invited her to watch cricket at the Wanderers in the firm's box which the cricket-mad senior partners used to entertain clients. Nick was young and attractive, with the fit figure of a sportsman, a broad smiling face, dark hair and dark eyes. Susie found him attractive, and wanted some variety in her life. It was a warm day and she wore an outrageously skimpy white sundress, which left on show her smooth, shapely back and shoulders, and much of her breasts and cleavage, shapely legs and voluptuous thighs. As he was meant to be, Nick was fascinated by the display, which was presented in a variety of poses and moves during the day. His main duty was to look after Susie, and it was not difficult to take more notice of her than of the cricket. Of course the subject of business from BAM was subtly in the air, and Susie found a moment to mention that she felt sure she could find a way of directing business to Nick, who knew that his firm needed it.

The game ended as the light was fading, and the Benchmark guests stayed for a last drink and a chat while the main crowd dispersed and the traffic congestion on the roads lessened.

Susie gazed into Nick's eyes, and said in a quiet version of her little girl voice: "Sweetie, that was such a lovely day. Thank you. Won't you come to my home and have a drink and some dinner with me. I can rustle up something very easily, and I would so like to thank you."

Nick was on the point of refusing, but she was insistent, so he said he would come for a short while. He telephoned his wife to say that he was entertaining clients and was not sure when he would be home.

At Susie's home, they sat on her veranda in the refreshing coolness which comes after a hot day, and chatted over a drink, while a light supper was being warmed up. Nick followed her into the kitchen and watched while she dished up the food. There was a gap against one wall, to which Susie drew his attention, explaining that that was where her old freezer had stood.

"It was so old that it stopped working and was not worth repairing," she explained, "so I had it taken away. I've been looking for a replacement and have found just the one I want at Freddie's. See, here it is, in this brochure. It's the one I've marked. I've checked, and they do have it in stock." Then, in the little girl voice: "It would be *so* nice to have it soon."

After supper she showed him the rest of the house. In her bedroom, she placed her arms around him and hugged. "You're so sweet, my darling," he heard the irresistible little girl voice say. "I just know we'll be able to work together."

She gazed into his eyes, willing him to look deeply into hers. She held herself close to him, so he could feel the voluptuous curves and smooth skin he had seen and been fascinated by all day. Nick was in no mood to resist the offer that was there. Soon they found themselves on her bed with no clothes on.

Susie's voice became deep and sensual: "You're so strong and exciting, my dear. I want you between my legs."

27

Every day was a working day for Geoff Loman, and he had no scruples about expecting that from all those who worked with him, especially when closing in on a deal. Families and private time were not to be considered. Over weekends it was relatively easy to assemble busy people, away from the pressing demands of their full diaries, telephones and offices. So it was that he had called a meeting of key executives and advisors, involved in the Morgen bid, at his home on Sunday morning, 28th October. It was a calm sunny highveld morning, so Geoff had instructed that tables and chairs be set out on the lawn in the spring-soft shade of two huge spreading oak trees. Some might have thought it strange to see casually dressed men and women sitting outside in those surroundings equipped with brief cases, laptop computers and mobile phones.

Geoff was briefed on progress with obtaining undertakings to vote for the proposed Morgen transaction.

"It's becoming more and more of a struggle now," said Stanley. "We'll certainly have a majority of the votes, but it's not clear that we'll be able to get to the seventy-five per cent we need. We've spoken to all the big players, and of course we're working on the smaller shareholders too. But it's hard work, and we've only been bringing in dribs and drabs the last three or four days."

Geoff asked, "What more can we do?"

"Apart from raising the price again, really only more of what we've been doing," answered James.

"No, we can't put up the price," said Geoff emphatically. "That would make the deal not worth doing."

James said, "So far as we can determine, Lucy Morgen is the only substantial shareholder who's not committed one way or another. Her three per cent of the votes could be critical."

"Then speak to her," said Geoff.

"She won't talk to anyone about it – even the Morgen family. She simply puts the phone down on us."

"Well then, somebody must get on a plane and go and talk to her. Stanley, you were married to her. Do you think she'll listen to you?"

"There is not the smallest chance of that," said Stanley. "But Geoff, she's on St Helena Island, where no planes can go. You can only get there by sea, and it takes a few days."

Geoff picked up his cell phone and called his secretary. "Jody, I need to get someone to St Helena Island as soon as possible. Can you see what can be done? ....I think it's in the Atlantic somewhere. I think you have to go by ship. Call me back as soon as you can.

"If we can find a way for someone to see Lucy, then who should it be if not Stanley? James, you were close to her once, and you're her brother-in-law. Do you think you could persuade her to vote for us?"

"Possibly, face to face, but not easily. She can be pretty stubborn, and she has basically run away from all of this."

The meeting continued. Then, a while later Jody phoned.

"Geoff, I've established that basically the only way to get to St Helena Island is to take the Royal Mail ship, RMS *St Helena*. The soonest sailing is from Cape Town next Sunday, the fourth of November. It's due to call at Walvis Bay on Wednesday, the seventh, and should reach St Helena Island on Sunday, the eleventh."

"That's five days before the meeting," said Geoff.

Jody continued, "Whoever goes will have to spend a week on the Island. The ship goes on to Ascension Island and picks up return passengers on its way back. It's due back in Cape Town on the twenty-fifth of November. That's three weeks away in all. I'll only be able to check with the shipping agents first thing tomorrow to find out whether they have accommodation for us."

"Thank you, Jody. Let me know in the morning." Then, turning to James: "It looks like a three week working holiday for you – with not much work. Lucky man!"

"I can't be away for three weeks, what with this deal and all"

"Nonsense. Stanley knows everything that's going on. When did you last take a break? Take Patsy with you."

"She won't want to be away from home and children for so long. Also, if I needed to work on Lucy, it would be better if Patsy were not there, but don't tell her I said that. I don't think I can afford to go away for so long."

"Maybe you can't afford not to go. It could mean a lot of money for all of us. It could mean a very large amount for you personally. We have to try to get her onto our side. She may hold the deciding votes."

Early the following morning, Jody contacted the shipping agents as promised. The ship was fully booked from Cape Town to Walvis Bay, but a good cabin was available from Walvis Bay to the Island and back. So it was that James prepared himself to fly to Namibia in time to board the RMS *St Helena* at Walvis Bay on Wednesday, 7th November.

James telephoned Lucy to tell her he was coming, but she put the phone down as soon as she recognised his voice. He sent an e-mail to her at her school's office, but she did not respond.

28

Susie Mack had been delighted with the new freezer that was delivered to her home soon after her evening with Nick Hunter. She telephoned him at once.

"Nick my dear, what a wonderful, unexpected surprise! Thank you *so* much. We had such a lovely time together. We must meet again soon."

She gave him a few small orders, but hinted that something interesting would come up soon. Then, while she was still having her breakfast early on the morning of Wednesday, 31st October, she received a phone call from Geoff Loman with carefully worded confirmation that "a critical period has begun and your project must continue immediately."

Susie phoned Nick and asked him to meet her for a quick cup of coffee before the stock market opened.

"Nick, I was almost certain I'd find something you'd be interested in, and I have. I just need to give you the background, so you'll know what to do, without our conversation being overheard or recorded."

Nick looked doubtful, but said nothing, waiting for her to speak again.

"You know, of course, about the Predvest bid for Morgen? Good. This Friday is the last day to trade for anyone wishing to be registered as a shareholder of Morgen, in time for them to be entitled to vote at the general meeting next month. Geoff Loman wants the deal to look attractive. As the price depends on that of Predvest, he wants us to make sure that Predvest trades, or at least ends each day, at or close to a thousand cents."

"It's about nine-eighty now."

"I'll give you orders in the normal way. Your job will be to execute them, so we get the level we want."

"I don't like it, Susie. We need business, but I'm not sure about manipulating prices."

"There's no risk whatsoever. All that's happening is that BAM is making an investment."

Nick looked doubtful. "I'll need to think about it, Susie."

"The matter's urgent, Nick." Then, in her little girl voice: "You did like our time together, my darling? Don't I make you feel good? It's our little secret, and we both want it to stay just between us, don't we?"

Nick was silent.

"I'll let you have the first orders to buy Predvest when I get back to my desk. There'll be a lot more behind them."

Nick nodded.

"Thank you, my darling. I just knew I could rely on you."

29

Neil flew from Johannesburg to Cape Town on Thursday morning, 1st November. He spent that afternoon and evening, as well as all of Friday, doing business, visiting Morgen offices and factories in the area. He found much the same apprehension there as in the Johannesburg head office and at Platberg. No violence had been done to Company property in the Cape, but everywhere he found people worried about their jobs, the security of their pensions, and the risks of the Company simply ceasing to exist after a possible takeover by Predvest. He tried to offer assurance where he could, but deep down he himself was now troubled, for he knew that Predvest was far ahead in the race for votes.

On Saturday, Neil decided that he was at last on holiday. After a leisurely breakfast, he took a drive into the beautiful Cape wine-lands. He began to relax as he explored historic wine estates with gabled white Cape Dutch buildings, beautiful gardens, and vast vineyards in fertile valleys, sheltered by tall rugged mountains. In the evening he enjoyed an excellent wine from one of those estates, while he dined in his waterfront hotel, idly watching the activity in the harbour, and enjoying the wonderful view across the city and up the steep slopes of nearby Table Mountain and Devil's Peak, soaring to more than a thousand metres above the sea.

Neil's travel information told him that he had to check in at the harbour at two o'clock in the afternoon for planned departure between four and seven o'clock on Sunday, 4th November. So it was that his taxi dropped him off with his luggage just before two o'clock at the Mission to Seafarers building near E-berth in the Cape Town docks. He and the other passengers were met by the cheerful and friendly representative of the shipping agents. She shepherded them into minibuses, while their luggage was loaded onto trailers. They were driven into a large warehouse, where the luggage was dropped off to be cleared through customs, loaded into cages and taken aboard ship, to appear in their cabins before departure. The passengers were driven on to the dockside, where they alighted near a narrow gangway leading into the side of the RMS *St Helena*. While waiting his turn to board, Neil took in the dark blue of the lower part of the ship, the white upper decks and square superstructure, and the mainly yellow funnel with a seahorse motif. Once on board, passports and departure forms were taken from the passengers, so the ship's staff could take care of the departure formalities, and passengers were shown to their cabins. Neil had a cheerful, comfortable cabin on the port side of A Deck, with a large curtained window from which he could then look out across the harbour. With time on his hands, he decided to explore the ship that would be his home for the next few days.

When the voyages of the Royal Mail ships of the Union Castle Line ceased in 1977, the sea link to St Helena Island was taken over by Curnow Shipping's St Helena Line under charter of the St Helena government. The present nearly seven thousand ton RMS *St Helena* was built in 1989 to replace a much smaller vessel of the same name. She was designed to carry cargo and up to 128 passengers. Neil was to find that she was beautifully fitted out as a comfortable passenger liner, notwithstanding her dual cargo-passenger function. Forward of his cabin, on the same level, he found a large and comfortable lounge, extending the whole width of the ship. It was warmly red-carpeted, with comfortable patterned red and green armchairs and light wooden round tables. Large, brightly curtained windows afforded views in three directions, though the forward view was then curtailed by containers forming part of the deck cargo. There was a bar, a library nook, and an alcove that could be curtained off from the main room if needed. One level up, on the Promenade Deck, Neil found a less formal Sun Lounge towards the stern. It was light and airy, with wicker-style chairs and green-topped little tables, a bar and a buffet serving counter. Large, curtained windows looked out to port and starboard, and also aft over an empty, covered swimming pool to a spacious "Sun Deck", temporarily cordoned off so the work of the crew would not be hindered. Neil found his way higher up to the blue-painted aft part of the bridge deck, where there was ample viewing space for passengers around the large yellow funnel.

Neil leant on the rail and looked past one of the bright orange lifeboats towards Table Mountain. Its top was covered with cloud – what the locals called its "table cloth" – which had been growing during the day.

"The weather's changing," said a friendly voice at his side.

Neil turned to see a comfortably proportioned gentleman in casual dress, who seemed to be quite happy in familiar surroundings. They spoke a few friendly words, from which Neil understood that his companion lived on St Helena and was returning home. Later Neil discovered that this gentleman was the Bishop of St Helena. His diocese was surely one of the smallest by population, but possibly the most remote and largest in extent, as it encompassed the far-flung and remote islands of St Helena, Ascension and Tristan da Cunha.

The first formal event for the passengers was the obligatory emergency drill. After being warned over the public address system, they heard the general emergency alarm signal (seven or more short blasts on the ship's siren, followed by a long blast), upon which they had to collect their life jackets from their cabins and assemble in the Sun Lounge. Neil found the lounge a crowded and cheerful sea of orange, as passengers put on their life jackets, with help from crew-members where needed. As people chattered away, Neil heard English spoken in a variety of accents, some Afrikaans and a little French. The passengers were introduced to some of the officers and staff and instructed in the ship's emergency procedures.

In the crush it was impossible for persons not to bump into one another. Neil was bumped by a tall lady who turned to apologise. He noticed a friendly smile, reddish hair, pale blue eyes, pleasantly freckled skin and shapely breasts. They introduced themselves while they waited for the crush to diminish as passengers began returning to their cabins. She was May Johnson, and she introduced her husband, Alan, when a tall, heavy, ruddy faced man with light brown hair and grey eyes joined them. They were English, with homes in Cape Town and Kent. They were bound for Ascension Island, from where they would fly with the Royal Air Force, which also carried civilian passengers to and from there, to attend a wedding near their northern home, before flying back to Cape Town for the best of the southern summer. Neil told them he was bound for St Helena "for some business and more holiday".

"What business would that be?" asked May.

"That's a long story" was all Neil could say then.

About six o'clock, with the help of two tugs, RMS *St Helena* slowly left E-berth and moved to another station in the harbour where she could take on fuel, an operation that, they were told, would take between four and five hours. The weather had grown cold, wet and windy, with low cloud obscuring most of Table Mountain. Neil had a shower and went to dinner, having asked to be placed in the first of two sittings, at a quarter to seven. The comfortable dining room was deep down in C-deck, decorated predominantly in blue, with pale wooden furniture, low lighting and elegantly set tables. Neil was placed at a small table with an English couple, and three other South Africans.

Neil discovered that the cruise had a musical theme. The Cape Town classical music radio station had arranged for a musical group, led by one of its knowledgeable musicologists, to travel to St Helena, with a series of concerts, lectures and musical events aboard ship and on the Island. Several of the passengers comprised that group. Three musicians accompanied them, and Neil listened to a concert in the main lounge, given by piano, violin and cello, before he went to bed.

Neil was wakened by the movement of the ship just after one thirty a.m. From his cabin window, he saw through the rain a green light at the harbour mouth. There was an increasingly heavy swell as the ship moved into open waters.

On Monday morning Neil woke to sullen skies, a strong wind and heavy swell. Old and young were doddering around uncertainly like drunken geriatrics as the ship lurched and swayed under their feet. Remembering that the Cape of Good Hope had formerly been called the Cape of Storms, Neil also reminded himself of the old adage of one hand for himself and one for the ship. Five or six dark-winged petrels flew over the wake, and two spectacular albatrosses over and around the ship. There was no land in sight. Not many passengers were about early that morning, but when Neil had a light breakfast from the casual buffet in the Sun Lounge (preferring that to a full breakfast in the dining room), he spoke to some of the friendly St Helenians, who were travelling home to the Island.

As the day wore on, the weather improved and the swell lessened. The noon report from the bridge informed them that they were travelling at thirteen knots. Neil went up to the bridge deck and leant over the side, fascinated by the movement of the ship through the water. The swell no longer flew over the bows onto the deck. The waves were smashed aside as they crashed into the bow and the sides of the ship, forming a bow-wave white and green with complex frothy lace patterns in the dark metallic grey water. It was beautiful and ever-changing. Neil felt a sense of purpose in the relentless forward movement of the vessel, but also a loneliness in the vastness of the ocean, and the feeling of a long transition to another world remote from his own. They still had several days to go. How would Lucy be, and how would she react to his intrusion into her far-away world?

The swell subsided and the ship became more stable, but the Captain's welcoming cocktail party was postponed to the following evening.

On Tuesday the weather continued to improve, and, with sunlight, colour returned to the sea. By afternoon it was glassy green like jade, but with some white caps whipped up by a cool wind. The swell and wind both came from the south, so the ship was far more stable as she churned her way northwards. She was now making a speed in excess of fourteen knots.

Late that morning Neil was sitting reading in a quiet corner of the main lounge. The music group had crowded into the curtained-off alcove to hear a lecture, but the murmuring which reached Neil across the lounge did not disturb him. After a while he became aware of May sitting down near to him. Her husband had joined the lecture group, and she had a book in her hand. They smiled at each other.

"What business?" asked May, as though continuing their conversation of the first evening.

Neil told her about Morgen and Predvest, and that he hoped to persuade an important shareholder to vote to block the proposed transaction.

"I own shares in Morgen," said May to Neil's surprise. "I don't think they've done much until recently. I remember a big envelope full of documents coming in the post, but I don't usually read that stuff. I tend to hold on to my shares for a long time and let them look after themselves."

"How many shares do you have?" asked Neil.

"I'm not sure. It might be twenty thousand."

"We could find out if necessary. Have you filled in a proxy form so you can vote at the meeting?"

"No, I've never bothered."

"Will you vote against the deal? We've still got until Wednesday next week to submit proxies."

"Perhaps, if you explain things very nicely to me."

"I'll do that."

Neill briefly outlined his argument. "I've got forms in my cabin. I'll get you one."

"I'll come with you."

Neil left the cabin door open while he sat at the little desk-cum-dressing-table and opened a folder to take out a proxy form. By accident or design, the door swung shut. May stood very close to him as he wrote down her exact personal details, so he could e-mail his office to establish the correct size of her shareholding, and in order to be able to fill in the form correctly. She pressed her thigh against his arm and put a hand on his shoulder. Then lunch was announced over the public address system. Neil noticed the sway of her hips as May coolly led the way to the cabin door.

The Captain's cocktail party was held in the main lounge between six o'clock and six forty-five that evening. Captain Rodney Young was there to welcome his guests. He was a St Helenian, and looked very smart in full uniform. Like the other passengers, Neil was introduced to him at the door to the lounge and was given a friendly greeting.

The lounge was already crowded, with nearly everyone dressed in their best, standing with glasses in their hands, talking to friends and family or making new acquaintances. One man had appeared in full Napoleonic uniform – one of the French people on a pilgrimage to the place of Napoleon Bonaparte's exile and death. That this was, in some ways, a very special cruise, was emphasized for Neil when he saw that some of the guests were very distinguished indeed. Not only was the Bishop of St Helena returning to his flock, but a new Governor, Andrew Gurr, and his wife, Jean, were also aboard and attending the cocktail party. The Governor-designate, whose responsibilities would also cover the Ascension and Tristan da Cunha islands, could more easily have flown to Ascension and taken the shorter sea journey from there to St Helena. However, it was deemed more appropriate for the Governor to enter his territories first through St Helena Island, and be sworn into office there, so he and his wife had taken the longer route via Cape Town. The Governor and his wife proved to be friendly and charming. Neil was nearby when he heard the Governor say, "The Bishop is wearing his dressing gown." Neil turned and saw the Bishop splendid and very bishop-like in a flowing red-violet gown with a gold chain and cross on its ample front. The Bishop might well be the Right Reverend the Lord Bishop of St Helena, Bishop John Salt, and the Governor might well be His Excellency Governor Andrew Gurr, but throughout the voyage and after, Neil was impressed by the way in which these people could be so friendly and accessible, and also be able to assume the dignity of their high offices, as occasion demanded.

Neil continued to get to know some of his fellow passengers: more returning Saints who could tell him about the Island; members of the music group; birders and nature lovers, hoping to see the unique birds and endemic plants of the Island; widely travelled people looking for a very different experience; an Afrikaans couple seeking to see where their ancestors had been held prisoner by the British in the Anglo-Boer War more than a century ago; two French couples on pilgrimage to the island prison of Napoleon Bonaparte long before that; some simply wanting to jump off the racing treadmills of their normal lives for a while; and a few looking to escape from who knows what hurt, sorrow, disillusionment or despair, by starting a new life far away – as Lucy had done, Neil thought.

At one time he was standing in the crush when he felt a body more than accidentally leaning against him. He turned to find the smiling full lips and sparkling blue eyes of May close to his face.

Neil's brief glimpse of Namibia was a happy interlude, a dream-like peep into yet another world between that he had temporarily left behind and the unknown one to which he was travelling. At eight o'clock on the morning of Wednesday, 7th November, the RMS, as she was affectionately called, was approaching Walvis Bay on the Namibian coast. At first the low land was scarcely visible in a misty haze. The ship slid slowly through a long channel marked by red and green buoys, turned around in the harbour with the aid of a tug, and settled gently against the tyres protecting her from damage against the quay. As the RMS would need a few hours to load and unload cargo, and disembark and embark some passengers, Neil had arranged to join a small group on an excursion to Swakopmund to the north.

They took the coastal road, with beach and sea to their left and sandy desert with dunes to the right. Swakopmund was a small coastal town with broad, extensive beaches; wide streets, shopping malls, and many restaurants with places to sit outside under trees and umbrellas; an interesting museum, a prominent lighthouse, and colourful public gardens watered by partly treated sewerage; a primary school which Neil saw had playing fields and grounds almost entirely of sand; a German flavour added to the overall African character, as seen in some interesting old German buildings, including the prison, in the German dishes served in some restaurants, and in the excellent beer.

They returned to Walvis Bay by a road inland from the line of high dunes, giving them a brief experience of the desert. They stopped at the large Dune 7, where a strong wind blew sand around them, and frantically waved the palm trees in a picnic area. They saw something of Walvis Bay on their way back to the ship, and Neil was left with impressions of what was essentially a port city, with palm-lined streets, some wealthy homes, and flamingos in a wide lagoon.

Neil was aboard RMS *St Helena* in good time for her departure, scheduled for five o'clock that afternoon. He was able to use his mobile phone to call his office, and to speak briefly to Lucy on St Helena Island. She was somewhat distracted and agitated.

30

It was a pleasant Tuesday afternoon. Formal lessons had ended for the day, but Lucy was in the library of Prince Andrew School, helping some of her pupils to source material for project work they had been assigned. The librarian helped with this in between checking books in and out for students returning or borrowing them. The afternoon light filtered through the trees outside the windows and gently illumined the library's pale green walls and warm wooden bookshelves. There was a pleasant buzz of ordered activity. Lucy was able to pause for a while to speak quietly with the librarian and one of the male teachers who had come to find a book.

A worried call disturbed the peace:

"Ma'am – Mrs Morgen – Katie's fainted."

Lucy turned to see Katie Thomas, one of her pupils, slumped with her head resting on an arm on the table where she had been working. An open reference book and a note pad lay under her arm, and the girl's long black hair hid her face and spread over the table.

"Keep away," warned Lucy as everyone in the library began to converge on Katie. Lucy reached her first of the teachers, who helped her gently raise the young girl into a sitting position. She was unconscious and was breathing, but Lucy quickly established that her heartbeat was faint and fluttery. Her brown face had grown pale and her lips had a slight blue tinge.

"Quick! I think I must take her to the hospital," cried Lucy, alarmed.

"No, call an ambulance," said Tony, the male teacher.

"I can get her there with one trip."

"But the ambulance people can stabilize her as soon as they get here."

"I'll dial 911," called Jenny, the librarian, running out to the office to telephone. "Stay here with her."

All this happened very quickly. Lucy put her arm around Katie's shoulders, gently stroked her face and spoke to her, trying to revive her, but without success.

"What happened?" Tony asked the other pupils. "Was she all right when she came in here?"

"She seemed normal. She was just sitting next to me at the table reading, and making notes, when she fell forward like that."

"Some boys were chasing her in the lunch break – only in fun. They made her run around a lot. She had difficulty breathing afterwards, and said she was feeling very ill. But then she sat down for a while, and seemed to be all right again."

Jenny burst into the room. "The ambulance should be here any moment."

"Shall I carry her to the entrance?" asked Tony, who was big and strong.

"Probably better to let them examine her here," said Lucy. "Jenny, please show them the way as soon as they arrive."

The ambulance men were soon there. They quickly examined the patient, and took her on a stretcher to the ambulance, which speeded off to the hospital in Jamestown.

Jenny had already telephoned Katie's mother, and now did so again to report that her daughter was on the way to hospital. Lucy dismissed the class, then rushed out to her car and drove in the direction of the ambulance.

The General Hospital was situated in the upper part of Jamestown at the end of Market Street. The two-storied, green-roofed, cream building with verandas and a pretty flower garden in front, had been built in 1955. It was part of a complex which also included a community clinic, dental surgery, administration offices and laboratories. The hospital had fifty-four beds, and was key to the sophisticated Island healthcare system which also included a number of rural health centres. The medical needs of the Islanders were generally well catered for, and large investments were made to improve the hospital facilities, and to bring appropriate specialist consultants to the Island for short periods. Lucy knew, for example, that an orthopaedic surgeon had recently been brought to the Island to perform a number of hip and other operations. However, with such a small population, some needs could not be fully met. These included cases of leukaemia, certain cancers, some heart conditions, and organ transplants. Such cases were sent abroad in the care of the ship's doctor to be treated, mainly to Cape Town but occasionally by way of Ascension Island to the United Kingdom. The infrequency and slowness of the shipping links between the Island and the outside world could be very serious for such patients, and reinforced the arguments in favour of an air link.

Lucy spent many hours at the hospital over the next few days. She arrived there at about the same time as Katie's mother, Jane Thomas, and helped to calm and comfort her. Katie's father was away, working at Stanley in the faraway Falkland Islands, but fortunately Jane had many relations on the Island and they rallied to give her support. There was much waiting to do initially, and news of Katie came through slowly. She had been stabilized, and recovered consciousness, but was very weak. Extensive examinations and tests had to be done. The doctors were very worried about her heart. It was not certain yet, but she might need to be sent to Cape Town for treatment.

At a time when the doctor was speaking to Jane, and Jane was allowed to see Katie for a short while, Lucy went out on to the veranda for a breath of fresh air and to calm her thoughts. She looked across the pretty garden in front of her to the jacaranda trees spreading themselves over the parking area. The most sheltered were already covered in blue flowers, while those further away still held only a few isolated bunches of blue. Across the road the tall silky oaks spread out their arms to show open hands of russet-yellow flowers. From behind the low white dental clinic building, the steeply sloping red roof of the red and brown stone St John's Church pointed encouragingly to the mountainside and sky.

What if Katie needed urgent treatment abroad? Suddenly the Island seemed very remote, something that had never worried Lucy, except perhaps for a while after Colin's departure. She could not help remembering the true story she had been told of a seven-year-old girl who had been diagnosed with leukaemia a few years before. Her parents had been away, working in the Falklands. The Island health authorities had radioed for passing ships to help. The nearest had been eighteen hours' sailing away and the cost of diverting her ran into tens of thousands of pounds. The shipping company never sent a bill, but treated the case like a ship in distress at sea. They took off the young girl, with two nurses, and three family members in order to match tissue for a possible bone-marrow transplant. Unfortunately she died about two weeks after reaching Cape Town. What if Katie needed urgent help off the Island? Would she reach it in time? "We're so far away," thought Lucy.

It was a terrible time. Irrationally, Lucy felt some personal responsibility, because Katie's collapse had happened when the girl had been in her care. She left the hospital when visiting hours ended at seven thirty that evening, but she could not get Katie and the incident out of her mind. Katie had always been a lovable young person. She was then fourteen years old, and had always been rather small for her age. She had a slim, fragile body, but was attractive with large brown eyes and long black hair. She was often quiet, and was gentle and caring, but could be full of fun, with a mischievous smile. She was a good student, and Lucy had become very fond of her.

The next day, Wednesday, Lucy had a free period just before the School's lunch break, and drove to the hospital. She was allowed to see Katie very briefly. Katie was very weak and pale, and hooked up to numerous instruments, but recognised Lucy and seemed quietly happy to see her. Jane Thomas told Lucy that the doctors continued to be worried. Katie was hopefully out of immediate danger, but her condition was serious and she would most probably need to be treated in Cape Town. Radio messages had been sent out to determine which ships were in the area, but there were none nearby. They would have to rely on the RMS *St Helena* which was due to leave Walvis Bay that evening, and would reach the Island on Sunday morning. It would be a further week before the ship left for Cape Town, after completing her return trip to Ascension Island. Hopefully Katie would not suffer a relapse, and could recover well enough to make the long journey. A watch would be kept for passing ships, though none was expected, and the option to send her to England by air from Ascension Island could be exercised if necessary.

After her last lesson that afternoon, Lucy briefly called in at her home before going again to the hospital. The telephone rang. It was Neil.

"Hello, Lucy. How are you?"

"Not too bad. Where are you?"

"I'm just about to leave Walvis Bay. I've had a good day today visiting Swakopmund. I just wanted to tell you, while I have a cellphone connection here in the harbour, that I'm looking forward to seeing you soon."

"Sorry I can't talk, Neil," said Lucy, distractedly. "I'm just off to the hospital to see a pupil who is seriously ill. She may need to go to Cape Town for treatment. Try to hurry the RMS, Neil. She may be needed for our patient."

Lucy rang off, leaving Neil feeling a little deflated. He fully understood the possible need of a patient on the Island, but he could not avoid the knowledge that Lucy did not want the RMS to make haste because she wanted to see *him*.

31

The RMS *St Helena* sailed from Walvis Bay on time and slipped quietly through the long channel towards the open sea, where she turned north-west towards St Helena Island still three days and four nights' sailing away. There was a strong breeze blowing, but only a moderate swell. Neil watched their departure from the aft part of the bridge deck. As he looked back towards the disappearing land, he noticed a familiar figure leaning over the rail on the Sun Deck below.

"James Bold!" he exclaimed to himself. "He must have come aboard at Walvis Bay. There can only be one reason for that. This could be interesting – and complicated."

Neil checked the passenger list and the dining room table allocations. James had been given the second sitting for dinner, and, as luck would have it, had been placed at the same table as May and Alan Johnson.

"That could be the end of my twenty thousand votes," thought Neil.

After dinner that evening Neil saw May and James sitting together in the Sun Lounge, away from the entertainment going on in the main lounge. Neil approached them and they exchanged greetings.

"This is a surprise, James. What brings you here? It's rather off your beaten track, isn't it?"

James looked at him coolly. "I decided to pay an old friend a visit on the Island. I think you know Lucy Morgen. I'm sure you're also here not purely for your health."

"I'm on holiday, but I may combine a little business with pleasure."

May broke in: "Neil, I was so surprised when James said he was going to the Island for the same reason as you. I told him I have shares in Morgen, and he wants to explain to me his side of the story."

"I'm sure he does," said Neil. "Remember you have my form, and you should vote against the deal."

"I'll get him to explain to me very nicely, and then decide which of you to support," she said with a happy smile.

Overnight the clocks were turned back two hours to Greenwich Mean Time, so on board ship they then kept the same time as in London and on St Helena Island, two hours behind Cape Town and Johannesburg.

Thursday, 8th November was a beautiful day. The seas were fairly calm, of the deepest dark blue, only touched with white here and there. The south-east trade wind blew them on their way, and the noon report revealed that they had averaged 14.6 knots since Walvis Bay. The sighting of two albatrosses just before lunchtime caused some excitement for the bird-lovers. At two o'clock Neil joined some other passengers on a tour of the bridge, where the equipment and workings of the control centre of the ship and its navigation were explained to them by the charming and petite lady second officer. Among other things, she was able to tell them that the nearest ship to them was 175 miles away!

Neil gathered that James Bold had not shaken off his big-city restlessness. He saw him on two or three occasions haunting the area around the purser's office, obviously making use of the e-mail and satellite phone facilities, and probably keeping in touch with his office. There were three or four public address announcements during the morning that there was "a message at the bureau for Mr James Bold". He also saw James and May talking confidentially to each other in the lounge. They carefully avoided acknowledging his presence, and he gained the impression that they were very interested in each other. On his way to his cabin after the bridge tour, he just caught a glimpse of them entering James's cabin.

James had of course spoken to May about the Predvest-Morgen deal and encouraged her to vote for it. He had also asked his office to confirm her exact details and actual shareholding in Morgen, and obtained the information early in the afternoon, when he found May reading alone in a quiet corner of the main lounge. He sat down next to her.

"I can fill in a proxy form for you to sign if you want, and then I can submit it in good time," he said.

"Oh, I know we still have plenty of time. I need to think about it." Then, leaning closely towards him and speaking very quietly: "I need more explanations from you, James. I'm sure if we go to your cabin you can tell me all about everything in private – and be very nice to me."

"What about your husband?"

"He's playing bridge. He won't miss me for an hour or two."

Together they slipped out of the lounge and went to the cabin. James locked the door and she put her arms around him.

"These beds are very narrow," he remarked as he responded to her.

"All the closer for our communications," she murmured.

James thought that twenty thousand votes were not all that many, but every vote counted, and there was no reason why he should not be happy in his work if the opportunity was offered.

Friday 9th November was partly cloudy in the early morning. After breakfast the sea was a deep blue ahead, but grey and silver behind them and to the east under the influence of the cloud and sun. By lunchtime the weather was clear and the sea all blue. Neil remembered reading somewhere that these seas were among the kindest of all, and so it seemed. They were still making a good speed of around fourteen and a half knots. There were children in the swimming pool, and passengers sunned themselves and enjoyed refreshments and lunch on the Sun Deck. The bishop appeared in baggy casual clothes and a camouflage-patterned sun hat.

Though it all seemed so far away, Neil was still aware that this Friday was the record date for determining who would be eligible to vote at the Morgen shareholders' meeting. He sent

Will a message to inform him that James Bold was aboard, and had most probably secured the twenty thousand votes of May Johnson. May had in fact not yet signed a proxy form, but was still concentrating on obtaining detailed explanations in private from James.

That afternoon Neil attended a showing, in the alcove of the main lounge, of a film about St Helena – its history, its people, its natural beauty and places of interest. There was time for questions and discussions afterwards. Much interest was shown in the unique character of the remote Island and its people, and the threats to that posed by the possible building of an airport on the Island, and plans for the establishment of a holiday hotel to cater for increased numbers of tourists drawn by easier access to the Island. Apparently opinions were divided amongst the islanders, and others who loved St Helena. Many wished to retain its isolation and existing character, while others felt change should be embraced with the benefits of easier physical contact with the outside world, including job opportunities created by an enhanced tourist industry, and more speedy access (by air) to medical facilities not available on the Island for certain serious emergency cases.

As he usually did, Neil went out onto the Sun Deck that night before turning in to bed. He liked to feel the motion of the ship, her progress through the water, pushing aside the waves and leaving a disturbed wake, with white touched by moonlight, disappearing into the dark sea. From the stern, the ship's lights were soft and comforting, suggesting a warm cocoon moving through the vast darkness of ocean and heavens. Only the wake and the low throbbing of the engines spoke of change, but their forward movement continued relentlessly. Neil thought about movement and change. Nothing in life stood still for long. Change had to be embraced, but was that always easy?

St Helena had been debating change for years. Some would resist it and others embrace it, but in the long run those changes would surely come. Already Neil could speak to Lucy by telephone, while satellite communications technology could link the Island even more closely to the remote outside world.

He himself should have recognized the need for change in his private life four years ago, when his marriage had been unhappy and Lucy and he had been so close. He had resisted change, in the name of his perceived duty to the woman he had married and to his children. So he had lost the love of his life, and this journey to meet Lucy again had a bitter-sweet quality. He would see her, and hopefully she would be glad to remember former times, but she could never be entirely his.

And what of Lucy? She had embraced change in her own way. She had handled the deep disappointments of her life by running away. After her failed marriage she had left the big city and buried herself in the quieter country environment in and around Platberg. She had found healing, peace and happiness. Then she and Neil had brought the deepest of love and joy to one another. When her pain and longing had become too great, and he had not been able to commit himself to her out of duty to his family, she had run away again. This time it was virtually as far as anyone could go, to St Helena Island. There it seemed she had once more found solace and peace and seemed to be very happy. Now she was resisting change. She did not want the world she had gone so far to escape to intrude upon her peace. She had not allowed herself to be involved in the Morgen-Predvest affair. However, the world was closing in, firstly with its ever more sophisticated communications, and now with talk of an airport. Now, too, he and James Bold, both from her past and with their own agendas, were moving across the ocean closer and closer towards her. How would she react to these intrusions?

Saturday, 10th November, would be their last day as sea. They were due to reach the Island very early the following morning. It was important that they were on time, for the new Governor had to be landed early to prepare for two important events scheduled for that morning. The swearing-in ceremony for the Governor was due to take place at nine thirty, and that would be followed at ten forty-five by a memorial service at the Cenotaph to mark Remembrance Day, 11th November.

The day was cloudy, but bright and pleasantly mild, with a calm sea. In the morning Neil watched a match of deck cricket, played on the Sun Deck with monkey-fist rope balls, and local rules, between the passengers and crew. Alan Johnson was playing for the passengers, and Neil noticed first James and then May slipping away quietly to take the opportunity for another round of explanations. These no doubt proved to be very satisfactory, for just before lunch May signed a proxy form, instructing that her votes should be cast in favour of Predvest.

Neil had a quiet day. Luggage was packed and collected during the afternoon for unloading the following morning, so passengers were left only with essentials and overnight bags for the last part of the voyage. A barbecue dinner (or braai, as the South Africans would say) was held that evening on the Sun Deck. There was a beautiful buffet laid out for the passengers, most of whom sat out on the deck and ate under the open sky. After dinner Neil went up to the bridge deck, where it was quiet, and spent a long time watching the movement of the ship through the water. He was now close to the Island and to Lucy. He felt an excitement he had not known for years as he keenly anticipated a new and special destination, which also held the promise of being again with the woman he had loved more than any other.

32

Friday, 9th November was the "record date" for the purposes of determining who would be eligible to attend and vote at the shareholders' meeting of Morgen Holdings to be held a week later. Usually purchases and sales of shares on the Johannesburg stock exchange were settled through the sophisticated electronic systems of the exchange a week (or five business days) after the transaction had been concluded. Transactions made on Friday, 2nd November, were therefore settled on the ninth, so when Morgen's transfer secretaries (the professionals who maintained the share register of the company by keeping the official records of all current shareholders and all changes of ownership) closed the records at the end of business on the ninth they reflected the result of all dealings in Morgen shares up to and including 2nd November. Only those persons then recorded as shareholders of Morgen were entitled to attend and vote at the meeting. Those who could not, or did not wish to, attend the meeting in person were entitled to appoint someone else, as a "proxy", to attend the meeting and to vote at it on their behalf. However, signed forms appointing such proxies had to be lodged with the transfer secretaries by the close of business on Wednesday, 14th November, less than two full days prior to the meeting.

By early Saturday morning, 10th November, both Morgen and Predvest representatives had obtained the latest list of Morgen shareholders, updated by the transfer secretaries the previous evening.

Will Morgen had called a meeting of key senior executives and advisors for Saturday morning in the boardroom on the top floor of Morgen House. The mood was subdued as the casually dressed group sat around the long table. Scrutiny of the shareholder register revealed no major surprises, but there were a few additional names to be contacted to try to obtain their votes. They were only small shareholders, however. The big picture did not look good.

"We've got undertakings for just over twenty percent of the votes in our favour," reported John Tshabalala of Ingwe. "Of course, sixteen percent is family," nodding to Will, Mark and Rob. "The rest seems small, but it's taken a lot of work to get there. We don't think much will change in the next few days, though of course we'll all keep working at it."

Will asked, "What percentage of the votes do we think will be present at the meeting? We'll need twenty-five percent of whatever votes are cast to defeat the bid."

"If it's eighty percent, then we already have enough," said Rob.

"I think it'll be nearer ninety percent," responded Carla Roodt, Morgen's petite, bright-eyed, dark-haired Group Companies' Secretary. "We all know that there are usually quite a number who won't attend company general meetings, for whatever reason, but, with all the publicity we've had, I think the turnout will be quite high. I was at the transfer secretaries yesterday, and they've already received a huge number of proxies – most of them with instructions to vote for the deal. I estimate that Predvest has close to sixty-four percent of total shareholder votes, which means, if only eighty-five percent are present at the meeting, they may already have enough votes to carry the day. We have to find more votes if we are to stop them."

Nancy Kawa asked whether there was any chance of persuading Patsy or Mary, who were family members and together held six percent of the votes, to change their minds.

"I've tried and tried," said Will wearily, "and so have Mark and Rob, but it's no use. Patsy is afraid of James, and Mary will not dare go against Adrian, who is after all Geoff Loman's son and a key person in Predvest. They won't talk to me any more. Family relations are very strained at present."

Carla said, "I've also seen the proxies they've submitted, both instructing the chairman of the meeting to vote for the resolutions."

"And Lucy Morgen?" asked Nancy.

There was a brief silence, broken by Will:

"She doesn't want to talk to anyone about it as she's cut herself off from her previous life. She's not interested, yet she's becoming our last hope. RMS *St Helena* only reaches the Island tomorrow. Thank goodness I told Neil to take his planned holiday. What we don't know is whether Lucy will see him, and whether he can persuade her to vote for us to save Morgen."

"We need her to vote for us," said Carla. "If she is represented at the meeting, I'm pretty sure her three percent will take us to an attendance of ninety per cent of shareholder votes. That'll mean Predvest will need sixty-five and a half percent, which they may not reach. We'll need twenty-two and a half percent, and Lucy's votes would take us over twenty three."

Will turned to Abe Levy, an excellent attorney, who, like his father before him, had represented the Company and several of the family members for many years. He was middle aged, round and avuncular, with wavy grey hair and grey eyebrows above grey-blue eyes. "Abe, is there any way we can arrange for Lucy to be represented at the meeting? Proxies need to be in by Wednesday, and I don't know if that leaves enough time for Neil to persuade Lucy, and for her to give us her instructions if she does decide to vote."

Abe thought for a moment. "I look after her affairs, so I do have her power of attorney. In terms of that I can, and will, submit a proxy on her behalf for me to represent her at the meeting. She must be represented in order to be able to vote. I don't think that will be acting in bad faith, and it does give us until the meeting on Friday to receive any instructions from her. However, in view of her attitude to this matter, I believe it would not be right for me to vote – either way – without her specific instructions. I'll tell her what I am doing, but I will not be able to vote unless she authorizes or instructs me to do so. That is as far as I feel I can go."

"So now we need to rely on Neil," said Will. "We'll send him a message to tell him that Lucy must vote for us. The matter lies in her hands."

"There's something else I think you should know," said Abe. "Late yesterday I tried to contact James Bold, on quite a different matter. His office said he was not available, and would be away for a few days. Apparently, he's aboard the RMS *St Helena*, bound for the Island."

Will said: "I was going to mention that. I received a message from Neil yesterday, confirming that. No doubt James will also try to see Lucy. Predvest must be unsure that they will win with the votes they have so far."

The next day, Sunday, a similar meeting was held under the oaks on the lawn at Geoff Loman's home. Much the same arithmetic was done. Predvest knew that they could count on just over sixty-four percent of the votes. They also expected a high representation of about ninety percent of potential votes at the meeting. While they might be able to find a few more votes from small shareholders, the only uncommitted large block was held by Lucy Morgen. To be sure of success they needed her to vote for them.

"Thank goodness we sent James to St Helena," said Geoff. "Get a message to him to confirm that Lucy holds the deciding votes, and that she must vote for us."

33

Neil was up early, at five o'clock, on the morning of Sunday, 11th November. RMS *St Helena* was sailing along the coast of the Island, its high cliffs looming in the early morning darkness – the first sight of land for several days. By five-thirty it was appreciably lighter, on a cloudy grey but mild morning. As the ship inched slowly towards her anchorage off Jamestown, a long blast from her horn seemed loud enough to awaken anyone still asleep on that part of the Island. Jamestown could clearly be seen in a narrow valley with steeply sloping sides. There were already several motor vehicles along the waterfront, behind which were some prominent buildings, houses and vegetation of light and dark green up the valley and the high hills behind it. Brown cliffs rose from the sea on both sides of the small town, while to the left was another little bay which Neil later learnt was called Rupert's Bay.

Neil had a light breakfast in the Sun Lounge, and then waited with the other passengers for their names to be called for disembarking. Then they donned life jackets, went cautiously down a gangway onto a pontoon moored beside the ship, and from there onto a motor launch which would ferry them to the shore. As all three (gangway, pontoon and launch) were moving in the swell, the passengers were helped by sailors to prevent them from falling. As the launch moved away from the ship Neil looked back somewhat nostalgically to the dark blue, white, and yellow-funnelled RMS *St Helena* which had been their home during their long voyage. Turning then to the Island, Neil saw the words "Welcome RMS St Helena" painted in large letters on the cliff face to the left which loomed high above them as they neared it. White terns flew about and roosted on the cliff, and waves broke into white as they crashed into its foot. The launch edged alongside the landing stage, rising and falling on the swell, so passengers again had to be assisted as they stepped off the launch onto a flight of steps which took them onto the concrete wharf. There they removed their life jackets and climbed into a bus which took them to the customs shed to be processed through the immigration and other formalities. Neil and others bound for the Consulate Hotel were met by a representative of the Hotel and driven by minibus along the waterfront, through an arched gateway, and a few hundred metres up the main street of the old town to the mid-eighteenth century building which was the Consulate Hotel on the left hand side of the road. They were met by a friendly receptionist, signed the register, were told about the hotel facilities, and shown to their rooms. To Neil's surprise it was still only half past seven in the morning.

34

Sunday, 11th November, 2007, was an important day for St Helena Island. Lucy was in bed at six o'clock that morning, awake but still dozy, when she heard the long blast from the horn of the RMS *St Helena*, carrying all the way up the valley to announce the vessel's arrival at the Island. Lucy knew she brought a new Governor, who would be ceremoniously inaugurated at nine thirty that morning, and who would attend a Remembrance Day Service at the Cenotaph soon after. She brought St Helenian passengers and crew who would be re-united, at least for a while, with their families and loved ones. She brought tourists to stay and explore and spend money for a few days. She brought essential supplies for the Island, and keenly awaited mail. She brought hope, thought Lucy, to fragile Katie Thomas, whose needs were such that she could now soon be taken off to Ascension Island and flown from there to England for the treatment she needed too urgently to wait for the RMS to return and take her to Cape Town.

Lucy put a dressing gown on and went out onto her veranda. It was a cloudy, grey morning, but fairly mild and with no real threat of rain. Lucy knew that there would already be many people at the waterfront to meet the passengers – Islanders and visitors – as they were brought ashore from the ship. She also knew that among the passengers were Neil Harrier and James Bold. She had mixed feelings, which she did not really want to confront. She felt some underlying excitement about the possibility of seeing Neil again, but was wary of being faced with the past she had fled, and of possibly opening up old wounds. She had no real feelings for James any more, but should probably try to be polite to him as her sister's husband. However, she did not want to be involved in the affair of Predvest and Morgen Holdings, particularly with those who sought to profit greatly from it. She knew both James and Neil had agendas in that regard, so she would try to avoid them, at least for now.

After breakfast Lucy drove down to Jamestown, and was early enough to find a parking space at the top of Main Street near the Consulate Hotel. She kept a wary eye out for Neil and James, who were both staying at the hotel, but whom she did not wish to encounter. Several "uniformed contingents" were to take part in the morning's ceremonies: the St Helena Police Force, Scouts, Rangers and Guides, Pathfinders, the Salvation Army Band, the Get-togethers Orchestra and a contingent of schoolchildren. Lucy was one of the teachers chosen to accompany the children from Prince Andrew School, so she was there early to meet her group and ensure they were in place, with the other contingents, on the Grand Parade near the Supreme Court at nine twenty a.m. While they waited for Governor-Designate Gurr and Mrs Gurr to arrive, as they did promptly at nine thirty as scheduled, Lucy scanned the waiting crowd to see whether she could see Neil and James. The latter was not within the range of her vision, but she felt a queer feeling in her stomach when she located Neil, tall and attractive in smart-casual open-necked shirt and long trousers. He was looking in her direction, and she thought he had seen her. Of a sudden she felt self-conscious, so she did not respond to his gaze, and forced herself to concentrate on the proceedings.

Neil was delighted to see Lucy. He had not expected her to be part of the ceremony. She looked very pretty with her auburn hair and neat figure. He could not be sure that she had seen him, for she was concentrating on the happenings before her. After unpacking his clothes and having a refreshing shower, Neil had taken a walk around the lower parts of the little town and along the waterfront, making sure he was in place in good time to witness the inauguration of the new Governor. Having met the Governor-designate and his wife aboard ship, he was very interested in the proceedings, but also because it was an important occasion for the Island. The ceremony was impressive, with the qualities of a long history behind it.

The stage was set on a platform and terrace in front of the Supreme Court building on the Grand Parade. There were flags and colourful bunting, and the front and sides of the platform were decorated with greenery and arum lilies. The male dignitaries were mostly in dark suits with red poppies, for Remembrance Day, in their lapels. The lady Sheriff of St Helena was dressed in colourful mauve with a hat that matched the blue of the jacaranda flowers on branches arching naturally above the stage. The Governor-designate and his wife arrived, and the two bands played the national anthem. The Chief Secretary read aloud the Royal Commission, signed by the Queen and appointing the Governor-designate to be Governor and Commander-in-Chief of St Helena and its Dependencies. He then presented the Sheriff to the Governor-designate. She administered the Oaths of Office to the Governor-designate, and then read an Address of Welcome, after which the new Governor replied.

There was of course great interest in the sixty-fourth Governor's speech. He offered guiding principles for his governorship which included transparency, openness and proper consultation. Change should have a sound rationale behind it and should not be pursued merely for its own sake. However, an unwillingness to change could be an obstacle to genuine improvement, and change needed to be accepted by the people in order to be successful. He wanted to reverse two trends, which he called "depopulation" and "dependency": depopulation, because the lack of opportunities on the Island led to persons seeking work elsewhere and so diminishing ever further the scale and viability of the economy; and dependency, because nobody likes to be continually reliant upon handouts which erode self-confidence and self-esteem. Many had already worked on the creation of a Sustainable Development Plan for the Island. Moreover, Her Majesty's Government would invest many millions of pounds in the building of an airport, providing the Island with a rare opportunity. He realised the airport was not favoured by everyone, but he believed it to be the best way forward to eliminate those two "D's".

He asked his audience to share in imagination his dream of the Island in fifty years' time. Cheap energy would be provided by investment in wind and solar power. Infrastructure would have been tastefully improved over the years, the education system would be excellent, and health services of the highest standard with the ability to provide speedy specialist treatment to all. There would be a tourist quota, and the pressure on it would be such that all accommodation would be fully booked three years in advance. It was desirable to have a vision for the future in order to raise expectations and work towards them. The airport was a challenge and would open up opportunities, but the bigger challenge would be to harness the abilities needed to realize the benefits.

The Governor was aware of concerns about possible changes to the Island's lifestyle and environment, but those challenges needed to be addressed in a positive manner. Was the outside world worth joining? He recognized that material wealth could be corrupting, and the modern world was deeply flawed. However, becoming self-sufficient would help families to be re-united, would open up opportunities for the future and widen the choices in education, healthcare and welfare. The alternative was the continuation of a decline which would see still more Saints forced to live abroad.

The ceremony ended with the playing of the national anthem, and a prayer and blessing from the Bishop. The uniformed contingents fell out, but Neil felt there was no point in trying to make contact with Lucy. She would be busy with her charges, and indeed, after a short break they would form up again to participate in a march down Main Street, through the Grand Parade and onto the waterfront to take their places near the Cenotaph for the Remembrance Service, due to commence at ten forty-five. Neil wandered down to the waterside, so he could find himself a good place to stand during the service. He had many thoughts in his mind as he looked out to sea. Inevitably, aspects of change had occupied his thinking recently, and the words of the Governor continued to resonate for him. Change for good reason was important: the right kinds of change. How to recognize, influence and embrace them was the great challenge – for himself, for Lucy, for St Helena, and also for Morgen. Lucy's concerns about the actual building of an airport now seemed rather irrelevant, for its coming appeared to be definite. The trick would be in influencing the changes and opportunities that would flow from it.

There were breaks in the cloud now, and the colours of the sea changed with the changing light. RMS *St Helena* dominated the bay despite the numerous small boats also on the sea. Her officers, in uniform, formed a group near the water so they could also attend the service and pay their respects to those who had died in the two world wars, and other wars including the more recent Falklands conflict. The short service was led by the Bishop, now looking and sounding very bishop-like indeed, with the participation of leaders of other religious denominations represented on the Island. The Last Post was played, there was a two-minutes' silence, and the laying of wreaths. It was a moving ceremony, and was followed by a parade of the uniformed contingents up the Main Street.

Neil allowed the crowd to disperse, and then wandered up and down the waterfront for a few minutes, not sure what to do next. He wanted to make contact with Lucy but recognized that she could still be on duty. Eventually he decided to treat himself to a cup of coffee, and made his way to the St Helena Coffee Shop, through the Arch and to his right, close to the waterfront.

Neil went to the serving window, ordered coffee and cake for himself, and looked for somewhere to sit. The place was fairly full, but he found an empty table under a white umbrella in a corner of the lawn furthest from the kitchen. It was a pleasant spot, with the low buzz of conversation unobtrusive in the open air. Shade was provided by umbrellas and some tall trees, including flowering silky oaks growing out of the old moat. Beyond and above the umbrellas the rocky brown side of the valley rose steeply, and Neil could see part of a stairway clinging to the hillside and climbing up to some old fortifications on top of the hill. Next to him, "yesterday, today and tomorrow" brunsfelsia shrubs made a pretty border for the garden, while their different coloured flowers filled the air with a beautiful perfume. Through a gap to his right Neil could see the bay, and RMS *St Helena* at anchor. White terns flew around, including into the tall trees. On the ground were cheeky, noisy Indian mynah birds; and the Island's gentle blue-grey peaceful doves, made soft 'whirrel' sounds as they foraged for crumbs fallen from the tables.

"Do you mind if we join you?" asked a pleasant voice.

Neil looked up into the smiling light blue eyes of May Johnson. With her red hair, friendly smile, low-cut neckline and good figure, she looked very attractive. She was accompanied by her husband and James Bold.

"Please join me."

The conversation was of a general nature, about the voyage, the morning's ceremonies, and the fact that the Johnsons would only be on the Island for a short time as they would leave with the RMS for Ascension Island on Tuesday afternoon. They were noticed by Lucy, who had finished with her duties for the day and had thought of having a cup of coffee to relax for a while. She changed her mind when she saw the little group at the end table in the garden. She was about to go away when she thought that she could not avoid James and Neil indefinitely, and that it might be a good idea to say hello and break the ice in the presence of strangers. She approached the table and paused for a moment before she was noticed. The men rose to their feet, and she shook hands pointedly, almost at arm's length, with both James and Neil, before being introduced to May and Alan Johnson.

"It's good to meet you, Lucy," said May. "You must be the important lady who owns a multitude of shares in Morgen Holdings. I've heard so much about you. These two men are both hoping to persuade you to vote for them. They've told me all about it. I own some shares in Morgen, and James persuaded me to vote for the deal. He has such a wonderful way of explaining things, I could not refuse," she ended almost wistfully.

Lucy looked for a moment at the attractive figure and beautiful breasts overflowing a skimpy top, then turned towards James thoughtfully. He took a sip of coffee and did not blush. May's husband took no notice.

"Of course Neil is also nice," added May. "I think you're so lucky to have two such interesting visitors, who've come so far to see you."

"Will you join us, Lucy? Can I get you some coffee?" asked Neil.

"No, thank you. I'm on my way to the hospital to visit a pupil there."

"How is she doing?"

"Her condition is stable for now, but she's very ill. She'll be taken on the RMS *St Helena* on Tuesday for treatment in England."

"I'm sorry about that. I hoped she'd be better by now."

There was a pause, and murmurs of sympathy. Then Neil asked: "Can I see you later today?"

"I was going to ask the same question," said James.

"I'm afraid I can't see anyone today. I'm busy all day, and all evening. Perhaps we can arrange something later in the week. I must go now. Good-bye."

She smiled at the group, turned away and walked a little self-consciously across the lawn and out on to the road. She drove to the hospital to visit little Katie Thomas for a while, then sought refuge in the quiet of her own home.

The quartet at the table on the Coffee Shop lawn settled down again and continued with their conversation. Neil allowed the others to chatter, forcing himself to concentrate on each sip of coffee and mouthful of cake, while trying not to be noticed. Externally he seemed calm, but inside he was a bundle of emotions. Seeing Lucy so close had suddenly reawakened all his emotions and memories of her with a vividness he had not expected, even with all his anticipation of being with her again. She was as beautiful as ever, with her auburn hair, enchanting green eyes and full lips curving upwards as she smiled. Her voice was still sweet and low. The fullness of her bosom reminded him of how he had so wanted to know the feel of her, and the way she moved as she walked away across the lawn told him that her figure was as graceful and attractive as ever.

Neil gradually forced his attention back to the talk at the table. James had arranged to hire a car and would soon be going up the main street to collect it. He was asking May and Alan, who had been to St Helena before, where they thought he should begin his exploration of the Island. The clouds were continuing to break up, and were high, so there seemed to be no immediate prospect of rain.

"It's a good day to go up to Diana's Peak," suggested Alan. "It's the highest point on the Island and the views should be spectacular. It's not far to walk from the road, but you can make your walk longer if you wish. If you have a map I can show you how to get there, and interesting ways to drive there and back."

"What are you planning to do? Do you want to come with me? Then you can navigate."

"That would be lovely," said May, with a glance at her husband. "Let's take a picnic."

So it was settled. James politely asked Neil if he would like to join them, but was secretly pleased when he refused.

"No, thank you. I just want to have a quiet time exploring in and around Jamestown today."

So the trio left Neil in peace once more, setting off, appropriately he thought, so James could climb as soon as possible to the top of the highest mountain. Neil wanted to compose his thoughts, imagine how it would be to be with Lucy again, and begin his exploration of the Island in a way that would give him a good feeling for her present environment.

Neil spent more time exploring along the waterfront, and then wandered around the lower part of the town. He went into the beautiful St James Church, to say a prayer and to admire the eighteenth century building, which was claimed to be the oldest Anglican Church south of the equator. Apparently there had been a church on or close to that site for centuries, and indeed James Valley had long ago been called "Chapel Valley". Then he was drawn to the nearby stairway up that side of the valley. It was called Jacob's Ladder, was 600 feet high and had 699 steps. Neil walked up part of the way and was soon out of breath, but with a bird's-eye view of the town, the waterfront and the bay with RMS *St Helena* prominent. He came down to street level again and crossed the Grand Parade to the Castle Gardens, just above and behind the Supreme Court where the inauguration ceremony had been held.

The Gardens were really a pleasant park, where one could wander along paths, enjoying the tall old trees, flower beds and lawns. Neil found a symphony of greens, reds and white, with some touches of orange, yellow and purple. He recognized salvia, yarrow, chrysanthemums, cannas, agapanthus and more. There was a fountain and an old ship's anchor, but he was most intrigued by the endemic St Helena ebony. It was as yet too small to be called a tree, but was an attractive bush with large leaves, reddish stems and large white flowers. Neil later learnt that the species was thought to be extinct for more than a century until George Benjamin found two plants clinging precariously to a cliff in November, 1980. The plant had been successfully propagated and even planted again in the wild. Ann's Place restaurant was accessed from one corner of the Garden, and Neil was enticed in to relax at a table on an extended veranda, whose shade was provided by a ceiling made from the flags of many nations.

Everywhere Neill inevitably had a sense of the long history of the Island. But everywhere he went things also spoke to him of Lucy. These were the places she walked, relaxed over coffee or a meal, shopped and went about the business that brought her into town. The same feelings came to him in the late afternoon when he went for a walk. If Lucy had not herself walked that exact route, she would certainly have driven it many times. In a way he was carrying her with him so she could show him her town.

Neil took the left-hand fork at the Tourist Office just above the Consulate Hotel and followed the road that clung to that side of the valley. Soon he was high up, looking down onto the little town. There were houses, a school and cultivated vegetable gardens. The valley curved to the right and what he later discovered to be the Briars area opened up, with a waterfall with a heart-shaped rock formation around it further on. The brown mountain slope that his road was climbing was heavily eroded in places, with the yellow-green of a sisal-like plant (called an "aloe") and some prickly pears. Almost every car that passed him had friendly smiling faces, whose owners waved in greeting.

At the intersection at the top of the climb Neil took the road to the right which snaked steeply back down into the valley, folding backwards and forwards upon itself many times as it criss-crossed the steep slope. The tooting of cars as they came to blind S-bends introduced Neil to the Island practice of hooting to alert other drivers when approaching a blind corner. There were some cotton trees on the way down, their pods bursting open. At the bottom of the valley, now in shade, the vegetation was prolific, with banana, pawpaw and avocado trees, date palms, frangipani and a few jacarandas and syringas. Then there was the sound of water and the clicking of frogs, and soon Neil crossed the stream at a weir. He found himself in a suburb of mostly small houses, painted in many colours – white, cream, yellow, green and blue – with flower boxes and red bougainvillea, and pretty little gardens with roses, geraniums, hibiscus and frangipani. One carrying the name "Pike Cottage" was pretty with velvet curtains and flowers in the windows. Neil passed the General Hospital, and found himself looking for Lucy's car in the small car park, until he realized that he did not know what she was driving on the Island. He passed three churches of different religious denominations, the primary school he had earlier looked down upon, and a playground named after Prince Phillip but looking somewhat neglected in the gathering gloom. A war memorial clock tower stood next to a now-closed but smart red and black market building, a short way before he closed the circle by again passing the Tourist Office and into his hotel for a drink, shower and dinner.

Afterwards Neil tried to phone Lucy, but without success. Either she was out or she was not answering her phone. He walked down the main street towards the waterfront. The atmosphere was calm and serene compared with the busy activities of the morning. Jacob's Ladder showed itself as two rows of bright lights against the black valley wall – climbing steeply like a veritable stairway to heaven. There were strings of coloured lights in the Grand Parade and part of the waterfront. The sounds of noisy music and chattering voices came from the brightly lit restaurant called Donny's Place, but it was quieter further away. The sea was calm, but still restless as it endlessly broke against the seafront wall and retreated, wave after wave. The wharf-and-warehouse end of the waterfront was brightly lit, as was RMS *St Helena* whose lights were reflected in the water, seemingly reaching out to Neil and the few other watchers. The task of unloading and loading seemed to be continuing, despite the late hour.

Neil leant on the railing and watched. He had come a long way, seemingly into a new world. He had only briefly seen Lucy. He would have to decide how to approach her the next day.

35

The dining room at the Consulate Hotel was a cheerful room, and full of interesting breakfast smells – bacon and eggs, fried onions, coffee and more – when Neil went in for breakfast on Monday morning. The red walls and dark wooden ceilings were brightened by the early morning light and there was a bustle of activity as hotel guests competed for space at the buffet, ordered cooked dishes and discussed their plans for a new day on the Island.

The room was nearly full, but there was space at a table occupied solely by James Bold. Neil decided that they could not avoid one another, though they were rivals in a sense, so he walked up to that table.

"Good morning, James. Do you mind if I join you?"

"Please do. How was your day yesterday?"

"Oh. I had a good time exploring in and around Jamestown. Did you go to Diana's Peak?"

"We did. It was a beautiful day and there were fine views in every direction. We had a great time. We walked a bit and had a picnic lunch. I also discovered that they have a system of 'Post Box Walks' here, and Diana's Peak was one of them. I left my name up there."

"How does that work?"

"Apparently there're several walks one can do. I'm going to the Tourist Office to get more details after breakfast. But there are instructions for each walk, to tell you where to go. There's a 'post box' somewhere on each walk – actually a weather-proof container with space for a notebook and pen, so you can record that you've been to that place. Maybe I'll see how many I can do while I'm here."

They were interrupted by a lady from the hotel office.

"Mr Bold and Mr Harrier? Good. I see I find you both together. We've received messages for each of you. The details are here" – she handed each a slip of paper – "but really you must both phone those numbers in South Africa urgently. I do hope you still have a lovely day."

After breakfast Neil went to his room, telephoned Prince Andrew School and asked to speak to Lucy Morgen.

"I'm afraid Miss Morgen is teaching. May I give her a message?"

"Could you please ask her to contact Neil Harrier. I'm staying at the Consulate Hotel. I tried to phone her at home, but could not get through. What time do lessons end for the day?"

"Miss Morgen will probably be teaching until three o'clock today."

Neil then phoned Will Morgen, who sounded as though he could have been in the same building, so clear was the connection. So much for those vast distances between different worlds, thought Neil ironically.

"Hello, Will. How're things going? Friday was your 'last day to register' to vote was it not?"

"It was indeed, Neil. We had a meeting over the weekend and reviewed the figures. Whichever way we look at it, it's clear that Lucy must vote for us. If she does, we'll win. If she doesn't vote, it'll be a lottery – too close to call. If she votes for them, they'll win. Everything depends on her, so we must rely on you to persuade her to vote for Morgen."

"I'll do the best I can, but it may not be easy. I don't think she wants to be involved, and she's already proving to be a bit elusive. I also think that James Bold being here has complicated things."

"Do what you can, Neil. We're depending on you. And enjoy the Island too. I believe it's a fine holiday place."

After breakfast James went to his room, telephoned Prince Andrew School and asked to speak to Lucy Morgen.

"I'm afraid Miss Morgen is teaching. May I give her a message?"

"Could you please ask her to contact James Bold. I'm staying at the Consulate Hotel. I tried to phone her at home, but could not get through. Could you please tell me when lessons end for the day?"

"Miss Morgen will probably be teaching until three o'clock today."

James then telephoned Geoff Loman. Jody, his secretary, recognized James's voice, and briefly asked him about his voyage and the Island before she put the call through.

"Hello, Geoff. I got your message. How're things going? Friday was the 'last day to register' to vote was it not?"

"It was indeed, James. We had a meeting over the weekend and reviewed the figures. Whichever way we look at it, it's clear that Lucy must vote for us. If she does, we'll win. If she doesn't vote, it could go either way: it's too close to call. If she votes for them, they'll win. Everything depends on her, so we are relying on you to persuade her to vote for Predvest. Thank goodness we decided to send you there."

"I'll do the best I can, Geoff. I don't think she wants to be involved, and she's already playing hard to get. Having Neil Harrier here is also a complication."

"Do your best, James, but it had better be a good best. We're depending on you."

"Don't worry, Geoff. I'm sure if I can just get her on her own, I'll be able to persuade her. I'll keep you informed."

"Please do. And knowing you, I suppose you'll find ways to enjoy yourself as well – lucky fellow!"

James had arranged for the Johnson couple to meet him at the Hotel at about ten o'clock. May wanted to see a wirebird, a small endangered plover, endemic to St Helena Island; Alan wanted to play golf; and James wanted to spend time with May and do another post box walk with her if he could not otherwise see her alone. After consulting the Tourist Office and a map, it was decided that James would drive them to Longwood, in what he dubbed the "middle-eastern" part of the Island. They would drop Alan off at the nine-hole golf course, and then proceed north to the end of the road, from where they could walk across Deadwood Plain and up the hill called Flagstaff.

James and May set off from their parking place along a clear vehicle track. They soon passed three wind turbines, but unfortunately one of them had fallen down, leaving a wreckage of tons of expensive equipment lying on the ground. They continued along an open plain, with pleasant views of quiet valleys and hills around them.

"I just love the expressive place-names on this Island," said May. "Like 'Deadwood Plain'. This all used to be forest, the Great Wood, but it was cut down for timber. The name apparently came from the many tree stumps that remained. This was also the site of a Boer encampment, where prisoners-of-war were kept during the Anglo-Boer War. It's difficult to imagine: it's all so peaceful now."

James caught a movement on the grassy ground. "Look! There's your wirebird. And another. And one over there too."

They kept very still and watched the little plovers. They were quite small with long dark spindly legs (which gave them their common name), dark eyes and dark, pointed beaks; a white lower body, and grey-brown back and wings; a grey-brown cap, and alternating white and grey-brown markings on the head. The birds stood very still, as though threatened by the presence of humans, and were then very difficult to see. Soon they resumed a pattern of alternately darting along the ground for short distances, and then standing very still again. Had it not been for the darting movement, James and May could well have passed by without seeing them.

"They're beautiful little creatures," said May softly. "I can't imagine how people used to eat them and their eggs. With that, and changes to their habitat, there're very few left now – only two or three hundred, I've heard – though they *are* now protected." They quietly resumed their walk. "My birding friends'll be very jealous when I tell them about this."

Pastureland gave way to bushes of furze or gorse, with yellow flowers, and then to forest. They kept to the edge of the forest and made their way along the side of a steep, eroded slope, from where they had views across yellow flowers, at their feet and on the upper ground, down to mainly brown, near-desert, lesser hills and valleys and the blue of the open sea. Then they had to turn to the right and pick their way through the forest, stepping over fallen trees, until they neared the top of the hill. Low cloud had formed to restrict their outlook, but from open spaces they were still held spellbound by views down green and flowered slopes, or steep cliffs, to the deep blue of the sea, white fringed along the coastline. They walked the last small rise up to the Flagstaff post box, on the summit, at the edge of a clearing, and sheltered by over-hanging branches.

James opened it, but there was no pen or paper in it. He exploded.

"What the hell! There's no pen and paper here. How can I be expected to leave my name here when there's nothing to write with?"

As he continued in this vein, May was surprised to realise that he was indeed very angry.

"Come on, James, surely it's not that important?"

"I've come all this way, I want to leave my name here – and at other post boxes too."

May felt for a moment in the small rucksack she had been carrying, and pulled out a ball-point pen and a small notebook from which she tore out a few used pages.

"Here, take these. You can start a new book with the date and your name, and we'll leave these in the post box for the next people."

After they had placed the pen and notebook, now with James's details entered, safely in the post box, May put her arms around him and drew herself close against him.

"Relax, James. I don't want to remember you like this. I want to remember you as a beautiful friend and lover. I know what they say about shipboard romances – ships passing in the night and all that – but I've loved our time together. Alan and I get along well enough, but I seldom have all I need from him, what with his golf and bridge and other things. Let me remember you as I found you..... How does it feel when I put my hand down here? .... Oooh! ... I can tell that feels very good... There can't be anybody for miles around, and I don't know when we'll meet again, if ever. Let's make love now, while we can... Mmmm... That's *good*...!"

Neil, meanwhile, was combining his exploration of the Island with some research into matters he believed to be of importance to Lucy. At the Tourist Office he picked up a brochure about The St Helena National Trust, one of whose projects – the care of the Millennium Forest – particularly interested him. The endemic St Helena Gumwood (*Commidendrum robustum*) was the Island's national tree and had been a dominant species in its once extensive forests. It had become rare and endangered, with fewer than a thousand trees remaining in the wild. To commemorate the Millennium, a conservation programme had led to the planting, in the year 2000, of a new forest of gumwoods on thirty-two hectares of the then barren Horse Point, which had once been part of the original Great Wood. Every school child had planted a tree, as had many other Saints and visitors, to raise the number of trees in the new young forest to over five thousand. Neil discovered that, for a donation to the project, he could arrange for further trees to be planted in his, or another, name. A trifle quixotically, but feeling that this was a worthy project which Lucy would surely support, he arranged for two trees to be planted in his and Lucy's names, to commemorate their past relationship. Then he donated two more trees, to mark his hopes for their futures.

Rather than hire a car, Neil thought it would be preferable to be shown about the Island by a St Helenian. The Hotel recommended the taxi service of one Hensel Peters, whose business card he had found on a table there. A telephone call resulted in the prompt appearance of a red car at the Hotel steps; a bald head, a correct but friendly greeting, and he was shaking hands with Hensel Peters himself.

"I'd like to see some of the Island," said Neil, "but could you possibly show me certain specific things on the way? I'd like to see the Millennium Forest, as I've just paid for four trees to be planted there, but more importantly I'd like to know where the proposed airport, and hotel and golf course, are planned to be built."

"I can do that. From the Millennium Forest I could point out where the airport may be built."

So they set off, climbing out of the valley and gradually winding their way eastwards through Longwood to Horse Point and the Millennium Forest. Hensel took Neil through the simple entrance building and then left him to wander about the area for a few minutes as he pleased. Most of the trees were still quite small and shrub-like, so the place still seemed wild and open, with a strong wind blowing. However, Neil was impressed by the scale of the project and the vision behind it. Later in the week he saw a few surviving gumwoods in the wild in Peak Dale. They were large trees with an attractive tracery of twisted branches, so Neil was then able to imagine a truly spectacular forest on Horse Point in years to come.

When he rejoined Hensel near the Forest entrance, Hensel pointed to the south-east, across "Prosperous Bay Plain", to a low dull-coloured ridge which hid the sea from their view, as the proposed site of the airport, indeed the only vaguely practicable site for it.

"Not too bad," thought Neil, "but of course construction would have to take place, and supporting buildings and infrastructure such as roads would need to be built."

They drove on, mostly high up, gradually winding westwards, negotiating the Island's high central ridge. There was a poetry in the place-names, which Neil dimly felt, but which struck him vividly when he later traced their route on a map: by way of Longwood, Halley's Mount, Diana's Peak, Sandy Bay Ridge, Bates Branch, Cason's Gate, High Peak, Broad Bottom, Horse Pasture, and through suburban Half Tree

Hollow down into Jamestown. It was a beautiful drive. Some of the roads were steep and very narrow, and, when they were, the vehicle driving up had right of way, "though often we go by the nearest overtaking place," Hensel explained. In the centre of the Island were high peaks and deep valleys (or "guts"). The two men stopped and got out of the car high up on Sandy Bay Ridge, and Neil gazed in wonder at the panorama that seemed to be nearly all around them. On two of the ridges running down towards the ocean were stone columns, called Lot and Lot's Wife. A cool, strong wind was driving clouds as mist in places over the highest peaks, and setting off rippling waves in patches of flax. Near Cason's Gate they looked across the quiet, grassy valley of Broad Bottom. Cattle were grazing, and it was a peaceful scene; but it had held a Boer prisoner-of-war camp during the Anglo-Boer War, and now there were plans to build an eighteen-hole golf course there, with a luxury hotel further down the valley towards the sea. Neil stood and looked for a long time, trying to imagine it. To give him a better look, Hensel drove him slowly around Broad Bottom towards Horse Pasture, where they saw no horses, but did see two wirebirds.

36

Lucy was hailed by the School secretary as she was about to leave the main building to go home on that Monday afternoon.

"Lucy, I do believe every man in or from South Africa is after you! Here's another one. He also wants you to contact him, and also says he can't get hold of you at home. Is your phone out of order?"

"No, I'm just playing hard-to-get."

"Here's your message, with his phone number in Johannesburg."

Lucy glanced at it and read the name and work number of her attorney, Abe Levy. She sighed.

"Thank you. I'm sorry you've been troubled. There are some who are trying to involve me in a matter I want no part of," she said somewhat mysteriously as she went off to her car.

As she drove home Lucy wondered whether Abe wanted to talk to her about Morgen, or about her own personal affairs. She put the kettle on to boil for tea, and then telephoned him.

After the usual pleasantries, Abe said: "Lucy, I know you haven't wanted to be involved with Morgen Holdings and its business, but please hear me out for a moment. The Morgen general meeting will be held on Friday morning, when shareholders will vote either to accept or reject the takeover offer made by Predvest. I was at a meeting with Will and others on Saturday, when we had a good look at the proxies we know about and tried to assess how the voting may go. It's too close to call, and your large parcel of votes is now the only one able to decide it either way, that is if you wanted to vote. It's not being too dramatic to state that you hold the fate of Morgen in your hands. From myself, who has represented the Company and the family for many years, and from your Uncle William, comes this request to you: please reconsider your wish not to be involved, and vote for Morgen at the meeting on Friday. I'm sure your father would also have wished it had he been alive today."

"Abe, I hear what you say, but you know that I came here to escape all of that, and I don't want to change my mind. Once I start to be involved, who knows where it will end? It will first be one thing, and then another, and another."

"I understand, Lucy, but ask you at least to think about it in the next few days. So you will have time for that, this is what I have done. By the way, I did try to contact you last night, but your phone was not answered. So this morning I lodged a proxy which will allow me to attend the meeting on Friday as your representative, and with the power to vote on your behalf."

"But Abe –"

"Please allow me to finish, Lucy. Because I know how you feel about these matters, I give you my word that I will not vote unless explicitly instructed by you to do so. The meeting begins at ten a.m. You may contact me at any time, at my office, or on my cellphone, to give me your instructions, especially should you decide you want me to vote. Please think about it, Lucy."

"Abe, I don't want to, but I'll probably be obliged to think about it. Neil Harrier and James Bold are on the Island, and I'm sure they're not here just to make courtesy calls, especially James. I'm sure they'll both want to tell me why I should vote one way or the other. I'll listen to what they have to say, and will let you know if I want you to vote. I can't promise more than that now."

"Thank you, Lucy. I look forward to hearing from you."

Lucy had just put down the phone when her doorbell rang. She opened the door.

"Hello, Neil! Hello, James! This is a surprise – a strange delegation indeed!"

However, if it were a delegation, it was not a united one. James had had lunch with May and Alan Johnson at Ann's Place, and had left them in Jamestown so he could drive himself alone to Lucy's home. He hoped that she would go home after school, and badly wanted to make contact with her. If she was not there when he arrived he would simply wait for her. She would surely go home eventually. Neil had had a snack at the Coffee Shop, relaxed for a while at his hotel, and then asked Hensel Peters to drive him to Lucy's home. He too hoped she would go home after school, and, if she was not there when he arrived, he would simply wait for her. She would surely go home eventually.

"Oh-oh, I think your friend has got here before you," said Hensel as he drew up behind a small white car standing at the gate to Lucy's home. "Well, here we are. What do you want me to do?"

James had only just arrived and was easing himself out of the car. Neil replied, "Somehow I don't think this will be a long meeting, with the two of us here at the same time. Could you collect me in about an hour? If I'm finished earlier than that, I'll walk back the way we've just come, so you'll see me on the road if you come that way."

Neil followed James up the steps to Lucy's front door, and they waited for it to be opened after James had rung the bell. Both men seemed resigned at having the other present. They both began talking at once in response to Lucy's greeting.

"Hello, Lucy – "

"Hello Lucy – "

" – you look well."

" – how are you?"

"I want to get together with you – "

"We need to talk – "

" – some time soon."

" – soon. Can we make a date?"

"Whoa! Whoa! Hold on," cried Lucy, raising her arms in mock defence. "I can't listen to you both at the same time. And I'm not used to being so popular." She regarded them, both now silently and a little uncomfortably waiting for her to invite them in. "I suppose I could offer you a cup of tea or coffee, if you want to come in, especially as you've come so far. I've just boiled the kettle."

They sat in the lounge, drank tea, and nibbled at some biscuits Lucy had produced. Lucy leant back in a comfortable chair and observed the two relatively powerful and usually confident men, both sitting forward in their chairs and pretending to be at ease with the chit-chat going on. She began to enjoy herself, keeping the conversation about family and friends, their journey, what they had done on the Island and whether they were enjoying themselves – indeed about anything but the Morgen-Predvest affair. Eventually she let silence reign, and waited to see what would happen.

Eventually James said: "Lucy, it's good to see you, but I think you must know that this is not only a social visit."

"Oh? I thought you wanted to see me."

"I do."

"Just for myself alone?"

"Yes, but not only that. I also need to talk to you about the Predvest-Morgen matter."

Neil said: "Lucy, I want to see you as a friend, but I also need to talk to you about the future of Morgen."

"I thought I'd made it clear that I don't want to talk to anyone about that."

"Lucy, we need your votes – "

"Lucy, we need your votes – "

" – so please give me a hearing."

" – so please won't you at least listen to what I have to say?"

"I can't listen to you if you both speak at the same time." Lucy looked speculatively at each man in turn. They were both interesting and attractive in their own ways, and, for the moment, they were at her mercy. She thought about her recent conversation with Abe Levy, and her promise to him.

"All right, I'll give each of you a hearing."

"Have lunch with me."

"I'm teaching."

"Dinner?"

"Exactly when is this meeting?" she asked.

"On Friday morning at ten o'clock," answered Neil.

Lucy looked again from one to the other. They both seemed to have kept themselves reasonably fit. She had known them both very well. She still liked Neil's blue eyes under dark hair and bushy eyebrows; and James was still attractive with his grey eyes and fair skin, especially as he was temporarily without his usual air of smug self-confidence. It might be fun to spend some time with each of them and see how things played out.

"I'll give each of you an afternoon and an evening, one on Wednesday, and one on Thursday."

"That'll be too late. Proxies must be in by Wednesday," said James.

"Abe Levy will represent me at the meeting. He won't vote, though, unless I instruct him to, and I'm still not planning to have my votes cast."

"I want to have Thursday," said James.

"Lucy, *I* would prefer to have Thursday please," countered Neil.

"Let's toss for it," suggested James.

"Hold on, both of you. This is *my* time you're talking about." She thought for a moment. Then she smiled as some mischievous devil emerged from somewhere deep within her. "I'll tell you how we'll decide it. We'll have a contest. You can race each other, and the winner will have the right to choose which of the two days he prefers."

"What sort of race?" they asked simultaneously.

"By now you must both know Jacob's Ladder, the steps out of Jamestown up to the top of Ladder Hill? Good. Then I'll meet you at the foot of the steps at four o'clock tomorrow afternoon. You will race each other to the top and back, and the winner can have first choice of which day to spend time with me."

Both men looked rather stunned, but they had little choice but to acquiesce.

"I'll try to arrange to get away from school as early as I can on Wednesday and Thursday," continued Lucy. "We can make detailed arrangements later, but I must lay down some conditions now. You will each take me for a walk, of your own choosing, because you have to see this beautiful Island while you're here. And you must each give me dinner. The rest will be up to you. Now I must throw you out, as I have important things to do. I'll see you at the foot of Jacob's Ladder tomorrow."

Lucy was smiling as she saw off her two visitors. She did not really want to spend much time with James, and she would like to see more of Neil on his own, but the realities of the situation dictated otherwise. She would at least be spending some time with Neil in the next day or so – and it could be fun making them pay for this intrusion.

However, her mood changed as she prepared to go out to the hospital to visit little Katie Thomas. Katie was still very ill, but the doctors were hopeful that she would be able to cope with her journey, and had fair prospects of improving health if she received the necessary treatment soon. This would be Lucy's last visit, for tomorrow morning, while Lucy was teaching, Katie would be taken aboard RMS *St Helena* and placed in the care of the ship's doctor. She would be accompanied by her mother and a nurse, who would help to care for their patient.

It was a bittersweet time. Lucy took some little gifts for Katie, who spoke quietly and hopefully about her coming journey, and the prospects of recovery it held for her. That was a positive development after her long wait in hospital. Lucy kissed her gently on the forehead, as she said her farewells. She was accompanied to the hospital entrance by Mrs Thomas, who promised to keep Lucy informed of Katie's progress. Neither of them knew how long she and Katie would be away, both for medical reasons and the difficulties of travel between St Helena and the outside world.

Lucy drove home, sombrely wishing, not for the first time since Katie's collapse, that they had an airport.

"It's a strange world, and I a strange creature," she thought. "Here I am wanting with a passion to preserve the Island as it is, yet now wishing for something that could change it dramatically, just because it suits me in this sad situation."

37

The following Tuesday morning dawned fair, though Neil hoped it would not be too hot by the afternoon. With the prospect of racing up and down Jacob's Ladder, he was not inclined to be physically very active until then. He thought he would make it a "Napoleon day", visiting the main Napoleonic sites, and obtaining a feel for that period of time and the last years of Napoleon Bonaparte's life, which were spent on St Helena Island. On Monday evening he consulted his tourist literature, and discovered that Corkers' Tours had just such a tour. He phoned Tracey Corker and was glad to learn that they still had space for him on their tour the following morning.

Neil did not see James at breakfast, and concluded that he was sleeping late to conserve his strength for the afternoon. A smiling Tracey met Neil and the others of the tour party at the steps of the Consulate Hotel, taking money and ticking off names. A minute or two before half-past nine there was a rush of noise and a most amazing vehicle drew up at the side of the road next to them. The driver, Colin Corker, with round face, green cap, white T-shirt and blue denim jeans, alighted and came to welcome his guests. The vehicle was a large open charabanc, its cover folded down at the back. It was predominantly a shiny green, with shining black front mudguards and radiator, and polished wheels and tyres. Colin told Neil later that it was a 1929 Chevrolet with a 1946 Bedford engine. It really was a lovingly cared for piece of history in its own right. Soon the ten passengers had climbed aboard and found seats, and were enjoying breezy but clear views as the charabanc slowly and noisily ground its way out of Jamestown.

There was much more history to follow. Napoleon first saw the forbidding cliffs of this remote Island, chosen as his prison because of the difficulty of rescue or escape, on or about Sunday, 15th October, 1815, for on that day the HMS *Northumberland* dropped anchor off Jamestown with him on board. He landed on the evening of 17th October and spent the night at Porteous House, a lodging house then rented out for the use of the French (destroyed by fire in 1865 and since rebuilt), in Main Road close to the Castle Gardens. The following day Napoleon rode, with escort, to inspect the house at Longwood earmarked for his residence. It was on a then bleak and windswept plain and needed much by way of alterations and repairs. On the return journey Napoleon discovered, and was enchanted by, the Briars Valley below the Heart-shaped Waterfall. The owner of the estate, William Balcombe, allowed him to take up temporary residence in the small summer pavilion (then just one room and an attic) on the estate, so he did not return to Porteous House. Napoleon stayed at Briars until Sunday, 10th December, when he moved to Longwood. Over the years the three main Napoleonic sites (Briars Pavilion, Longwood House and his tomb) had been acquired by the French Government and lovingly restored and maintained.

The charabanc first took Neil and his companions to Briars. There they walked up onto the smallish spur on which the Pavilion was situated, in pleasant gardens and with attractive views. It was a small white and green house, with green and white also predominating in its restored main room. Neil tried to imagine the once seemingly all-powerful man, with the palaces of an empire at his disposal when not on campaign, reduced to living in that small place.

They went on to Longwood House, which had been much improved by the time Napoleon moved there, but which was still in a bleak and windy location. However, the gardens (partly designed and laid out by Napoleon himself) were now beautiful and inviting, Neil's first impressions being of Norfolk pines and agapanthus in full flower.

Near the entrance to the house they encountered a Frenchman resplendent in full Napoleonic dress, including three-cornered hat, dark long-tailed coat, white breeches and long black boots. He was one of the pilgrims who had come with Neil aboard the RMS *St Helena*. He had been at Longwood House the day before and assured them that he would be there again the next day.

"Our Emperor Napoleon made St Helena famous. He is what everyone knows about St Helena, is that not so?"

As at Briars, green was an important colour in this Longwood residence: in the latticework of the entrance veranda, the window shutters, interior walls, curtains and soft furnishings. Neil was especially interested in some of the little details: the sunken paths in the gardens, the peephole in a shutter allowing the former emperor to see out without himself being seen, and the fact that he sometimes watched the races on Deadwood Plain from the veranda through his telescope. This was a man, thought Neil, who once bestrode much of the world as if it were his own.

Napoleon died at Longwood, of stomach cancer, on Saturday, 5th May, 1821. He was laid to rest in the Sane (or Geranium) Valley, just below Longwood to the west. He had liked to walk there, enjoying the clear spring and its stream, the willow trees, the flowering cannas, begonias and geraniums, and the long view along the valley to the sea. He had requested that he be buried there if his body were not permitted to be taken from the Island. There he lay until his remains were exhumed and taken to Paris for reburial in 1840. Neil walked from the charabanc down a pleasant shady path between flowerbeds and trees to the site of the grave. It was a quiet and beautiful garden, with many trees and lush vegetation, which now restricted the view. Neil could not see the sea, but could see a long way down the valley to a distant hill. Ironically, he thought, men and time and nature had created this beautiful, peaceful memorial to a man of war.

Relics of French imperialism were supplanted by images of British imperialism as the charabanc continued on its way. It made a brief stop at Plantation House, the home of the Governor. Its passengers strolled to a vantage point from where they could look across a lawn to see and admire the Georgian-style building which had been built in 1792. Its light cream colouring and beautiful proportions made it stand out in an appropriately distinctive way. It had two storeys, with shuttered windows and a triangular gable accentuating the small entrance porch in the main facade.

Of almost equal interest to some were the large tortoises which they were fortunate enough to see on the lawn. The oldest bore the name of Jonathan and was then thought to be about one hundred and seventy-five years of age. He had been brought to the Island from the Seychelles in 1882, and was reputed to be one of the oldest of living animals.

"How amazing!" thought Neil. "This Jonathan was born not long after Napoleon's death, and while he was still at rest in Sane Valley. How many empires have risen and declined, how many monarchs and governments have come and gone since then? We humans have our good and bad times, our struggles and worries and loves and pleasures, our projects and plans and strivings to all kinds of ends, while Jonathan here quietly munches and sleeps his life from age to age."

The tour continued over some of the most scenic parts of the Island, until the charabanc came to a stop at the top of Ladder Hill, next to the old fortifications there, and just before the steep and winding descent into Jamestown. Neil and his companions stood at the top of Jacob's Ladder and looked out on the spectacular views. In the bay RMS *St Helena* was preparing for departure, its attendant vessels fussing around it to perform their last minute duties. Behind the white-fringed waterfront the streets and buildings of Jamestown, made small by height and distance, streamed between the dark steep sides of the narrow valley. Neil allowed his eyes to look down the steps immediately in front of him. The way was steep and long and, involuntarily, his stomach churned and he began to feel queasy. He needed to begin to concentrate his mind on how to race up and down as fast as possible later that same afternoon.

38

Lucy left school as soon as she could and drove straight to the waterfront in Jamestown. Some of those who had come to see the departure of loved ones aboard RMS *St Helena* were beginning to leave, so she was able to find a parking space. She stood at the white railing and watched as the RMS churned her way purposefully northwards in the direction of Ascension Island. She was already quite far away, and Lucy watched the vessel seeming to grow smaller with every passing minute. Lucy's prayers for Katie and her mother followed the departing ship, hoping fervently for the restoration of the attractive, gentle, fun-loving girl who had collapsed while in her care. At least Katie was now on her way to the treatment she needed. In two days' time she would arrive at Ascension Island, and hopefully she would be on a flight to England soon after that. Lucy watched until she could no longer be sure whether the little black dot in the distance was real or imagined. Then she turned away, walked slowly through the Arch, and made her way to the foot of Jacob's Ladder. She had now to turn her mind to other things.

Lucy crossed part of the Grand Parade and took the short narrow road between the Museum and another building. She stopped involuntarily outside the door of the Museum and looked with fresh eyes at the stairway climbing steeply up the dark, rough, rocky valley wall. It certainly was impressive. Its 699 steps (200 yards, or 184 metres high) had originally been built in 1829 to allow goods to be hauled between Jamestown and Ladder Hill Fort. It was now an impressive pedestrian way of rough stone steps, with smooth metal railings running along each side, and rough stone paving outside the railings. Lights were set at intervals in the paving to illuminate the steps at night. There were four or five pedestrians on the stairway, and those near the top appeared as small dots. Lucy had only climbed it once, shortly after her arrival on the Island. She had found it quite taxing, even though she had taken her time to climb up and down. Now she wondered whether she had been foolish in instigating this race. What if one of the two had a heart attack?

Lucy arrived close to four o'clock, more or less on time. Initially she could see neither Neil nor James. Then she was surprised to see both of them warming up for the race, jogging gently up and down the road, each trying not to take too much notice of the other.

"They *are* taking this seriously," thought Lucy, somewhat amazed. "It obviously means a lot to both of them. I wonder why? Is it all for money, or something besides? They must seriously believe that the last impressions will be better than the first in persuading a lady to do their bidding. But this lady intends to stay out of it all, and let all those many other Morgen shareholders decide their matter."

The two men jogged over to her when they saw her. They greeted her, and she had no doubt about the admiration and interest of both of them as they briefly appraised her attractive figure, in yellow slacks and blouse, brilliant in the sunlight. Both were sweating a little, fair skins glistening in the sun, and appearing to Lucy surprisingly fit and attractive in running shorts and T-shirts. Neil wore blue shorts and a white T-shirt proclaiming the Harrismith Mountain Race to be "the toughest in the world". James wore red shorts and a T-shirt of the Rand Athletic Club's 32km "Tough One".

"Are you trying to out-tough each other?" asked Lucy. "Have you both actually run those races?"

Neil replied. "I did the Mountain Race two or three years ago. It's up and down the Platberg, as you know, and I was in the area. It was a challenge – very tough – but I managed to finish reasonably well. I was fitter then."

"I ran the Tough One about three years ago," said James. "I do an occasional five-K time trial at the Club on a Tuesday evening when work allows, so it was a challenge to do thirty-two kilometres. It was hot, and very hilly in the second half, but I finished. I was fitter then."

"I had no idea," said Lucy.

"I've been working too hard to do much in the way of training, and then haven't been able to run while at sea," said Neil, now silently thankful for the many steps he had had to climb on the RMS and at the Consulate Hotel. "James may be in a similar position?" he enquired hopefully.

"I am."

"Are you both ready? Good. I'll set you off in a moment. There're not many rules. You go to the top and back to street level here as fast as you can. At the top you must touch the wall of the Fort before you begin to descend. Please remember this is a public thoroughfare, so have respect for other pedestrians."

Sensing that something unusual was about to happen, a few curious bystanders had begun to collect around them while Lucy was speaking. As Lucy, James and Neil moved closer to the foot of the steps, they saw a youth speeding down, not on foot but sliding down, face-up with his arms and legs draped over the railings on each side of the stairs. It seemed a very efficient mode of descent. They made way for him as he jumped onto the road and sauntered off.

"I presume we're allowed to do that?" asked James.

"If you can."

James said nothing, but could scarcely conceal a smirk. The others need not know that he had noticed the technique and had spent some time that morning taking lessons and practising.

"Okay, line up here," ordered Lucy. "I'll give the usual three commands."

The two men stood at the foot of the steps. They both breathed deeply. Their eyes were drawn irresistibly up the long stairway. Then they leant forward, waiting for the start.

"On your marks... Get set... Go!" – and they were off.

"What are they doing?" asked a spectator, who happened to be one of Lucy's pupils.

"They're racing to the top and back."

"What for?"

"For me. They both want to take me to dinner on Thursday, and the one who wins will do that."

"Oh?" Then after a puzzled pause: "Why not let both of them have dinner with you on Thursday?"

"I don't think either of them wants that."

All the while Lucy was watching the two figures, one in red shorts and one in blue shorts, racing up the stairs. Somehow it was exciting to have two men fighting over her. It was like two knights of old jousting for the hand of a fair lady. Had those ladies sometimes felt this same thrill of excitement?

James had set off very fast, determined to establish a commanding lead. Neil kept to a more sedate pace, trying to keep to a steady rhythm, and trying not to worry about the rapidly opening gap between the two of them. Soon their breathing became laboured, especially that of James who was moving faster. He soon found himself heavily into oxygen debt. He tried to keep going, but was forced to stop to recover his breath. Neil saw him leaning over a railing, taking in great gulps of air, and the gap began to close. When it was only two or three steps, James set off again, almost as quickly as before, gradually widening the gap again. He was determined to be at the top first, to give himself time to get into position to slide down the railings, and then to do so without having to overtake Neil on the way down. However, he was forced by the intensity of his effort to stop to recover his breath from time to time. He was doing the equivalent of a series of sprints, or spurts, with forced rests in between. Neil was trying to keep a more measured pace, working hard, but trying to keep just on the right side of severe oxygen debt, which would force him to make stops as James was having to do.

Lucy watched, fascinated, from below. Both men were now hauling themselves up the stairs, each pulling with both hands on the railings. As they receded into the distance, the two figures grew smaller and it became difficult to distinguish much in the way of detail. The neutral colours of their T-shirts did not show up well, but she was able to tell the two men apart by the bright colours of their running shorts. The red shorts were leading, but every time they paused the blue shorts closed the gap. The blue was never allowed to overtake the red, which began to move up again as soon as the blue came close.

Three local youths decided to join in the fun, and set off after the two contestants at what Lucy thought was a suicidal pace. Gaps opened up between them, but all three were young and fit and accustomed to using the steps, so they all continued to gain ground on James and Neil at a rapid rate. In trying to stay close to James, Neil's breathing grew more and more anguished, so that he too was forced to stop for breath a few times in the last third of the climb. He tried to limit these delays by climbing hard for twenty steps, and then pausing for a count of ten seconds to recover some breath and rest the fatigue in his legs. James was hanging over the railing and Neil stooping with hands on knees, both gasping for breath, when first one and then another two locals cruised past them, all breathing heavily but comfortably.

"That's fitness, and that's how to do it," thought Neil.

James was spurred into action again and continued hauling himself up, trying in vain to keep in touch with the last of the trio, but somehow managing to increase his pace. Neil resolved to let him go if he had to, and reined back his pace so he would not need to stop again. James took two more stops, and Neil closed a little each time, but James reached the top a few metres ahead.

Lucy saw her two competing businessmen being overtaken by the three local youths, one of whom disappeared beyond the top, presumably into the suburbs. The other two turned at the top and began to descend at a great rate, comfortably and rhythmically jumping steps, two small dots bobbing up and down as they did so. They passed James and Neil, before the latter two reached the top, and continued down. One of the locals opened up a gap, and after about halfway, where there was a break in the railings, draped his arms over one railing behind him, and his bent knees over the one he was facing, and came rushing smoothly to the ground at great pace, much to the admiration of Lucy and the other spectators. He waited for his friend to reach the road, they shook hands with each other, and then turned to watch the second half of the descent of the two visitors.

Lucy had seen the red shorts reach the top, disappear while James went to touch the fortress wall, and emerge again at the top of the stairs just as the blue shorts arrived there.

"See you in Jamestown," said James, as Neil went to touch the wall. Ignoring the view which had opened out as they climbed, James draped himself over the two railings, as he had been practising that morning. He was a little awkward using the novel technique, but managed to start sliding down before James reappeared at the top of the steps.

"Bloody hell!" exclaimed Neil in astonishment. "He's been practising."

He watched James slide away from him, quickly but a little uncertainly, as he began his own descent. Neil tried again to get into a rhythm, trying not to fall, and trying to make his tired legs move as quickly as possible. The problem now was not lack of breath. He remembered the Harrismith Mountain Race: how he had tried so hard to gain places on the climb, only to lose them to seemingly fearless youngsters who came flying past him on the steep, rough downhill. They had not seemed to know that they could be hurt if they fell, he had thought at the time, but as you grew older you knew that you could be badly hurt. He concentrated on the descent of the stairs, but could not help every now and again raising his eyes briefly to take quick glances at parts of the view he had had time to appreciate a few hours earlier.

Suddenly Neil realised he was catching James. James had fallen off the railings and was picking himself up off the steps. He gingerly took a few steps down, and then decided to revert to the sliding technique. While he clumsily got himself into position over the railings, Neil made more ground on him, but then James was on his way, opening the gap once more. This happened again, and then Neil burst out laughing as James came crashing down a third time. He had forgotten the gap in the railings, or had remembered it too late and had been unable to stop himself in time. He landed in a heap, and lay for a time, trying to recover the breath that had been knocked out of him. Then he got up, feeling the pain in his body, and assessing how badly he had been hurt. He remembered the race and began painfully to descend the steps in more normal fashion. Before he could pick up speed or get into the sliding position again, Neil flew past him.

"If you want to slide again, I won't move aside for you," said Neil. He continued on his way, with James following somewhat deflated. James got into the sliding position again, but was shaky after his fall and fell off before he could catch Neil. He gave chase, but his race was over. Neil kept his tired legs moving as fast as he could, lightly brushing the railing with one hand so he could catch himself if he stumbled. The figures on the ground grew larger and larger. Neil's eyes found Lucy, all in yellow, at the foot of the steps. He looked at her every time he raised his eyes, willing himself to reach her as soon as possible. Soon he could distinguish her sun-burnished auburn hair drawing him on. A few more painful steps, and at last he thankfully landed next to her. He turned to see James only ten or fifteen metres behind. They shook hands, and then stood exhaustedly, bent over with hands on knees, trying to recover.

There was a buzz amongst the spectators, and a few hand-claps as the two men finished their race. Realising that the fun was over, the onlookers began to disperse. Lucy remained, looking at the two glistening wrecks of men, bent over with hands on knees, and then slowly straitening and dazedly looking again up and down Jacob's Ladder, before turning towards her. Lucy's emotions were mixed and complex. The last vestiges of lingering guilt were swept away by the excitement of being the cause of the contest. She had a great feeling of power over the two men, but also a growing admiration for each of them.

"I'm sure you could do with some refreshment," she said. "Let's go up to the Consulate, and I'll buy you a drink."

The three of them made their way slowly up Main Street and paused at the entrance to the Hotel.

"I'm sure you want to put on dry clothes. I'll order the drinks and you can join me in the courtyard, or on the little lawn beyond it. What'll you have?"

They both asked for their favourite beers, and then went off to change their clothes.

The table on the lawn, in a quiet little space backed by shrubs, was vacant, so Lucy waited for them there, idly watching the bubbles rising in the three long glasses of cold amber liquid. In the shade, the air was pleasant after the warm afternoon, and Lucy relaxed with a languid sense of temporary repose, combined with an underlying anticipation of what could lie ahead.

Neil came first, with James only a few seconds later. Both had had quick showers and looked refreshed and spruced up with slightly damp combed hair. They all raised their glasses and said "Cheers!" The liquid was cool and welcome, even to Lucy who had grown thirsty in the warm sun. There was not much conversation for a while as Neil and James thankfully sat back and relaxed. Lucy quietly appraised each of them. Neil wore a bright blue summer shirt which lit up the blue of his eyes. James wore a knitted golf shirt of shades of grey which complemented the attractive grey of *his* eyes. She was aware that she too was being carefully observed. Her yellow blouse was cut low, subtly suggesting the beautiful curves of her breasts. James was openly gazing at her, and Neil more subtly eying her over his tilted glass as he drank from it.

After a while of comfortable quiet Lucy said: "I'm quite impressed. I think you both did very well, and I can't help being proud of you."

"I think those three local youngsters showed us up, and showed us how it should really be done," said Neil. "We can't crow too much."

"But I think you did well for two businessmen, no longer in the first flush of youth," she said with a teasing smile. "You certainly showed yourselves to be very competitive."

"That's how we live," said James. "In the rat-race, it's the survival of the fittest."

"I'm glad I'm out of it," said Lucy. "However, I must listen to each of you, seeing I've forced you to run up and down Jacob's Ladder. Neil, as the winner of the race, you have choice of days. Which will it be?"

"I'd like Thursday please, Lucy," replied Neil unsurprisingly.

"So we'll meet tomorrow, James," she said smiling at him. "I've done some switching of lessons and free periods with colleagues willing to help me, so I should be able to leave school about two thirty on both days. If you'd each like to come to my house at about three on your particular afternoon I should be ready for you, and we'll take it from there. I'm not sure what you have planned, but I'm happy for us to use my car where that will help."

They finished their drinks, and Lucy left them at the Hotel. She walked down to the waterfront to her car, reflecting on the day as she walked and as she drove home. The departure of RMS *St Helena* with Katie carried both sadness and hope. The race and its aftermath had been fun. She would listen to James and to Neil as she had promised them and Abe Levy. However, she fully believed that she would keep out of the Morgen-Predvest matter. There were many others whose votes would be counted to decide what would happen. She did not want to be involved, except to the extent she had to be by the presence of James and Neil on the Island. Her chief interest was not in their arguments, but in how each of these men from her past would go about trying to persuade her.

Meanwhile she had work to be done, particularly as her free time would be occupied for the next two days. However, there was an unusual letter in her letterbox when she arrived home, and she sat down to read it before doing anything else.

The envelope was addressed in awkwardly-formed handwriting to: "Mrs Lucy Morgen, Saint Helena Island, South Atlantic". It had presumably arrived on Sunday with the RMS, and the Island postal service had quickly and correctly delivered it to her. There was a letter inside, written with obvious difficulty in the same unformed handwriting. The spelling (not replicated here) and grammar were imperfect, but the meaning was clear:

Mrs Lucy, I hope you are well and I hope you get this in time. I am all right and also Jacob and Julia. They still go to school.

Mrs Lucy we are suffering and we need you to help us. You won't be happy if you are here. A company called Predvest wants to buy Morgen. We hear they will close the factory. Also Morgen Farm and the shop. Our people will have no jobs. They will also stop pension or make it smaller. Then what will I do and how will I keep Jacob and Julia?

Mrs Lucy, we are suffering. Can you help us? Please can you stop them.

I am,

Patience Dlamini.

Lucy was moved. Patience had probably only had about six years of school learning, and English was probably only her third language. She sat for a long time with the letter on her lap. Here indeed was an appeal from her past, reaching somehow from the Free State platteland across the vast ocean to her little Island refuge. She had so far resisted all appeals to become involved in the Morgen-Predvest affair. She could refuse to speak to people on the phone. She could be polite to the emissaries in the shapes of Neil and James, and even toy with them – have fun with them – since they had invaded her space. She had left her past behind and would resist being drawn into it again. She wanted to make no exceptions and set no precedents for future appeals for her involvement in what she had escaped. How then was she to view this letter from Patience Dlamini? She thought of the slim dark young lady she had spoken to Neil about; whom she had helped to be part of the home crafts project; who had trusted her; and whom she had assured that Morgen would continue to care for through their pensions system and the crafts project. Geoff and Will, and Stanley and James and the others, and even Neil in this context, were easy to dismiss as people fighting for wealth and power, regardless of the consequences for others, and despite the good things her father and others had done through Morgen. Surely it was not for her to become involved in that struggle? Surely it was not her responsibility to protect what her father had built at such cost to his family relationships? Surely it was not for her, from so far away, to concern herself with the collateral damage from the power struggles and greed in the commercial and financial markets? Surely she did not have to continue forever helping those whom she had assisted long ago in another life in another world? So how should she view this despairing human plea, which had somehow seeped through a tiny crack in her fortifications?

39

Lucy worked until late that Tuesday night, until she had all her school work up to date and organized, so she could experience the next two afternoons and evenings with a clear conscience. She was tired when she went to bed, but her mind was still active and she found it difficult to go to sleep. When at last she did, her sleep was restless, with troubling dreams.

Katie came to her. Suddenly she was in Lucy's room, slim, fragile and ill, with dark, gentle eyes and long, black hair flowing over her shoulders and halfway down her back. Katie was pleading for an airport. If she had an airport she could fly away to Cape Town for treatment. Miraculously the airport was there, and Katie's brown eyes became the large brown eyes of Patience, also slim and dark but with short hair. Patience had flown into the Island to plead for Lucy's help.

Then suddenly the Island was overrun by people flying in: tourists with golf clubs hacking divots out of Broad Bottom, drinking cocktails on the main pool terrace of a monstrous high-rise hotel dominating the view from the sea off that shore, trampling and destroying sensitive vegetation, ordering wirebirds' eggs for hors d'oeuvres at dinner, extending the desert areas made by goats and foresters of old – but keeping the golf course green and cut with the sounds of sprinklers and mowers all day long.

Tourism creates jobs, so masses flew in for that reason: Saints coming home, and all the Morgen employees who had lost their jobs, banging on her door, demanding work. Big Joe and her father had made jobs for them, so why not Lucy? She saw Big Joe on top of Morgen Koppie, gazing out over the hills and mountains and conceiving his dream of the future. Then she was alone on the same mountain top as a young girl, and later with Neil's arms around her. Morgen Koppie transformed itself into Diana's Peak on a clear day. Standing alone, she saw the Island spread out around and below her, an emerald set in bronze, tranquil and beautiful. How could she keep it like that? And what should she now think of Morgen Koppie and the dream that began there? Her grandfather had built Morgen. Her father, too busy to come to her twenty-first, had built Morgen. They were in her room, pleading with her. Then her Uncle William and Neil were beating on her door, and Geoff Loman and James were trying to pull them back and get to her themselves.

Suddenly a host of Morgen shareholders, hundreds of them, like ants, were racing up and down Jacob's Ladder to decide the fate of Morgen. They resolved themselves into Will and Neil, and Geoff and James and Stanley. They were racing towards her as she stood at the bottom watching, while her grandfather held her hand. Someone tripped on the stairs, and brought all of them tumbling down to the ground in an ugly heap. Big Joe Morgen vanished, and Lucy saw Morgen crashing at her feet.

Lucy was suddenly awake, shaking, perspiring, her heart jumping. She was very disturbed. She sat up in bed and turned on the bedside light. She breathed deeply to calm herself, looking at the comforting familiarity of the things around her. She knew she should not again have become involved in Morgen's affairs. She did not want to be disturbed and upset in that way. In her nightdress, she walked out onto the veranda. She stood there in the darkness looking out into the night. It was calm and tranquil. There was only a little breeze to gently ruffle her hair and the skirt of her nightdress. She let the peace of the Island seep into her, calm and restoring. A few clouds played gently among the stars. The lights in the valley below twinkled in the darkness. This was the peace she wanted. This was why she had come here. She would keep to her chosen way, and would help to preserve the Island if she could.

40

Johannesburg was anything but peaceful. It had been a sultry day and, unusually, the normal coolness of evening was absent. It remained oppressive. Dark thunderclouds built up in the sky and blotted out the stars. Thunder began to rumble in the distance. Then in the early hours of Wednesday morning, an almighty storm broke over the city. Lightning flickered and flashed and spat with menace, and nearly simultaneous thunderclaps woke the city. The storm was frightening. A few heavy drops of rain fell. There was a momentary silence, then more lightning and thunder as the skies opened. Rain and hail came slashing down in great noisy torrents, trying to drown out the thunder, and lit by the wild light of the lightning. Eventually the rain and hail stopped as suddenly as they had begun. The storm moved away to the north. The lightning only flickered occasionally, and the rumble of thunder became a distant grumble.

Susie Mack got out of bed even earlier than usual that morning, as she had not been able to sleep after the storm. At first light she went into her little garden to assess damage. Fortunately it was not too serious. Some unmelted hailstones still lay white on the ground, a few small plants had been flattened, and twigs and shredded leaves lay beneath her trees and shrubs. She went inside to make her morning coffee, and was just sitting down to drink it when her telephone rang. She was not surprised to hear the voice of Geoff Loman.

"Hello, Susie. I thought you'd be awake after that storm."

"Hell-oo Geoffie. I thought it might be you. Did you suffer any damage?"

"Fortunately, nothing serious. I trust you're all right. Susie, you know the meeting's on Friday. Your project's going well, but I just want to confirm that I want you to keep up the good work until after the meeting."

"Geoff, we've had to buy a lot of shares the last few days. I think GAIM are doing most of the selling. They know we'll be there near the close each day so they're unloading quite a lot of stock."

"Well, keep going. Do the best you can. It you can get the price up a bit that will also help. The thousand cents has been a ceiling for a few weeks now."

"I'm scared to push too hard. That might bring out more selling. Also David and Harry are starting to worry about the volume of shares we're acquiring. They'll have to report to the Board eventually, and there'll be hell to pay if the Predvest share price falls once the excitement is over."

"They should know Predvest's a good investment. But I'll talk to David Goldberg and square things with him. They know they need me. We might be able to place some of the shares in certain of my portfolios later on if really necessary, but I can't do that now. I need help from a 'neutral' party, because officially none of this is happening. So carry on Susie. You know I won't forget you."

"I know that, Geoffie darling."

The streets of Sandton still glistened in the early morning half-light as Will Morgen drove himself to work that Wednesday. The city was always restless. Some of the many cars were already being driven fast and impatiently, as many came into the business centre early to avoid the daily crawling congestion soon to clog the roads. The car tyres hissed through standing water in places. Shredded leaves lay under large trees, and the way sand, mud and bits of vegetation lay in and near the gutters, and sometimes across the road, told of the earlier rushing torrents of storm water. The gleaming wet buildings of the business district stood proudly tall, most of them also lit from within. Will turned into the entrance to Morgen House and drove into the basement parking area, mildly surprised to notice a few people already outside the building's main entrance. He took a lift up to the still deserted ninth floor, walked somewhat wearily to his office, took off his jacket, and sat down at his desk to work. It was the one time of the day when he could usually work without interruptions and be very productive.

Just after seven o'clock his secretary brought him an early morning cup of coffee, as she had done voluntarily and faithfully for a number of years. This morning Judy looked as elegant and attractive as ever. Her face lit up gently as she smiled her greeting, but Will knew her every expression, and as the smile faded he was aware of some anxiety and weariness behind her lovely grey eyes and in the slight furrowing of her brow. They worked very closely with one another, and had become valued friends as well as trusting colleagues. They could often steal a few moments at this time of the morning to chat, and perhaps to discuss the programme for the day.

"Would you like to sit down, Judy? Did you survive the storm?"

"Yes, but it woke up the whole family. I couldn't go to sleep again. My mind just kept racing on. I can't help feeling that the real storm is about to begin."

"Perhaps, but we must try to win through."

They were quiet for a while. Then she asked: "Will Lucy vote?"

"I still don't know. She promised Abe she'd think about it."

"Couldn't you talk to her again?"

"I may, but at the moment I think to try will do more harm than good. Neil phoned. He's going to spend the afternoon and evening with her tomorrow. It's last minute stuff, I know, but I think it's our main hope."

"I didn't sleep, not only because of the storm. I'm worried about my job, and so are most of us here."

"Don't worry yet. We must still hope. If we do lose, I would like you to stay with me in the new dispensation, or in whatever I do later. They'll need me for a time, and I'll stay to try and lessen the damage and save as many jobs as possible. The trouble is that I can't see myself working for long in an environment controlled by Geoff Loman." Will gestured towards the portrait of Joe Morgen on the wall. "I hate to think what my father would think about the present situation, but I do know he would fight to save the Company."

A short while after Judy left him, Will's telephone rang. It was Geoff Loman.

"Geoff! This is a surprise. Are you calling off your bid?"

"I'm not in the mood for jokes. I want you to call off your pickets, and immediately."

"I haven't the faintest idea what you're talking about."

"Am I to believe that you don't know that there's a demonstration going on outside Predvest Building? There're a whole lot of people holding placards with all kinds of nonsense. 'Save Morgen'. 'Save Morgen jobs'. 'Save Morgen pensions'. That sort of thing. I want you to call them off at once."

"Are they peaceful? Are they stopping anyone from going in or out of your building? Are they trespassing?"

"Well, no. They're on the pavement in front of the building. But it's bad publicity – a dirty trick. The journalists will have a field day, and the market won't like it."

"Oh, I have a feeling your share price will close the day around a thousand cents as usual. I don't know anything about that demonstration, and I don't know what I could do about it. You say it's peaceful, not causing a nuisance, and I must say that I have sympathy with their sentiments. I'd be interested to know who's behind it, so I'll make some enquiries. I can't say more than that."

As Will put the phone down, Judy walked in to tell him that Building Security had just reported a peaceful demonstration outside Morgen House. Will stood up, and walked past the offices of Mark and Rob. The latter was in and Will asked him to join him. They went down to the ground floor and out through the front entrance. A peaceful group of Morgen employees, like that described by Geoff Loman, was there. Some of the placards were similar, but there were others, including "Say NO to Predvest".

Some other Morgen managers were already there. Will spoke to the demonstrators. He assured them of his sympathy, thanked them for their support, and assured them that everything possible was being done to fight off the Predvest bid. He hoped that after the meeting on Friday he and they would be pleased with the outcome. He learnt that the demonstration had been quietly organized by the trade union members in order to reinforce the points they had been making in their discussions with management, and to gather support from shareholders and the general public There would also be demonstrations at other Morgen offices, distribution centres and factories, and at Predvest headquarters, on the Wednesday, Thursday and Friday mornings.

Will returned to his office. Judy had telephone in hand as he passed her desk. "Hold on a moment. He's just come back," she said. She placed her hand over the speaker and said to Will, "It's Andries, from Platberg Factory, asking for you."

"Good morning, Will," said Andries. "I couldn't get hold of Rob, so I'm troubling you directly. I think you should know that we've a work stoppage here. The union's called it until ten this morning. The staff are all outside, in front of the factory, protesting about the possibility of a takeover by Predvest. As you know they're very worried about a possible closing of the factory, as well as their jobs and pensions. It's probably illegal, but it's all peaceful, and we're handling it as best we can. They've told us they'll stop work again tomorrow morning between eight and ten, and on Friday from eight until they hear the result of the meeting."

41

Lucy was both excited and apprehensive when she drove home from school that Wednesday afternoon. She was excited, as she would often be at the beginning of a holiday, a longed-for excursion, or an adventure into the unknown. She was a little apprehensive because she had not been alone with James since he had taken her home from the Magaliesberg that day when he had tried to coerce her into making love to him. She had ended their relationship the next day. How would he be now, and how would he treat her? It would be interesting to see. If they were playing a game (though admittedly with some serious implications), they were playing on her ground. Also, he needed her, so she should be able to exercise sufficient control of the situation if necessary.

She made herself ready as soon as she reached home. It was a warm day, so she changed into an attractive T-shirt and shorts – she knew she looked good in shorts – and put on thick socks and her walking boots. She packed her light rucksack with a light rain jacket, sunhat and water bottle. "Would James think of bringing any refreshments?" she wondered. Not sure, she also packed two cool drinks, some biscuits and dried fruit.

James drove up to her front gate on time at three o'clock. He was confident and looking forward with zest to the afternoon and evening. He was in pursuit of a deal, which was always exciting. In this one he needed to rely on his way with women, and he was very confident of that. Lucy was a strange and uncooperative woman, but he believed that, if anyone could win her over, it would be he. Lucy again noted that he looked good in T-shirt and shorts, and that he wore running shoes. She also noticed his appraising and approving glance at her smooth, shapely, bare legs and attractive figure.

"Hello, James. Would you like to come in for a cup of tea or coffee, or shall we be on our way?"

"I've just had something, thank you. I think we should go for our walk."

"Where are we going?"

"I'd like to do another post box walk. I've done Diana's Peak and Flagstaff, so I thought the Peak Dale walk sounded interesting."

"That's a good choice. Then I can also show you the proposed site of the golf course and hotel. If we take two cars, we can leave one at each end of the walk. Let me get my car out and you can follow me."

They set out, with Lucy leading the way. She stopped near Cason's Gate, and parked her car close to where their path joined the road. Taking her rucksack with her, she approached James's car which had stopped behind hers.

"Get out for a moment, James. I want to show you something."

She led him a short distance down the road, and then stopped on the grass verge beside a barbed wire fence. She waved her arm to indicate a broad, grassy valley. "*This* is planned to be a golf course; and the five star hotel will be built lower down," gesturing to their right.

She let him look for a while without her saying anything more. From a little way below where they stood one of a complex of little valleys made its way down to join the main one, which was wide and green, and ran down to their right, to be obscured by a grassy ridge sloping down to meet it. It was a peaceful scene. Nearby, cows were grazing calmly. There was a water trough and a few struggling trees.

Lucy continued: "That is Broad Bottom. On the other side of the valley, over there, is the site of a camp for Boer prisoners-of-war in the Anglo-Boer war. The buildings you see are the remains of an old flax mill."

"It's a pretty spot," murmured James cautiously.

Lucy turned on him. "James, can you imagine all this being turned into a tourist area? Can you believe anyone would want to turn this into a golf course?"

James privately thought it could be turned into a very interesting golf course, but kept his thoughts to himself.

"Can you imagine a great big hotel down there, with access roads and sewerage needs and goodness knows what else? It will completely ruin this part of the Island. And can you imagine the amount of water it and a golf course would consume? The Island only has limited water supplies. Even to think of doing this is sacrilege. It must be stopped."

"Then we'll stop it," said James firmly.

"Do you think you can?"

"Vote for us and we'll stop it as soon as we're in charge of Morgen."

"Will Geoff Loman agree to that?"

"He will. He'll do as I say, so long as he gets the deal. I'm here to represent him. I'm sure he'll agree to stop this project." Privately James was thinking that the project was very risky and that there was no way that it could be profitable, or profitable enough to satisfy Geoff's or his own views of an adequate return on investment.

Lucy felt more hopeful as they got into James's car and he drove on along the road under her direction. Further on they passed, on the left, on a grassy slope with trees behind, the St Helena and the Cross Church. It was an attractive white building with a dark grey roof, round-arched windows and a portico entrance. A small dark car was parked amongst the scattered headstones of the unfenced graveyard, and a grave-digger was digging a grave. "This is where all our struggles end," thought Lucy. "This is the last change, which cannot be denied."

She shrugged off such thoughts. It was a beautiful day, to be enjoyed. It was very windy as they approached Thompson's Wood, and Lucy remarked that strong winds often blew around Thompson's Valley. She showed James where to park, close to where their path left the road to their left.

They set off on the path which zigzagged fairly steeply down through long grass.

"What did you do this morning, James?" asked Lucy.

"I went to Briars, and Longwood House, and briefly to Napoleon's grave. It was interesting to follow his history on St Helena. I like powerful men, but it was sad to think of the great man reduced to being Emperor over only his retinue in a small house and garden."

They turned onto a rough vehicle track and followed it through some eucalyptus trees. The going was easy and they could chat as they went. The vegetation was lush. Every now and again there were spectacular views, across the varied greens of plants and trees and, beyond them, down through steep arid valleys of brown rugged desert, to a blue-grey sea. After a while they reached an area of surviving gumwood trees. There they came to a small wooden building in an open grassy space, and beside the structure was the "post box", actually a pole with a red cap on it.

"Let's stop here and have some refreshments," suggested Lucy. "It's a long time since lunchtime, and then I worked most of it."

"Good idea. I want to record my name in the post box."

James did that, with evident satisfaction, while Lucy found a pleasant shady spot, sat down and unpacked the refreshments she had brought. James had brought cool drinks and some small cakes, so they had fare for a pleasant little picnic

"I thought of bringing champagne, but then I remembered we'd be driving," he said.

They sipped and munched in silence for a while. Then James said: "I can't help remembering our last outing together. I've often thought of it."

"You've a cheek even to mention it. You only wanted to have sex with me."

"I asked you to marry me."

"You were only interested in my money – and some sex I suppose. I don't think you loved me."

"Of course I did, but perhaps I was tactless, for which I apologise." Then, after a pause, he said, "You must remember that you promised to make love to me."

"That was under duress."

"I wouldn't have harmed you, and a promise is a promise."
He paused. "Tonight would be a good time."

Lucy did not answer. Instead, she pointed to the gumwood
trees, growing in front of them. They were quite large –
survivors in the wild. Lucy told James about them: that they
were endemic to the Island, and had become endangered; that
the Millennium Forest project aimed to re-establish a
gumwood forest.

"Come and have a look," she said, standing up.

They walked about, looking more closely at the
gumwoods. The branches were crooked and most of the leaves
made up little curved, mini-umbrella bunches at the ends of
main branches. So in places they could look all the way down
to the sea through a twisted tracery of branches below a curved
leafy canopy.

Lucy and James packed up the remainder of their picnic
and continued on their walk. Lucy told him more about the
endemic species on the Island, the need for conservation, and
the work of The St Helena National Trust and others to that
end.

James listened. When she paused, he said: "Well, we've
already agreed on the hotel and golf course. Perhaps Predvest
would make a substantial donation to the Trust. I could even
do something myself if the deal is consummated. I'm certain
we would if you voted for us."

They continued on their way, not speaking for a while.

It was a beautiful walk. The terrain through which they
passed was open sometimes, and closed in on them in other
places. There were some more spectacular views down to the
sea to their right, and, on the other side, breathtaking views up
the mountain slopes on which they were walking to High Peak
and Mount Vesey above them. They passed through an avenue
of erythrina, or African coral trees. There were yellow woods,
arum lilies and much more. At length their path climbed up to
the road near Cason's Gate, where they had left Lucy's car.

Lucy drove them back to the beginning of their walk. She
went very slowly past Broad Bottom to make sure that James

would see it again. "Don't forget your promise," she reminded him.

James had arranged for them to have dinner at the Consulate at seven thirty. He offered to pick her up at her home, but she declined, arranging to meet him at the Hotel at seven o'clock for a pre-dinner drink. She told herself that it would be best to have control over transport of her own.

James was waiting for Lucy on the lower veranda, close to the Hotel entrance. When he saw her parking her car in the main road, he came across, opened the car door for her and escorted her into the hotel. They took their drinks to the upper veranda and sat in a quiet corner, in the cool of early evening, looking out onto the street, idly watching the activity there. It was peaceful, with only the unhurried restlessness of a few people and vehicles passing by.

Shortly after seven thirty they went in to dinner. The dining room was normally only open when RMS *St Helena* was in port, or when her passengers were staying on the Island while she did her round trip to Ascension and back. Lucy always liked dining there. This evening the lighting was subdued, and the dark wooden ceiling, wooden columns made from old ships' masts, an old ship's wooden steering wheel and other artefacts, all worked to create the feel of a ship's elegant dining room. There were white tablecloths and tall candles on each table, most of which were already occupied. There was a lively but unobtrusive buzz of conversation, which meant that Lucy and James could talk comfortably without being overheard.

James was at his most charming. He talked of many things: Patsy, his wife and Lucy's sister; his own and the Morgen families; South Africa, and especially things he and Lucy had done together before he had married; his impressions of St Helena; and their walk that afternoon. Lucy found herself well entertained, so she did not need to contribute much to the conversation. It was clear that James was making every effort to please her. She found him interesting and attractive, but perhaps a little too smooth. He seemed to be trying just a touch too hard.

While they were waiting for their main course to be served, Lucy said: "I had a dream last night. It was partly about Morgen employees losing their jobs. Also about someone I know from Morgen Farm who wrote me a letter I received yesterday. I think you should read it, James."

She gave him Patience's letter and he read it in the light of the candle. He handed it back to her.

"She has no need to worry. Pensions and jobs will be safe. I'll confirm it with Geoff tomorrow. If you don't hear from me, consider it decided. Geoff wants the deal, so he'll agree. He's already said they'll take any actions necessary in a humane way. He'll agree – so that will mean that any loss of jobs will be by natural attrition."

After a pause, Lucy asked: "What if I didn't vote?"

"It's too close to call. If they win, we lose the deal, and can't try again for a year. Who knows what things will be like by then? If we lose you'll be in their hands, and there'll be no donations to the Trust. If we win and you don't vote, you also can't expect much from us, because you'll have left things to chance without helping us win the deal. You must vote for us. It's a good deal for you, quite apart from all the things you've made me promise. You'll benefit from the growth of the Predvest group and your shares will increase in value."

"Let's talk about other things. I have until Friday morning to decide."

After their dessert plates had been removed and coffee served, James sat back in his chair, looked directly at her, and said: "I want to make love to you."

"Why?"

"You promised, you're beautiful, and –" he added with a mischievous a smile "– I want to make you feel good so you'll vote for me."

"Sex and money: simple motivations," said Lucy. "I let you have sex with me, and out of gratitude I ensure that you make a few millions. How much am I worth to you and to

Predvest at this moment, and how much will I be worth after Friday?"

"Have you had a lover since you came to the Island?"

"I can't see what business that is of yours. However, I haven't in fact had a lover for a long time."

"You must be frustrated after all those years. Let me make you feel good again – and at the same time keep your promise to me, as you want me to keep those I made to you today."

"What about Patsy?"

"She won't know."

"And what about that May?"

"What about her?"

"I met her. She assured me your explanations were irresistible. Did you seduce her to get her votes?"

"I explained everything to her. I was nice to her and she was very grateful."

"And am I another May? Do you think you can make love to a supposedly frustrated lady – to make her feel good, as you said – so I will give you my votes out of gratitude?"

"I wouldn't put it like that. I really would like to make you happy – "

"And yourself too."

" – especially as you promised to make love to me. And I *have* made promises about the hotel and golf course, and retrenchments, and pensions and your Patience." James assumed the pleading expression of a little boy, all the while trying to hold with his her green eyes, deep and shining in the candlelight.

Lucy was amused, more than anything else, by James's performance. She tried to hide her amusement, but it probably showed in her eyes. She wondered whether he would keep all those promises if she walked out on him now, leaving him frustrated and with wounded pride. Probably not, but perhaps she would not vote, so the matter could be irrelevant.

However, Lucy was also full of curiosity. What would James be like as a lover? It might be fun to know more about this man she might have married. He was an attractive man. She had thought so before, though she was glad that she had not married him. He was trying all he could to please her, though with mixed motives. She had not made love to anyone since Colin had left the Island. It might be interesting, pleasant, even amusing, to let James have his way. She returned his gaze, looking thoughtfully into those grey eyes she had always liked. Then she smiled.

"Where do you suggest?" she asked.

Lucy went ahead of James up the steep, carpeted steps to his room, so he could see her attractive figure as he followed. The bedroom was spacious, pleasantly decorated in light colours. James had put the two single beds together. A large window was curtained, from ceiling to floor, in a light floral material. It let in some light from outside, and James had augmented that by artfully using the bedside lamps to create pleasantly subdued lighting. Lucy noticed two wine glasses, and a small bottle of champagne in an ice-bucket, on the dressing table.

They put their arms around each other. James held her as he had done that day when a waterfall plunged into a clear pool at the end of a narrow gorge in the Magaliesberg. Again she felt his strong body pressing against hers, and saw the grey eyes close to her face as he kissed her. This time James was more cautious and patient, "playing me carefully so I don't take fright or offence and change my mind," Lucy thought.

Soon they had helped each other out of their clothes. Lucy knew that she was in good shape and very attractive, and James obviously appreciated the curves of her figure and the smoothness of her skin. She thought he looked good too, fit and strong, though just a little softened by good living. Curious to see how he would be, and what he would do, she let him take the lead.

His hands felt good on her body, her breasts, between her legs. Nevertheless she felt the foreplay was relatively brief and perfunctory; gentlemanly, but with no real tenderness. As with Stanley, she had a sense of a mission to be accomplished. James entered her, moved with a somewhat military precision, and soon climaxed. He lay on her for a while, breathing heavily at first.

"That was good. I enjoyed that," he said.

"I can see you did."

"You did too?"

Lucy smiled, but gave no other answer.

James opened the champagne bottle with a loud pop, and poured out two glasses of the golden, bubbling liquid. Lucy said she would only be able to have a few sips as she still had to drive home.

"You're welcome to stay the night if you wish."

"No thank you, James. I have to teach tomorrow."

They sipped in silence for a while. Then James said: "Will you ask your attorney to vote for the deal?"

"I promised to hear Neil before deciding."

"Surely you'll vote for me? Lucy, we've been so very close, and you must know now how much I love you."

"Yes, James. I have a very good idea of how much you love me."

Lucy thought of the evening as she drove herself home along the quiet, dark roads. Perhaps in some genuine way James really had wanted to make her feel good – happy and satisfied. It had been an interesting and pleasant experience, but she was left with a sense of unfulfilment, vaguely frustrated and dissatisfied. She could not escape the feeling that, for him, she was a goal achieved, a notch on his gun, his signature left in an Island post box, an item to be ticked off a list.

42

In Johannesburg another hot day was followed by another warm night. The build-up of typical cumulus clouds during the afternoon led to a spectacular sunset. There were storms during the night, but nowhere near as bad as the night before. Thunder grumbled away, there was lightning, but very little rain.

Will Morgen drove early to work as usual on Thursday morning. Morgen House glowed in the half-light as the interior lights shone through the large glass windows. As he drove into the entrance, employees were already beginning to assemble in front of the building for the promised demonstration.

"They've certainly attracted attention," thought Will. "I wonder whether it'll help us."

The demonstrations of the previous day had been reported on radio, television and in the newspapers. They had apparently created public sympathy, and a far greater degree of public interest in the Morgen/Predvest affair than would normally be expected. However, it was the shareholders who would decide, and decision-time was now close. Today Neil would have a chance to persuade Lucy to become involved and vote for Morgen. Will had listened to news reports, including about the Predvest bid, on his car radio, and more reports and comments confronted him in the morning newspapers. These could perhaps be summed up by an extract from Jennifer Rogan's column in *Daily Business*:

> Much public interest is being shown in the tussle between Morgen Holdings and Predvest Ltd for the ultimate control of the Morgen group which should be decided tomorrow. The interest has been heightened by reports of peaceful demonstrations

yesterday by Morgen employees outside the Predvest and Morgen headquarters in Sandton, as well as at other of their factories, distribution centres and offices. There have also been reports of work stoppages at several of Morgen's factories.

Morgen staff, like their directors and management, are clearly opposed to the hostile takeover bid made by Predvest, and are determined to make their voices heard.

However, the matter will be decided by Morgen shareholders at a general meeting tomorrow morning. Word is that Predvest has garnered a large proportion of the votes, but it is not certain that they will be able to achieve the seventy-five percent majority needed for the bid to succeed.

It should be an interesting meeting.

Geoff Loman was also at his desk early and was also aware of the various reports of demonstrations, and the speculation about whether Predvest would clinch the deal at the Morgen meeting the next day. He was irritated by the negative publicity, particularly as another demonstration had been forming outside the Predvest Building when he arrived there. He had just finished reading Jennifer Rogan's comments when Jody put through a call from James Bold.

"Good morning, James. What time is it there? This is devotion to duty."

"It's six o'clock, Geoff, but I wanted to speak to you before you became too involved with other people. I want you to know that I think we have a done deal. I had a good time with Lucy, I left her very happy, and I'm sure she'll vote for us."

"How sure?"

"At least ninety percent. But I had to make some promises on your behalf. I said I'd check with you, and if she didn't hear from me today she could take it that you agree."

"What promises?"

"First of all she wants us to stop the luxury hotel and golf course project that Morgen's involved in. Having seen the place, I'm sure you will at least want to pull out of the consortium promoting the project."

"Okay. No problem."

"I said if Lucy voted for us Predvest would give a substantial donation to the St Helena Trust for conservation purposes."

"How substantial?"

"You can decide."

"Okay. What else?"

"Pensions are to be left intact, and there will be no retrenchments. Jobs will only be reduced by natural attrition."

"We'll see. But there'll be no harm in letting her think that that's how it will be. You don't need to talk to her again."

43

Meanwhile Neil had not been idle. At breakfast on Wednesday morning he had overheard James ordering dinner for two for that evening, so he resolved to dine at Ann's Place and keep out of the way of James and Lucy. He had asked Hensel to show him parts of the Island he had not yet seen, so after a leisurely breakfast the little red car called at the Hotel and he was driven out of the Jamestown valley to cross the high central mountain ridge. On the way they stopped to see the graveyard at Knollcombes where Boer prisoners-of-war, who had died on the Island over a hundred years before, had been buried. Then they made a brief stop at St Paul's Cathedral, the seat of the Bishop. It had been built in 1851, and Neil saw a weathered grey-brown brick structure with pointed arches and an impressive bell-tower soaring heavenwards. They drove on, and once more Neil asked Hensel to stop high up on Sandy Bay Ridge, so they could again appreciate the glorious view. It was a clear day, so the sea was blue in the distance as they looked down the long valley with the complex ranks of ridges running down on either side. The high mountains behind them were green and unclouded.

The narrow road twisted and turned its way down Sandy Bay Valley. They stopped at the Baptist Chapel, a small stone church with red roof and pointed windows and door, but impressive nonetheless against a protective hillside, and with the great grey stone column of Lot looming behind it. They went on and entered a desert of grey, brown and dark sand and stone, with rocky hills and mountains. This was relieved by a narrow oasis on a tenuous watercourse along the valley floor, where there was a strip of farmland of incongruous green, and even a few date palms.

The desert ran down to the sea, so there was much sand at Sandy Bay, but ironically the beach itself was nearly all pebbles. Neil walked on them, listening to the rush of the waves breaking on the shore, and the crackling noise of the pebbles as the outgoing water rolled them upon one another. The rocky arms which formed the bay were very dark, almost black, and the sea was a beep blue in the clear light. Neil put his hands in the cool water and looked out to the south-east through the opening of the bay. His home was thousands of kilometres away in that direction.

Neil indicated that he would like to walk part of the way back into Jamestown, so Hensel took him to Prince Andrew School – interesting of course as Lucy's place of work – and showed him the start of a path which led from the edge of the School grounds down and along the valley below the Heart Shaped Falls. It was a pleasant and interesting walk. The steep bare rock of High Knoll, crowned by its fortress, rose out of the valley vegetation and loomed over him. There was only a thin stream of water dropping down the centre of the falls, but the brown and grey of the cliffs on each side, together making up the shape of a heart, were impressive. White terns hovered above the branches of trees next to the path, but always moved away too soon to be photographed. The valley was joined by another running down from the direction of Briars, and then there were views to the narrow strip of rich farmland on the valley floor above Jamestown itself. Neil joined the winding road he had taken back into town on Sunday evening, crossing the stream, passing the hospital and Pike Cottage, and walking down along the urban roads to his hotel.

Neil also spent a lot of time talking to St Helenians and canvassing their opinions. This was easy, for the Saints were unfailingly friendly and ready to exchange a smile and a word with a visitor. So Neil was able to engage people in conversation at the Consulate, the Coffee Shop, Donny's, Ann's Place, in shops and at the museum, and of course he had long conversations with Hensel as they drove about the Island.

The debate about change inevitably began with the airport. Some were in favour of it: for better access to the Island, medical emergencies, stimulation of the economy by tourism, the creation of jobs, attracting back and keeping Saints on the Island, helping to keep family structures intact, and so on. Others were against it: a sea link would still be necessary for heavy cargoes, an influx of tourists would change the culture of the island, and they feared the importation of drugs, HIV/AIDS and other diseases. Many were ambivalent, typified by one lady who told Neil:

"Personally, I would not want the airport and the changes it would bring. I would like the Island to stay as it is. But from a medical point of view it is necessary. And we need to stop the young people from leaving the Island. I hope we'll attract the right kinds of visitors, and I don't think there will be great numbers."

Neil also had a long and interesting conversation with a gentleman he described to himself as an elder statesman of the Island. He told Neil:

"The question of the airport should be seen in the context of the history of the Island, which has been used as a staging post and has never been financially and economically independent. I believe that trying to create an entrepreneurial society too fast will harm the Island. For example, many islanders buy plots, and build homes bit by bit with the help of friends when they can afford it. Therefore about eighty per cent of islanders have their own homes. A developer/builder/estate agent system would make homes too expensive to acquire. I'm not a socialist, but I would not want to lose a caring social environment.

"The airport will not solve all problems, but it's the main focus of attention now, so other things may be neglected. I don't like the idea of a large hotel with an eighteen-hole golf course. That would take up a large proportion of scarce arable land, and consume scarce water resources. I would prefer a number of small environmentally appropriate lodges around the Island, and the attraction of the right kind of tourist.

There's danger in too fast a transition, but I suppose it'll be years before an airport is actually operational.

"Prices are already rising. Low wages for locals mean they have to leave to make a living. Shortages of medical staff, teachers and others have to be met by contract at much greater cost than locals' salaries. Paying decent salaries and wages would keep people on the Island. The Island's main sources of revenue are remittances from abroad, and from the British government. Tourism will be relatively small, and won't be the answer to all problems."

On Wednesday afternoon and evening Neil could not help thinking from time to time about Lucy and James. How were matters going, both on a personal level and in relation to Morgen? Neil had decided to come to St Helena well before Lucy's vote had become critical to Morgen. He had come to see Lucy. He had loved being on the Island, but he could not escape the thought that so far he had come a very long way to see very little of Lucy. Perhaps tomorrow would compensate for that. He placed his head on his pillow that night, thinking that he would at last have time to spend alone with her.

44

Lucy slept well on Wednesday night. She had not slept much the night before, and had had a long day of teaching, walking, talking, some lovemaking, and driving home late at night. She awoke refreshed, but rather cynical about James, whom she inevitably thought about as she dressed and had breakfast. She had obtained some possibly useful promises from him, but could now well leave him behind, except to be polite to her sister's husband.

She now looked forward to having time alone with Neil. She was both excited and apprehensive, but in different ways from the previous morning. She and Neil had loved one another very deeply and had been as close as any two people could be. There had been a long separation since the prospect of never having him to herself had hurt so much as to drive her away. How would they react towards one another? Would there be strain in their relationship?

The weather had turned cool and windy, with low cloud over the Island, so Lucy had to dress warmly. Ironically, she could not show herself off in shorts as she had the day before. Lucy was watching out for Neil just before three o'clock that afternoon. She came to the gate as Hensel's red car drew up beside it. Neil got out and greeted her.

"I took you at your word that we could use your car this afternoon. Is that still OK?"

Lucy nodded assent, and Neil arranged for Hensel to pick him up again at Lucy's home at about a quarter to six that evening.

"You're looking good," said Neil as soon as they were alone. "I thought we could walk on Diana's Peak, because we both loved the mountains so much, but I'm not sure now. It looks as though it'll be misty up there."

"Let's go anyway. I'd like that. I know the paths. They're very clear, so we'll be quite safe."

Lucy did not have to drive them very far. They were still below the clouds when she found a safe place to park beside the road between Rose Hill and Black Gate. They walked up a broad grassy path, from where there were views of rolling green hills and valleys over the ferns, and then flax, growing along the side of the path. Then they were closed in by a steep bank on one side and very tall flax plants on the other.

"There's a lot of flax here," remarked Neil. "It doesn't seem like a national park."

"The encroachment of alien species is a massive problem," said Lucy. She told him that the surviving ancient tree fern thicket, and all its related species along the high ridge, were both unique and endangered. There were projects in place to remove the harmful aliens – flax and buddleia and others – to preserve the remaining original fern thickets, and to propagate and replant various endangered endemic species in what was now a national park.

Soon they were in thick mist, with only a few metres of visibility. They came to some wood-protected steps cut into the hillside, and turned up them. They climbed in the clouds onto the high ridge of the Island. The first peak they reached was Cuckold Point, with a huge Norfolk pine on the summit. The path continued steeply down, through a saddle, and then up to Diana's Peak, the highest point on the Island. There they stopped beside the weathered wooden signboard proclaiming "Diana's Peak 823m". Ironically, it stood amongst flax plants beside the path. Lucy noted that Neil was taking in all the details of his surroundings, but ignored the post box. It was wild and windy up there so they moved on, down through another saddle and up onto Mount Acteon, distinguished by two large pine trees just below its summit. They followed a path down the ridge for a while, but when they came to an area of flax they decided to turn around, climb up onto the ridge again, and return the way they had come.

"I'm sorry you're missing the views," Lucy remarked early in their walk. "They can be spectacular from here."

"I'm not worried," Neil assured her. "Fortunately, I've already seen so many beautiful views on the Island. I know I'd love to have the long views from here, but I always think the mist brings something special with it. It makes you concentrate on the smaller things, the plants and flowers and trees, and there is so much that is special here."

Indeed they walked in a ghostly wonderland. In exposed places the wind raged, and drove the mist around them. In more sheltered parts it was calmer and the cloud had a more gentle touch. The ancient fern tree thicket was very special. Lucy did not know the names of all the species, but structure was given to the ever-changing shapes looming out of the shifting mist by the tall tree ferns, seeming to semaphore with their outstretched arms, and the black cabbage trees with dark branches and canopies of large green leaves highlighted by clusters of white flowers. Masses of ferns and other plants filled in the spaces. The ghostly shapes changed before their eyes with every step they took and with every darkening or lightening of the swirling mist.

There were some aliens too, apart from the flax and the three tall trees marking two of the summits. When Neil remarked on the red spots of flowering fuchsias, Lucy told him that they had spread from domestic gardens and were now a nuisance, spreading and preventing the germination of some endemic species. Later they discovered a beautiful bank of arum lilies. Ironically, that species had originally been imported to be cultivated for cattle feed; the island had later exported the bulbs; and then the arum lily had been adopted as the national flower.

The mist also produced a feeling of intimacy between the two isolated people. There was no one anywhere nearby, and they had the mountains to themselves, but the restricted visibility emphasized the near and now. They instinctively drew closer to one another in the misty cocoon in which they were contained even as they walked. It was natural to hold hands when the path was wide enough. There was no strain at all between them. They could speak or keep a comfortable silence, all the while sharing their experience. They felt no need to be polite or to make small talk. It seemed right to be together.

"I chose this walk because we loved the mountains so much," said Neil. "I'm so glad to be sharing this with you. I hope we can now both add Diana's Peak to the hills and mountains we've shared and loved: Morgen Koppie, Platberg, and so many in the Drakensberg."

They found a sheltered spot, sat on the grass and made a little picnic. Lucy had brought hot coffee in a thermos flask, and Neil had brought some of the traditional hiking food they had enjoyed in the past: dried fruit, nuts, biscuits and chocolate. They sat close together and sipped their coffee as they watched the mist and the ferns and trees that sheltered them. They were fully clothed against the wind and the damp. Neil pushed back his hood and Lucy looked at his tousled hair, bushy eyebrows and kindly blue eyes. She could not resist leaning over and kissing his cheek.

"I'm also glad we're sharing this," she murmured. "I'm remembering how and why I loved you." They were silent for a while, and then she continued: "Do you remember the time we went high up Sterkhorn in the Berg, and had to turn back early because the mist came down? I remember how cold it was. We had a warm shower together as soon as we got back to the hotel, and then made love so beautifully under a warm duvet. This could also be a duvet day."

"I'd like to do that again," said Neil. "Make love, I mean."

"Let's wait until tonight and see how we feel."

They sat, leaning against each other, with their own quiet thoughts for some time. Eventually the silence was broken by Neil:

"I can't help thinking about time when I think of St Helena. I've read that this vegetation and some of these species go back for millions of years, as does the Island itself of course. Then in human terms we think of the Island's long history, just over five hundred years, and the changes that have occurred. That's long for you and me, who have so little time in this world, but it's really less than the blink of an eye in geological time."

"I sometimes have such thoughts," said Lucy. "But I think of how small we are, and how unimportant. Here we are, two tiny dots on a tiny dot of an Island in a vast ocean on a tiny dot of a planet in a vast and not very significant universe amongst only God knows how many others."

"We have our little space and our little time. We need to use it as best we can. We need to make memories, even if only for ourselves."

"I'll remember *this*," said Lucy, leaning closer to him.

Neil knew of course that James had given Lucy dinner at the Consulate, and so wanted to do something different for her. He told Lucy he had tried to book at Wellington House in Main Street, where the man who was to be Napoleon's conqueror at Waterloo had stayed in 1805. "I was met at the door by a beautiful lady who stepped out into the sunlight to talk to me: a golden lady with lovely golden eyes and golden skin in the golden light. Unfortunately they're closed for alterations, mainly to the kitchen." So he had made further inquiries, and booked for dinner at Farm Lodge. Lucy and Neil agreed to meet there at seven thirty.

Farm Lodge Country House Hotel was at Rosemary Plain, about fifteen minutes drive south-west from Jamestown. It had been built in about 1750 as an East India Company planter's house. It was situated in quiet countryside in its own extensive tropical gardens, where some of the best coffee in the world was still grown. The small hotel was run by Stephen Biggs and Maureen Jonas. It was comfortably and elegantly furnished, and the dining room had an enviable reputation.

Lucy was parking her car when Hensel's red taxi drew up next to it with Neil aboard. Neil was not sure what transport arrangements to make for later on, so he arranged to telephone Hensel by nine o'clock if he wished to be collected and taken back to Jamestown. If Hensel did not hear from him by then, he would know that Lucy would give Neil a lift.

The couple held hands as they made their way to the hotel entrance. They were greeted heartily by their host and were made comfortable in the elegant lounge, where they chatted over a drink until dinner was served and they were escorted to their table in the dining room. They were happy with each other, and comfortable in the elegant surroundings. Lucy noted approvingly that Neil was dressed smartly, and that his eyes took a deeper blue from the blue of his shirt. Lucy herself wore green, with emerald and diamond earrings, which emphasised the green of her eyes, which smiled with the smile that played about her lips. She wore a gold chain that Neil had given her long ago, and her skin was smooth and creamy. They reminded each other of their first dinner date at Susanna's. They talked of previous times together, of the Island, and their walk that afternoon. Eventually, and inevitably, they had to talk about Morgen.

"How did you get on with James yesterday?" asked Neil.

"Quite well. He says he'll stop the big hotel and golf course."

"How?"

"Geoff will do it. James says Geoff will do as I ask, if I vote for them, because he wants the deal."

"They'll probably withdraw from the consortium. It will almost certainly not come up to Geoff's idea of profitability. But Lucy, they're only part of a consortium. What if the other parties want to continue? You'll have given away Morgen and will still end up with the hotel and golf course."

"I received a letter from Patience Dlamini – you remember her? I showed it to James. Here, read it."

Neil read the letter carefully, and then read it again. Thoughtfully, he folded it and gave it back to Lucy.

"James says Geoff will keep pensions intact, and jobs too. There'll be no retrenchments, but they may not replace people who leave."

"Do you trust them?"

"They want the deal, and they've promised, if I vote for them."

"And after the deal is done, what's to stop them doing exactly as they like? Lucy, if Morgen wins you'll have all these things without destroying Morgen. Morgen will keep pensions and the pension funds secure. Jobs will only be lost by natural attrition. Morgen Farm will still be important. And pursuing expensive property developments in St Helena will not happen, because Morgen has to improve its profitability and restructure its shareholding in the next year before Geoff can try again."

"What will happen if I don't vote?"

"It's too close to call."

"But if Morgen wins, there's no problem. If Predvest wins, James has promised they'll address my problems –"

"If you can trust them."

" – though I suppose I would have to vote."

"But you *can* trust Will and Rob and Mark. Geoff only wants what he can plunder. He's the ugly, greedy face of capitalism. After all, how rich do you need to be? Geoff simply wants more and more. His greed is insatiable. He doesn't care about any collateral damage: lives destroyed, jobs lost, pension funds raided, and so on."

"I came here to escape all of that. Why should I become involved to make one person or another a few million here or there?"

"You might be needed to save Patience and her dependents, and many other real, helpless people who could suffer. But Lucy, your grandfather demonstrated capitalism with a kind face. He built Morgen that way. We need to save it from the Geoff Lomans of this world."

"But Morgen is also seeking to make profits."

"Morgen needs to be profitable to survive. Companies need to make profits, ethically we hope, in order to survive, and then to be able to do good works."

They were interrupted by the serving of the deserts, and the conversation turned to other things. Neil glanced at his watch.

"I told Hensel I'd phone him before nine o'clock if I would need him to take me back to Jamestown," he told her, half-inquiringly.

"You don't need to call him. I'd like to take you home to my place for coffee or a drink. Then you'll be my prisoner until I decide to take you back to your hotel."

Lucy and Neil sat on the front veranda of Lucy's home. They had placed their chairs close together, half-turned towards one another, so they could easily see each other and also look out over the Island. Lucy had provided coffee and liqueurs, which were on the table in front of them. She had taken the telephone off its hook so they would not be interrupted, and had switched off the veranda lights. The air was mild as they were sheltered from the south-east wind, which seemed to have abated but which was probably still blowing on the high mountain ridge. The sky had partly cleared, but there were still clouds being driven from the southeast across the stars, which seemed very bright to the couple sitting together in the dark. Some of the landforms loomed out of the dark night, and the lights of homes on some slopes, and far down in the valley, twinkled in harmony with the stars. Lucy and Neil sipped their drinks, enjoying being in repose and at peace with one another. They could quietly think their own thoughts without feeling any need to speak.

Eventually it was Lucy who broke the silence. "I love it here, and I'm loving sharing it with you, Neil. It's so peaceful. I don't want it to change." She thought for a while, and then continued, "When Katie sailed away on RMS *St Helena*, I found myself wishing for an airport so she could have been taken off the Island to be helped much sooner. I do see that need, but I don't want things to change. I don't want the culture and the beauty and the peace to be spoiled."

"But Lucy, change is happening all the time. Think only of the history of the Island. And now I can telephone my office from here in a moment. You have satellite communications. I've seen at least two Cable and Wireless Internet kiosks. I've seen live sport from across the world on TV in the Consulate bar. So far St Helena has escaped much of the worst of the outside world, and people are right to be worried about some things. But St Helena also needs the outside world – for supplies, for certain kinds of medical help, for subsidies, for tourists to come and help make job opportunities, to bring families and the big St Helena family together."

Lucy was listening carefully. "So what is the answer?"

"The answer is to accept change, to embrace it as you did yourself when you went to Platberg, and again when you brought yourself here. Use your influence to control change, to make it the right kind of change. It seems the airport *will* be built. Why not accept its benefits? Why not accept tourism, but with smaller eco-friendly lodges, attracting the right kind of persons to the Island? Numbers should be limited anyway."

"I suppose so. And what about Morgen?"

"I've been thinking that St Helena and Morgen are two characters in our story. We can help them, or destroy them, or just turn our backs and leave everything to chance.

"Lucy, the people who came to St Helena in the early days might have been ignorant in our terms, but they plundered the Island and used it for what they wanted with no thought for the consequences. They cut down whole forests without replenishing them. They set goats free to run wild and breed, so they would have a supply of fresh meat when they called again, but the goats multiplied and ate until they produced a desert. You and the Trust and others are now trying to repair or reverse the damage done to the Island and conserve the best of what is here. That's good. Preservation and conservation are important and must be balanced against change.

"Geoff Loman is like those seamen of old, taking possession, taking what they needed or wanted, but he's worse. He's trying to take possession of Morgen, but he has no need. It's only greed that drives him. He will do the equivalent of cutting down forests and making deserts. He will destroy Morgen, and will not care one bit about the damage to people's lives. He is a destroyer. Your grandfather and father were creators. You want to conserve what is good on the Island. You have it in your power to be an influence for good. You also have it in your power to conserve all that is good in

Morgen, and the good works it does. If you turn your back tomorrow, you will not be using that power."

They were silent for a long while. Eventually Lucy stood up. "These are deep waters. Let me see how I feel in the morning."

She leant down and kissed him on the lips. "I'm going to keep on kissing you now, so you won't be able to talk any more tonight." She kissed him again, long and lingeringly.

"Would you like some more coffee, or something else?" she asked softly.

"I think I'd like some of the something else," he replied.

"Then wait here for a moment please."

Lucy cleared the table and took the tray of cups and glasses to the kitchen. Neil heard her moving around inside, and then she came back onto the veranda. She took his hand and pulled him to his feet. They stood close together, having a last look out into the peaceful night. Then Lucy took him by the hand and led him to her bedroom.

She had lit two candles and placed them on her dressing table, so Neil was reminded of the first time they had made love. In a way this was another 'first' after a separation of years. They stopped in the space between the door and the bed, held one another closely, and kissed.

"Are we going to play the undressing game again, or shall I take off your clothes?" Neil asked.

"Let's do as we did that first time. I'll take off my earrings first. You take off your shoes."

So they played an undressing game, gradually revealing each to the other.

"You are still a miracle," said Neil in wonder, as he took in Lucy's beauty. "Turn around for me so I can appreciate all of you."

She did as he asked, with no embarrassment, knowing she looked her best, and still comfortable with her body.

So they learnt anew about each other's bodies as they made love unhurriedly, but with growing passion, feasting their senses, especially of touch and sight. Neil was caring, tender and passionate. Lucy always had the feeling that he genuinely cared for *her* and not just for himself, clearly wanting to ensure that her experience was at least as good as his own.

"You're still a beautiful lover, Neil," she said at last as they lay close together, blissfully exhausted. "All day I've been remembering the things that made me love you, and they're still there." She paused. "And do you know again the feel of me?" she asked with a mischievous smile.

They lay close together, drifting in and out of sleep, but always keeping close contact.

"It's so lovely to have someone to be close to sometimes," murmured Lucy, partly to herself.

45

As the bedroom curtains began to brighten in the light of early dawn, Lucy woke again. Neil was still deeply asleep next to her. She half sat up, still keeping her body in contact with his, and watched him in the dim light. He lay on his side, dark brown hair tousled, and face dark with the prickly stubble of a day and night's growth of beard. He breathed deeply and evenly, seemingly trustful and vulnerable at the same time. She felt an almost motherly tenderness as she watched over him.

Lucy's mind ran over the happenings of the past few days – and nights, she thought. She had undertaken to listen to both James and Neil, but had thought she would still not vote in the Morgen matter. Now she was beginning to feel that Neil was right, that sometimes one could not turn one's back and leave the fates of vulnerable people like Patience to chance when she had the power to make a difference. If she took sides, she must stand behind Neil and for his values, which were in truth similar to her own. She let her thoughts wander as it grew lighter and Neil continued to sleep. She thought that his own job might also be at risk if Predvest took over Morgen, but he had not used that as an argument. She could not see him working under Geoff Loman. What would he do? It would be wonderful to have him here, but that was not practicable. At least they would have two more days and nights together before Neil would be taken away aboard RMS *St Helena*.

"What are you thinking about?" She found that Neil was now awake and two deep blue eyes were looking at her quizzically.

"I'm thinking how wonderful it's been to have you here to be close to. I hope we'll have more time together before you go on Sunday. I'd like to have you always, but, Neil, I can't leave the Island, I don't want to turn back, and I don't think you would be happy here. What would you do?"

"I know, Lucy. I lost my chance when I decided to stay with my family. But I could still visit you here, and you could come to South Africa for holidays."

"I'm not sure that I would."

"Not even to stand with me on top of Morgen Koppie and Platberg again, and to walk with me in my beautiful Drakensberg?"

"That would be possible, I suppose."

"And if you have an airport here I'll be able to come and see you much more often, and make you feel wonderful."

"Now that really is the best reason for the airport that I've heard. Change may have its advantages after all. You lie here while I make coffee and breakfast."

It had been a quieter night in Johannesburg than the previous two. There had been a brief storm in the northern suburbs around Sandton in the early hours of the morning. A sharp shower of rain had cleared the air, so it was cool and clean and fresh as Will made his early way to work on Friday morning. This was the day of the meeting, and he felt apprehensive. He had heard nothing from Neil or Lucy, though admittedly it was still very early on St Helena Island. Abe Levy had already phoned Will at home to ask whether Lucy had given any instructions. He had not heard from her, but would try to contact her a little later when she should be awake.

A large demonstration was forming outside the front of Morgen House as he drove onto the property. His morning newspapers were already on his desk, and he noticed that the demonstrations, combined with the imminence of the meeting, had received a place on the front page of *Daily Business*. An article, under Jennifer Rogan's byline, quoted "usually reliable sources" as saying that Predvest were now confident that they were assured of the remaining votes they needed to clinch the Morgen deal.

"What can she know that we don't?" wondered Will.

Judy was at work even earlier than usual and brought Will his morning coffee early.

"I couldn't sleep," she said, "so I came in early. I thought you would need this now. Have you heard from Lucy?"

"Not a word. I tried to phone her last night, but couldn't get through. I suggest we wait until eight o'clock, and then would you please try to get hold of her for me. I need to talk to her before the meeting."

"Is there anything else we can do? Do you think Mary or Patsy would change their votes?"

"I tried both of them again last night. Adrian answered the phone when I called, and wasn't very pleased. He grudgingly let me speak to my own daughter, but I suspect he was hovering over her while we talked. Mary's afraid of him, but I think she may really have been persuaded that it'll be a good deal. She won't change her mind."

"And Patsy?"

"Patsy refused to discuss the matter, except to say that Neil would kill her if she voted against him, especially as he's gone half way round the world to secure the deal. I'm afraid we're in Lucy's hands."

Just then Rob walked into the office. "Morning, Will. Morning, Judy. It's D for Decision Day at last, thank goodness. Will, just to let you know we're receiving reports from all over the country about work stoppages and peaceful demonstrations on our premises. We'll send you the details once we've collated them. For example, I've just spoken to Andries at Platberg. Everyone's lined up outside the factory, and there'll be no work done until they have a positive result from this morning's meeting. If it's negative we don't know what will happen. And I might add that it's not only staff there. There are several worried pensioners, some of whom have walked for hours since the early hours of the morning to be there. Andries says they're looking after them, serving them coffee and something to eat, that sort of thing."

Geoff Loman was of course also in his office early. Hopefully the morning would see a positive decision on the Morgen deal, on which they had worked so hard and long. It was irritating that another demonstration was forming outside Predvest Building, and that they were now receiving front page coverage in the newspapers. It was good though that Jennifer Rogan had acted on the leak, engineered by Predvest's public relations officer, that James Bold (unnamed, of course) had secured the remaining votes they needed. Geoff hoped that James was right, but at worst the story might swing any remaining waverers at the meeting to vote for Predvest. And Susie had managed to get the Predvest share price up to 1030 cents, which would make the deal seem even more attractive. While that was positive, Lucy's vote remained critical.

Lucy and Neil had a leisurely breakfast, and then washed and dressed.

"I'll have to leave for school in a little while," said Lucy. "I have to be there by nine o'clock today. I'd like to leave in time to take a detour to Jamestown to drop you off at the Consulate."

"Thank you, Lucy. I must ask, though, whether you've thought about voting at the Morgen meeting. It's at ten o'clock this morning, and you'll need to phone Abe Levy."

"Yes, Neil, I do want to vote. I want to support you and the principles you stand for. There's plenty of time. It's only ten past eight now, so I'll phone Abe before we go and ask him to vote for Morgen."

Neil suddenly froze. "Lucy, I've just had a terrible thought. We've been so bound up with each other that we've forgotten the time difference! Jo'burg's two hours ahead of us. It's already after ten o'clock there. The meeting's probably in progress. Hurry, Lucy!"

"Oh, shucks!" Lucy ran to the telephone and picked it up. "It's been off the hook all night. I remember now. I wonder who's being trying to phone us." She dialled Abe's cellphone number, but could not get through. She dialled his office number. They had been trying to contact her. He had gone to the meeting. They would try to get a message to him. Perhaps she could try his cell again.

Lucy dialled once more, with Neil watching in stunned silence.

Abe Levy was a worried man as he arrived at the offices of Merchant Attorneys, where the meeting would be held, just before ten o'clock that morning. He was directed to the spacious auditorium, at the entrance of which Morgen's Company Secretary, Carla Roodt, and a representative of the transfer secretaries, were screening would-be entrants to the meeting. Such meetings were not usually well attended, but the fact that it was a hostile takeover attempt, and the publicity it had received, meant that a substantial number of shareholders or their representatives were there. Abe found a seat next to Will in the front row.

"Have you heard from Lucy?" Abe asked.

"Not a word. We've not been able to contact her. The phone just gives an engaged signal. I've tried her school, but it's early and they assume she's still at home."

"That's my experience too. I've tried since last night, with no result. I would have thought that, even if she were not going to vote, she would have confirmed it with me."

"Can't you vote anyway?"

"Technically, I can, as I am her proxy here. But ethically I cannot act against my client's specific instructions."

The Court had appointed one of the partners of the firm, Merchant Attorneys, to be the Chairman of the meeting. He was a respected elderly lawyer, with sparse grey hair, a wrinkled face, and reading glasses perched on his nose, so he could look over them whenever he wanted. Such meetings were usually very formal and of short duration, after all the discussions, negotiations, dissemination of documents, the appointing of proxies and the instructions about voting on most of the proxy forms.

The Chairman began to race through the formalities. There was only one resolution before the meeting, incorporating the approval or rejection of Predvest's proposed Scheme of Arrangement.

"Does anyone want to say anything before I put the resolution to the vote?"

A man in jeans and a neat open-necked shirt stood up. Will recognized him as a senior trade union official. He had not been told that he would attend the meeting.

"Mister Chairman," he began, "I represent the thousands of workers in the Morgen organization."

The Chairman interrupted, "Sir, I must remind you that this is a meeting of *shareholders*. Are you a shareholder of Morgen Holdings?"

"I own one hundred shares, and I have a right to speak."

"I'll allow you two minutes to make your point. I believe all shareholders are by now fully aware of all the issues which have been documented and canvassed over the past few weeks and months."

The trade unionist began to speak passionately about the harm that could be done to workers' interests if the Scheme of Arrangement were to be approved and Predvest began to lay off staff.

Abe had his telephone on silent mode in his pocket. He kept fiddling with it, hoping for a vibration that would warn him of an incoming call. He whispered to Will, "Keep them talking as long as you can. I'm going to try Lucy again." He slipped out of the door and dialled Lucy's number, which was still engaged: then again and again with the same result.

Meanwhile the Chairman swiftly steered the meeting to voting on the resolution.

"Could we see a show hands please? Those in favour please raise your hands."

Will stood up. "Mr Chairman, we'd like to request a poll please."

(In a show of hands each shareholder had only one vote. In a poll all the votes of every shareholder present in person or by proxy are counted.)

"Does anyone object to deciding the matter by poll? Good. I believe the transfer secretaries, represented by Mr Herbert here on my left, have tallied up all the votes made on valid proxy forms. Are there any additional votes from the floor?"

Will was becoming desperate. How could he delay matters until Abe reappeared? He stood up again, "Mr Chairman, I believe the meeting should appoint scrutineers to count the votes."

That caused some discussion and bought Abe a little more time. Mr Herbert assured the meeting that all the votes had been tallied correctly and had even been audited. He suggested that the meeting appoint him as a scrutineer, and another to help him check the addition of any further votes to his lists. That was agreed and done. Then voting papers were handed out to the few shareholders who had not yet voted by proxy. Will optimistically took one for Abe.

Abe was about to give up and return to the meeting when his phone suddenly came alive in his hand. It was Lucy.

"I'm sorry, Abe –"

"Lucy, we'll talk later. Do I vote or not?"

"Vote for Morgen please."

Abe ran into the meeting, just as the Chairman was saying, "….. may I take it that all the votes are now in?"

"Sorry Mister Chairman. One more please. I've just been instructed by my client."

He hastily took the voting paper from Will and completed it. He stepped up to the front desk, and handed in the deciding votes.

46

Morgen was saved! Lucy's votes ensured that Predvest did not achieve the seventy-five per cent of the votes it needed to take control of Morgen. The news spread from the meeting with extraordinary speed. There were cheers from the demonstrators at Morgen House, the Platberg factory and throughout the country as they heard the news. Their jobs, benefits and pension funds were safe. At Morgen Farm, Patience Dlamini shed a tear as she turned towards the mountains and said a thankful prayer. Morgen would continue to care for them.

Morgen was saved, and it did use the opportunity to ensure that in future its majority shareholding remained in friendly hands, supportive of the family and their ideals. It did improve its profitability and its financial strength, but in a caring way as Will had promised. Though the Geoff Lomans, James Bolds and Stanley Vanes still lurk in the financial jungle, Morgen is safe from them. It continues to operate with the ideals of its founder to be a rewarding investment and a force for good in the world.

Lucy and Neil spent two more wonderful nights and days together before Neil had to board RMS *St Helena* on the Sunday evening. By then they were fully committed to each other, despite knowing that they would have to be apart for long periods. Lucy continues to be happy on the Island, and works to influence for the best those changes that are occurring. Neil values and enjoys his work in South Africa, and Lucy understands and supports the good that Morgen does. With modern communications Lucy and Neil are able to keep almost daily contact with each other. Once or twice a year they have been able to be physically together for extended periods, and continue to make wonderful memories to treasure. Parting is still always difficult, but the airport will enable them to see each other more often, and it seems inevitable that one day Lucy and Neil will find a way to be together always.